Praise for the Novels of Laura Bickle

NINE OF STARS

"Bickle does an excellent job of letting her characters speak for themselves and blending realistic, grounded conflicts with her supernatural plot . . . Also of note is Bickle's respectful treatment of Native American spirituality . . . Bickle is well on her way to establishing her work as a cornerstone of her genre."

Publishers Weekly (*starred review*)

"Following the prequels *Dark Alchemy* and *Mercury Retrograde*, Bickle's series launch mixes alchemy, folklore, and Native American traditions with a wintry Western landscape that will intrigue fans of the Weird West subgenre."

Library Journal

"Full marks to Bickle for . . . this . . . consistently engaging series. Our protagonist is as likeable and resourceful as ever . . . The way the series sticks to a single source of the supernatural while still managing to come up with a wide range of manifestations . . . is very compelling."

"Readers who like no-nonsense characters, the occult, Native American myths, and the modern Wild West will enjoy this. The writing is fun, compelling, and straight from the hip, with no apologies as to language used."

MERCURY RETROGRADE

"This wonderfully unusual Weird West novel combines the best of contemporary fantasy with metaphysical magic and mayhem, and even a bit of romance. Bickle has a knack for creating atmosphere, and she fills the fast-paced narrative with vivid scenes of wonder and a poignant story of death and rebirth."

"Petra's adventures in a magic-choked version of Yellowstone continue to balance nicely with a sense of fun, well-done and subtle world-building and characterization, plus some serious stakes. The series feels like it's building splendidly, and there's certainly room for expansion."

RT BOOK reviews

"Bickle's world and characters are enjoyably complex, sinking the reader happily into this contemporary fantasy landscape."

Omnivoracious

DARK ALCHEMY

"This fun adventure in modern-day Wyoming introduces Petra Dee, a geologist looking for her missing father and trying to make peace with her past. Bickle (*Rogue Oracle*) adds a dash of romance to the charming adventure, wrapped up with a perfect ending."

Publishers Weekly (*starred review*)

"Mix in some Native lore, great characterizations, a gift for bringing a setting to life, and a plot that eschews any hint of the tiredness of too much contemporary fantasy, and *Dark Alchemy*'s a winner on all fronts for this reader. Bickle writes with an individual clarity and style, leaving the reader to appreciate a dark sense of wonder that's all her own. Highly recommended."

Charles de Lint, *Fantasy & Science Fiction*

"*Dark Alchemy* reads like a stand-alone work, but Petra is such a likable protagonist and the slightly off-balance world in which the town of Temperance exists is so well drawn that it's hard not to hope we'll see more of Petra's adventures. There are elements here that easily could have shaded into standard tropes, but Bickle is skilled enough to put her own spin on them, and she has a clear, clean sense of plotting that gives the novel a wonderful pace and sense of completeness. More, please."

RT BOOK reviews

"If *Dark Alchemy* was a movie, it'd pass the Bechdel Test and more than passes equity tests . . . *Dark Alchemy* was a compelling read with a satisfying conclusion promising more Petra Dee stories set around Temperance. I'm hooked."

Dark Matter Zine

WITCH CREEK

By Laura Bickle

WITCH CREEK

A WILDLANDS NOVEL

LAURA BICKLE

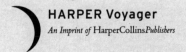

HARPER Voyager

An Imprint of HarperCollinsPublishers

WITCH CREEK. Copyright © 2018 by Laura Bickle. All rights reserved. Printed in the United States of America. No part of this book may be used or reproduced in any manner whatsoever without written permission except in the case of brief quotations embodied in critical articles and reviews. For information, address HarperCollins Publishers, 195 Broadway, New York, NY 10007.

First Harper Voyager mass market printing: March 2018

Print Edition ISBN: 978-0-06-256731-4
Digital Edition ISBN: 978-0-06-256732-1

Cover photographs by © Fernando Cortes / Shutterstock; © Hills Outdoors / Shutterstock (river)

Harper Voyager and the Harper Voyager logo are trademarks of HarperCollins Publishers in the United States of America and other countries.

HarperCollins is a registered trademark of HarperCollins Publishers in the United States of America and other countries.

FIRST EDITION

18 19 20 21 22   QGM   10 9 8 7 6 5 4 3 2 1

For Jason, wrangler of cats and mermaids.

CONTENTS

WITCH CREEK

CHAPTER 1

The Forgetting Place

What's gone was never forgotten.

Not really.

Some things were best buried. Ignored. Set aside in some dark corner of the mind. These sharp things should be bundled carefully in the cushion of ragged memory and tucked away for some later date, like leftovers in a refrigerator. Petra Dee told herself that this was for the best. She had far more immediate matters on her mind, starting with trying not to throw up.

Again.

She stared up at the dark ceiling of the hospital room, trying to breathe deeply and force the bile back down. A dim light emanated from the open bathroom door at her left, illuminating her feet encased in plastic massage booties to increase the blood circulation in her feet. Right now, the sensation was making her seasick, adding to her nausea. She lurched forward to pull them off, and her stomach sloshed.

She reached for the plug of her IV pole and yanked it out of the wall, even as bile burned up her esophagus. She snatched the pole and dragged it to the bathroom, one hand over her mouth.

She made it in enough time. Almost. Yellow fluid leaked between her fingers before she let go, retching into the toilet bowl. Good thing she'd left on the bathroom light. Not that she had much choice; she was either hurling or shitting every hour on the hour for the last three days.

Chemo was a bitch.

With her clean hand, she grabbed what was left of her hair to keep it out of the way. Some of it still stuck to her cheek as she threw up. When her stomach quieted, she flushed the toilet and washed her hands, mindful to keep her right arm—the one with the IV attached—lower than her heart so it didn't start beeping and summoning the nursing staff. As bad as she felt, she was determined not to have some poor patient assistant come running to wipe her extremely sore ass or ask her if she needed anything, like more ice chips.

She sure as hell needed things, but ice chips weren't one of them. She needed sleep.

She needed chemo to be over.

Petra splashed some water on her face and reached

for her toothbrush. She was almost out of toothpaste. She'd have to ask the nurse for more the next time she checked on her, which was pretty much every two hours. That, and toilet paper and . . . she glanced around the little tiled bathroom. Maybe more washcloths. One could never have too many washcloths.

She wrapped her fingers around the IV pole and walked it back to her bedside, hating how much she needed to lean on it. She plugged it back in, then climbed back into bed before pulling the cotton blanket up to her neck. Her fingers chewed on the hem of it.

Outside, a soft spring rain pattered against the window. The silhouettes of tree branches moved in the parking lot light, their new green leaves twitching in the rain. Petra hadn't been outside in weeks. It seemed like the season had changed without her even knowing it, the world outside her little white room prying off winter's last hold and spring finally settling in.

It wasn't just the weather, though. Everything in the world was moving beyond this still capsule of her corner room. This late at night, after shift change and before the phlebotomist came in to take her blood at 4:00 a.m., strange things invariably happened. Fights. Fires, sometimes, in the utility room. There was an old man in the next room who everyone was waiting on to die, but the Reaper hadn't come to collect him just yet. Instead, it was a constant litany of sobbing and shrieking through the walls, some of it from his relatives, but just as much from him. He was a pitch-perfect asshole to the staff during the day, but at night . . . the fear set in. He'd cry. He'd howl. Last night, he'd gone off the rails—or over the rails of his bed, as it were—and security had to tie him down. He was fighting Death, but it was going to come for him anyway.

Just like it felt as if Death was coming for her.

Petra cringed in her bed, staring at her closed door. She had never felt this afraid before. And she'd had a lot to fear since she'd come to the tiny town of Temperance, Wyoming, nine months ago. She'd been held prisoner by a drug-dealing alchemist. She'd fought a basilisk *and* the gang of biker women who worshipped it as a goddess. She'd battled a hundred-fifty-year-old ghost bent on wiping out Yellowstone's wolves. And the undead . . .

She squeezed her eyes shut. She would not think of *him*.

Would.

Not.

But in the dark hours, in the silence surrounding her, she couldn't help it. Gabriel, the man she loved, had stared down death in all its guises. He'd been hanged from the Alchemical Tree of Life nearly two centuries ago, and been resurrected to serve the land's masters. He'd been taken apart again and again by time and night and circumstance, and always rose to greet the dawn. Even when the magic of the tree, the Lunaria, had drained away and left him an ordinary man, he'd faced death and come out the other side. Half-blind and lame, certainly, but he had survived.

Or so she had thought. He had vanished at the end of winter, right before she was to go to her first chemotherapy session.

Her hand with the IV balled into a fist. He would not have left her. Not if he could have helped it. He'd been a wanted man, sure, but . . .

The IV pole shrieked, and she stabbed the RESET button. It quieted down, and Petra snorted back a sob and a string of drool. Dammit—he was supposed to be facing this with her. They'd been married. Sure, a marriage of convenience for many reasons, but wasn't he supposed to be here? Even if just to be her friend? Just to . . . just to brush what remained of her hair and maybe hold her hand once in a while?

She sucked in a breath. She'd looked for him. She'd gone to the Rutherford Ranch, the site of the Alchemical Tree of Life, and found nothing. She'd filed a missing persons report, even threatened the sheriff, who surely wanted him dead. Nothing. It was as if he'd never existed. As if she'd just imagined him. She was supposed to assume he was dead, that he'd walked off the edge of a flat Earth and been eaten by dragons. Gabe had confronted many kinds of death, most stranger and more violent than that.

But Gabe had never faced death like this. Sterile as saline water. With machines and lack-of-sleep hallucinations. The sheer . . . helplessness of it all. Maybe it was best that he wasn't here.

She closed her eyes.

She didn't believe that for a second.

"Where are you?" she whispered over lips that felt gummy and tasted like wintergreen toothpaste.

Her father had forbidden her from trying to enter the spirit world while she was undergoing treatment. She ignored him. She'd been trying hard to get there to look for Gabe, thinking that if he were dead, at least she'd know for certain. But she couldn't get in, no matter how hard she tried. She'd asked for her father's help. He was an alchemist—he could open the door. She had begged him.

Her father had looked as if he was ready to cry.

"You might not come back," he'd said, reaching out to touch her thin hand. "You have to hang on to this world."

And she had come to admit that he might be right. Chemo wasn't going well. She'd gotten badly dehydrated this last round, and they'd had to stop. Her kidneys had started to shut down, and there was worry about infection and what her liver was—or, more to the point, *wasn't*—doing.

She couldn't help it, though—she felt the veil close at hand. She wasn't sure how to explain it, just that she felt . . . a stillness nearby. There was no fear in that place, just a background white noise like the hum of a refrigerator that was constant in wakefulness and in sleep.

She exhaled and drifted away. Sleep slid through her fingers and tangled around her wedding ring, which she now wore around her index finger so that it'd still fit on her withered digits. She dreamed disjointed dreams of disembodied needles that poked through her parchment-like skin to find no blood. A raven came screaming through her hospital room, flinging itself against the glass of the window. Petra scrambled to open the window to let the poor thing out, to discover that it didn't open.

The bird slammed itself again and again against the glass, needing out. Petra reached for the visitor's chair at the foot of the bed, struggling to slam it against the glass. It tangled with her IV line and ripped it out. The glass cracked, and a pane fell to the floor in a staccato crash. Blood gushed out of her arm, and the raven clawed its way into the world outside.

Petra instinctively brought her hand to her arm to stanch the bleeding. When she looked down, a feather had stuck to the blood. She plucked it up and smoothed its ruffled vanes. Somewhere beyond the glass, she could hear the raven cawing . . .

. . . and the cawing became the agitated beep of her IV pole.

She opened her eyes.

She'd turned over onto her left side in her sleep, and she'd actually torn out her IV. Blood trickled down into her palm. She gazed at it dispassionately. It looked like ordinary blood—red and healthy. No trace of leukemia.

A nurse opened the door and rushed in. She saw what had happened and immediately reached into a drawer for a handful of gauze to press against the inside of Petra's elbow. She muttered soothing things as she assessed the damage.

"That vein's pretty well blown out, sweetie. It's okay, though. We can put the IV in the other arm. I'll go get a kit." She reached forward to smooth the hair from Petra's brow. "What else can I do for you?"

Petra sucked in her breath. "I want out of here."

THERE WAS NO escaping this place.

He had known darkness, to be certain. He'd flown in the blackness of moonless skies, slept wrapped in the tendrils of the Alchemical Tree of Life. He'd faced his demons and peered into the motivations of his own evil acts, always finding himself sorely lacking. He was guilty of murder, of the crime of indifference, of things that had ultimately caused the undoing of all he held dear.

But there was no darkness like underground. Underground was beyond the reach of light, sound, warmth . . . even the touch of life. Sensations bled together and faded away, leaving him suspended, in pieces, in this place.

He'd started out running. Gabe had always fled to the underworld beneath the Rutherford Ranch when he needed to retreat, to heal and regenerate. But that had been when he was a supernatural creature, not an ordinary man. Once upon a time, this warren of tunnels winding miles into darkness had been his kingdom. Lit by the Alchemical Tree of Life, the Lunaria, and by his own preternatural senses, he'd been able to see unerringly in the dark, master of all the shades of black under the dripping earth.

No more. As an ordinary man, he was blind. Literally blinded in one eye, and lame in one leg, he'd stumbled into the dark, fleeing the new heir to the Rutherford Ranch, Sheriff Owen Rutherford. Owen had followed him beneath the tree to the winter earth, bringing with him a new order. Gabe could taste it, the bitterness telling his tongue of how the land had turned away from him to serve a new master. It even smelled wrong; instead of the softness of rich loam, the world underground now smelled like freshly cut metal, cold and sharp.

The land had never rejected him before. Not ever. It had always been his safe place to fall, through generations of Rutherfords. But the magic of the Lunaria had been drained. And Gabe had allowed the Hanged Men to kill its last ruler, Sal Rutherford. Owen surely wanted him to suffer for that, despite all his lip service he'd given about wanting to uncover the ranch's secrets. Revenge was an atavistic state, much more so than curiosity. And the land had shifted, recognizing Owen's authority and plunging Gabe into the black.

Gabe limped down a tunnel, grip tight on his pistol. He knew most of these by heart, by the counts of steps as he ran, his breath ragged in his throat. But the tunnels had clearly shifted, too. He tripped more than once on a jutting rock, slammed into a wall that wasn't there just months before, and yet was forced to plunge ahead, his arm before him, scraping in the mud of the tunnel walls. Parts must have caved in; he turned left, then right, careening into the black.

Behind him, a flashlight beam bounced off the ice-slick walls with cold blue halogen light.

"You won't get away from me." Owen's voice was gaining. As was Owen. "You can't."

Maybe not. But he was sure as hell going to try. Underground was a big place, miles and miles unwinding beneath the placid fields above. Owen was still too new to know exactly how big, and how many bodies were buried here—of men and things much more terrifying than men.

Gunfire exploded in the close space, and Gabe instinctively ducked. White muzzle-flashes illuminated staccato bits of darkness, dirt spraying into his face. He pivoted to return fire, ears roaring. He couldn't see or hear if he hit anything. He bet not, though, since the star-like distant flashlight advanced upon him, washing over his face.

He flung his arm up, lunging away . . .

. . . and he fell.

The ground beneath him sloughed away, splintering like rotten barn wood. In that ringing silence, he slammed down, down at least twelve feet, landing hard on ground that drove the breath from his lungs.

He rolled over, wincing. He realized immediately that he'd lost his gun. He scrabbled for it, fingers rolling around in smooth, damp gravel. A veil of cold velvet moisture fell over his face. The gun had to be here, somewhere. He cast about, searching as the roar of gunfire receded in his ears. It was replaced by the rush of water, and he stumbled back, up to his ankles in water. His hands sought an escape in the blackness. He hoped to feel the movement of an air current against his face, one that would suggest a passageway from where he might get free of Owen.

But his fingers found only mud walls . . . all around him. Cold silt ran between his fingers. He'd fallen into a sinkhole, and he was trapped.

Owen's light shone down from above, a searing glare that caused Gabe to shield his eyes with a grubby hand.

"You're coming with me."

"No," he said. "You're gonna have to shoot me."

Owen blew out a breath that sounded like exasperation. "Jesus Christ."

Lightning struck. A blue-white light arced out from above and slammed into Gabe's chest. He felt a shout freeze in his throat and his heart stop as he toppled over, his face crashing into the shockingly cold water.

Darkness fell over him in a sizzling shower of sparks.

THEY COULDN'T DO anything to stop her from leaving. Not really.

The nurses made her wait until the doctor wrote her discharge order the next day. They'd pumped her full of antinausea medications in the meantime, double what she'd been given. Her oncologist, to put it mildly, had not been pleased at Petra's decision to leave.

"An interruption will greatly reduce your chances of survival," he said bluntly.

"My chances of survival are not great to begin with." Petra sat up in bed, her back aching against the rubber mattress stretched over an uncomfortable adjustable frame. "You said that it had spread to my lymph nodes. Which is why we can't do surgery. So . . ."

"Radiation might still be an option," he suggested.

"We talked about this. You'd have to irradiate half my body. I'd lose my thyroid and a whole lot of other stuff that I'd kind of like to keep." Her voice was raspy, burned from too much bile.

"You need to decide if you can commit to this. It isn't easy, under even the best of situations. And your blood work hasn't improved yet, but it still could." His gaze was direct, but tired. Petra couldn't imagine doing what this guy did for a living, parceling out hope to dying people and trying to corral them into coloring within the lines. Petra had never been any good at coloring within the lines.

"I need to think." She'd pulled her legs up against her chest and looped her arms around her knees, a gesture that was both self-protective and one that soothed the cramping in her gut. The decision to undergo chemo had been so clear to her months ago.

There really had been no other choice. But now, the reality was not squaring with what she'd expected. She was having a really bad trip in chemo-land. Much worse than anyone had anticipated.

And it sure seemed like a waste . . .

"I need to step back and decide."

"Decide . . . what?" The doctor's brow wrinkled. "We can try a new cocktail of drugs. If there's some more information or tests that I can run for you . . ."

She blew out her breath. "I need to decide whether I want to die like this, in a hospital, barfing into a plastic dish or shitting myself to death. Or whether I want to do it at home with a cup of coffee in hand watching a sunset."

The doctor blinked. Probably people weren't that blunt with him. "That's a fair assessment. From what I've seen of the progression of your disease, I can't say for certain that chemo is going to work for you. Even if we do make some progress, your projected five-year survival rate is much lower than the average."

"So this is really going to be about how I want to go out, isn't it?"

"You always have the final decision-making authority on your care. You can decide to stop at any time. I don't advise it, but you can do that."

She inhaled deeply. When her breath stilled, she listened to her belly gurgle and the blood thump in her chest. She shifted how she sat; bedsores were beginning to set in on her thighs. Her mouth was raw and oozing from the stomach acid, and she didn't want to think about the hemorrhoids growing underneath her print hospital gown. She felt weak. Her fingers in her lap were spidery and pale, her arms spindly. She wasn't in control of her life. She was submitting to a procedure that seemed designed to kill everything it touched, and if anything of Petra remained after the razing, then that was considered a success.

She thought of herself as a tough woman. But she just couldn't do this anymore.

"We need to stop," she said at last. "I need to go home."

"All right," he said. "We'll get you stabilized as much as we can, and as long as I'm satisfied, then we can discharge you."

"Thanks." She wanted to thank him for *all* his efforts, even though they hurt like hell, but she didn't know what to say about the failure. Was there a Hallmark card for this type of thing?

Dear Doctor,

Thanks for the chemo, but it's not working. I've barfed up my last toenail. I appreciate your expertise, but I think I might want to die at home and look at the stars while I'm doing that. Better luck with the next patient?

The doctor gathered his paperwork and left the room, leaving Petra to gaze at the blossoming tree outside her floor-to-ceiling window.

Petra always thought that she could withstand nearly anything. And in most cases, that had been true. She'd suffered all kinds of physical and psychological damage in the last couple of years, scars that laced around her arms and haunted her dreams. Unlike others, she had walked out alive through fire and mercury and venom. Chemo should have been manageable, much more manageable than getting bled out by a drug dealer or losing people she loved.

But the truth was, she just couldn't do this anymore without Gabe.

They'd released her in "fair condition." That's what it said on her paperwork, anyway. Petra dressed slowly in clothes that felt too big for her now: a T-shirt that hung on her body, a jacket that had once been a bit too tight around the shoulders but now swallowed her, and cargo pants that she had to safety-pin together to keep from falling off her hips. Though her body was likely now the ideal of some fashion magazine somewhere, she frowned at how light and delicate it felt, like skin stretched over bird bones. She yearned for the tanned, solid strength of her old body, a body that climbed mountains effortlessly and drank in sun on its freckles. Even her freckles seemed to have paled. She hated that.

She felt weak, and she hated that, too.

She pulled her dark blond hair back and tied it with a ponytail holder. It used to take three twists of the elastic to hold all of her hair. Now, it took four, and it was still loose. She jammed a baseball cap over her head. She had six bottles of pills on her night-stand: antibiotics, antiemetics, painkillers, antidiar-rheals. She scooped them all with the paperwork into a messenger bag and dug for her keys.

It was time to go. But she hesitated, looking out the window at the spring-blooming tree, all pale green in the pink morning light. She had felt a curious in-timacy with this tree during her time in the hospital. It had stood silently, bearing witness to her struggle without sympathy or comment.

And she knew that, no matter what, no matter how sick she got, they wouldn't let her die in here. They'd keep her going with drugs and chemicals, hanging on to the last dreadful minute. She'd be sick enough to want to die, but they'd keep her going, even in a comatose state. There was no safer place on earth than in the hospital. Safe and hellish.

A wail emanated from beyond her door. Petra opened it a crack. The relatives of the man in the next room were huddled in the hallway. It struck Petra for the first time that she had never seen them before, only heard them. Odd. And yet, they were as she imagined—wiping tears from behind glasses and clutching at shirt collars.

A gurney with a sheet over it was wheeled out of the old man's room. He'd passed. Finally.

The family followed the gurney down the hallway, sobbing.

And then there was a curious silence settling over the place, like the dark hours of the night.

Something tapped at the window. Petra turned. The tree. A breeze had pushed its branches into the unopenable panes, and they scraped the glass.

She shouldered her bag. Time to go.

Time to find Gabriel.

And time to get down to the business of dying on her own terms.

CHAPTER 2

The Loss of the Raven King

Daylight felt incredibly bright after the soft artificial light of the hospital.

Petra squinted behind the sun visor of her 1970s-vintage Ford Bronco, peering through the smears that freshly hatched bugs made as they splattered on the windshield. The sun shone cheerily through the streaks, which remained, despite her efforts to squirt windshield washing fluid on them. She dug around in the glove box for a pair of sunglasses, managing not to run the Bronco too far off the rumble strip at the shoulder of the road.

Though she'd been a few weeks in the hospital, things had changed since she'd last been outdoors. Petra had pretty much decided that an hour in a hospital was equivalent to a day on the outside. Grass

had begun to spring through cracks on the pave-
ment, and trees had started to flower. The leaden sky
of winter had given way to the thin, wispy clouds of
early spring that stretched high above the mountains.
Bits of color were emerging in the landscape, green
and white that replaced the blue shadows of cold.
Winter salt on the roads had been rinsed away by
spring rain. Petra had even lowered the window on
the Bronco. The air smelled like fresh rain. Life was
stirring all around her.

But not in her, she knew. She sucked on an ice chip,
trying to drive the chalky taste of an antacid from
her mouth. Her stomach gurgled. Part of her wanted
nothing better than to go home and sleep in her own
bed. But first things first.

The black ribbon of road churned west and north,
and she followed it to the Red Rock Indian Reservation. The blacktopped road dropped off to gravel, and
Petra tooled through the town, past the hotel and the
casino, through the main drag with its shuttered ice
cream shop.

She turned off at a stand of houses, pulling up
before a small yellow bungalow. She shut off the
engine, popped the door, and climbed out. In the
yard of the bungalow, a garden had begun to sprout.
Looked like kale and onions. Maybe cabbage. Pie pans
and metallic streamers were strung up to ward off
the crows.

She climbed the porch to the front door. She was
just about to lift her hand to knock when the screen

door exploded open, and a grey furry mass knocked her on her ass.

"I missed you, too," she wheezed, gazing up at the coyote standing on her chest. For the first time in a long time, she was truly happy.

Sig slobbered on her face, knocking her hat from her head. He whined and snooted at her ears, whimpering and slapping his tail against his legs. Petra rubbed his ruff and sides, noting that he'd plumped up. Maria's cooking, no doubt.

She glanced up over his shoulder, seeing Maria standing in the doorway. And she looked pissed.

Her dark hair was flung over one shoulder, and her fingers drummed an elbow covered in embroidered velvet. Her brows were drawn together. "What in the hell are you doing here?"

"Erf," Petra gasped as Sig planted his foot on her stomach. "I thought I'd pick up Sig and . . ."

"That's not what I meant. What are you doing out of the hospital?"

Sig did Petra the honor of stepping off her belly, and Petra climbed to her feet. "Well, it wasn't going well."

Maria looked her over, head to toe. "Obviously. You look like hell."

"Yeah. I feel like it, too."

"Get in here before you catch cold." Maria leaned down to grasp her elbow and drew her inside.

Petra started to protest, but gave up. She needed to go to the bathroom, anyway, and was pretty sure she deserved whatever tongue-lashing Maria was going to give her.

Petra stepped inside the door and stooped to take off her boots. The place smelled like fresh paint, and the interior walls were a warm yellow color. The pictures that had been on the walls were now arranged in stacks against the couch and coffee table, wrapped with quilts and crocheted blankets.

"Wow," she said. "You painted. Looks nice."

"Wasn't me," Maria said. She hooked a thumb at a young woman standing in the hall. "Nine has been busy."

"Hi," Nine said. The young woman was dressed in a T-shirt and paint-spattered overalls. Bits of yellow paint were in her ponytail, the silver hair a sharp contrast to her unlined face. "What are you doing back?"

"You did a good job," Petra said, dodging the question. Her stomach gurgled audibly. "Um, hey . . . can I use your bathroom?"

"Sure," Maria said. "I'll put some soup on and . . ."

Petra lurched to the bathroom and barely closed the door behind her before retching into the toilet. She didn't remember the last time she'd had anything to eat, but she had never managed to hit the dry heaves. Ever.

She flushed the toilet, washed her hands, rinsed out her mouth, and washed her face before rejoining the women and Sig in the living room.

Maria and Nine had been whispering when she arrived, but stopped as soon as she rounded the corner.

Sig sat on the couch and turned to face her. A small grey and white cat seated in the catloaf position on the back of the couch flicked her ears in Petra's direction.

"Oh, hey, Pearl," she said to the cat, rubbing her ears. "You made friends with Sig. Finally."

The elderly cat emitted a rusty purr and closed her eyes.

"So, what are you doing out of the hospital?" Maria asked again.

Petra made a face and dropped onto the couch beside Sig. The coyote snuggled up next to her. "I told you—it wasn't going well. The chemo . . . it just isn't working."

Maria sat in a chair opposite her, and Nine sprawled on the floor. Petra had yet to see the young woman look comfortable in a chair. Nine's nose twitched. "You smell sick. Really sick. Like death."

Well, there was no sugarcoating things. "Yeah. I just . . ." Petra took a deep breath. "I wanted to spend the time I've got doing something other than rotting in a hospital bed. Like finding Gabe."

Maria nodded. Petra expected a fight that might end up with the two women dragging her back to the hospital, kicking and screaming. But Maria surprised her.

"We'll do whatever we can to help you."

"Great. I think that—" She stood up, far too quickly. The bright yellow living room swam around her, a swirl of patchwork and light.

She sat back down again.

"That's what I thought," Maria said, and her surprising support crashed down on Petra with its intended lesson. "You're in no condition to go charging off into the sunset with a gun on your hip." Maria stood over her, took Petra's chin in her hand. "But if you're going to do this, this last quest, you need to rest. Get that stuff purged from your system. Get strong. We'll plan, and *then* we'll act."

"I don't know that Gabe has that kind of time," Petra protested.

Maria's mouth thinned. "We *are* looking for him. I've put the word out among the Arapaho to look for him. Mike is combing Yellowstone with the rangers. Things are happening, even if you can't see them."

Petra slumped deep into the couch cushions. Sig crawled into her lap.

"I don't even know if he's alive," she said finally.

"Gabe has survived a lot," Maria said. "Don't underestimate him. He's been around for a hundred fifty years."

Nine nodded. "He is, after all, the Raven King." Nine had a peculiar way of naming people. Perhaps it was her time among the wolves, and her need to assign people to a hierarchy. There was something about that title, something she divined when she first saw him. Perhaps it was still some of that animal instinct in her, from when she had been a wolf. But her character assessments were always spot-on.

Petra smiled thinly. "He has no kingdom, now, though. No ravens. It's just him. Wherever he is."

GABE AWOKE IN an aching darkness.

There was no sign of the blue lightning, but his body still throbbed from its touch. He tried to sit up, under the weight of a thundering headache. His ribs ached, as if he'd been dragged two miles down white water in an inner tube. He was able to sit up, but as he moved his good leg, he heard the rattle of a chain. He reached down to feel a manacle around his leg.

Shit.

"Good. You're awake."

A cigarette bobbed in the darkness, red as a coal.

A light clicked on overhead, a bare bulb buried in a half-rotted wooden ceiling. Owen stood over him, in a clean sweatshirt and jeans. They were indoors, Gabe realized. Far from the elements. Stacked boxes and wooden shelves surrounded them. A desk with a sheaf of paper and a chair were pressed against the wall. A bucket sat beside the desk. Gabe's eyes traveled along the chain. It was short—too short to fight with. Four feet and it disappeared down a floor drain.

"Ain't no use thinking you'll get that chain free. It's tied to the iron pipes below." Owen exhaled a ghost of smoke. "You know where you are?"

Gabe turned his head away. "Sal's basement."

"No. It's *my* basement, now."

Gabe flexed his cold fingers. "What do you want from me, Owen?"

There were a lot of possible answers to that question, apparently. Owen seemed steeped in thought, pausing to drag on his cigarette with his left hand. His beard was poorly trimmed. His eyes slid left and right, as if he saw things flitting around him. Owen was crazy. And Gabe had also killed his cousin. And Gabe was, indirectly, responsible for the loss of two fingers off the sheriff's right hand. Lots of perfectly good reasons for Owen to want to snuff him out. But not to drag him out of a pit and install him in the basement of the Rutherford Ranch. That seemed sort of excessive.

Owen leaned forward, his eyes narrowed. "I want to know what you know."

"I would have told you what you wanted to know. Without all this pomp and circumstance." Gabe gestured to the musty basement and his chain.

Owen's mouth turned upward. "You haven't got anything keeping you here."

"You had my word."

"Not good enough." Owen stubbed his cigarette out in an empty tuna-fish can full of butts.

Gabe felt something crawling along his spine. "You're lying. You want something else."

Owen snorted. "Let's just start with what you know."

"I know you went back on your end of the deal. When you and Petra and I were on the mountain, we made an agreement. You were to leave Petra alone, and I was going to reveal the secrets of the ranch to you. Why should I bother holding up my end of the agreement now?"

"Things have changed." Owen looked a little dazed, dazed in that slack-jawed look that men under hypnosis got.

Gabe narrowed his eyes, and he began to guess what had happened. "You said on the mountain that you'd spoken with the Mermaid. I told you to leave her alone, that she—"

"Let's be clear on a couple of things." Owen reached into his belt for a black plastic device. He flipped the switch, and blue light sparked at the wires at the edge. "One, you already got a taste of."

It was with some measure of relief that Gabe realized that Owen hadn't become a proficient practitioner of the magical arts. The man just had a stun gun. That much was manageable.

"Two. Your wife. Cooperate with me, and I *will* leave her alone. Fail, and any number of bad things could happen to her."

Gabe lifted his hands immediately. "I'll do as you ask." There was no choice in this.

"Good." Owen gestured to the desk. "I got some paper for you. Pencils. Write down what you know about the ranch. That tree. All the magical shit underground. I want to know it all."

Wincing, Gabe hauled himself to his feet and trudged to the folding chair. He sat and spread a piece of paper before him. He picked up a mechanical pencil.

"Where do you want me to begin?" he asked.

"Start at the beginning," Owen said. "When you first came to the ranch."

MARIA STOOD, KISSED the top of Petra's head, and moved to the kitchen. She plucked some jars of herbs off a shelf and headed to the bathroom, where Petra could hear water running.

When she returned, Petra eyed the herbs. "Are you making a potion?" She was only half kidding.

Maria pulled a mason jar full of dried plant matter from the counter and began pouring vodka into it. "I'm making you some things that will make you feel better. They'll help you sleep, quiet the nausea, muffle the pain. You'll feel stronger, more able to chase after Gabe. Thing is . . . they won't cure you at all. It's just an illusion, and they *will* burn you out." She turned to look at Petra. "Is that what you want?"

Petra took a deep breath. It sounded like a shorter time than she would otherwise have had, but it would be time that she might be able to put to use. Right now to her, an hour in bed was worth five minutes standing. She didn't ask all the good questions that a scientist was supposed to ask, things like: *What's in that? How much? How often? What about side effects? Any interactions?*

Instead, she said, "Yes. Thank you."

Maria nodded and screwed the lid on the jar. "All right, then." She put the jar in a dark cabinet and headed down the hall toward the sound of bathwater.

Nine sat opposite Petra on the floor, playing with the tassel of a rug. She gazed up at Petra through a thick fringe of eyelashes. "Sig missed you."

That might have been an understatement, because even as Petra sank further into the embroidered pillows on the couch, Sig had tried to get his entire body onto her lap and had installed his muzzle underneath her arm.

"I missed him, too." A lump rose in her throat. She couldn't imagine what would happen to him if she was gone. But she couldn't imagine dying without him, locked away in a cold white room. "Look, if stuff doesn't go well . . ."

"I'll take care of Coyote. We both will." Nine nodded fiercely. "He will always have a home."

Petra smiled. Nine never called him Sig, and that was somehow charming. "Last time I talked to Maria, she said that you were doing some work for the animal shelter on the reservation?"

"Yes." Nine picked at a bit of fringe, lining it up with others on the scarred hardwood floor. It struck Petra as a transplanted sort of grooming ritual. "There are so many dogs, there. They just need someone to listen."

"They call her the Dog Whisperer," Maria said from the hallway. "She can calm down any wild one. Even one that came in feral last week. He's now following her around like a puppy."

Nine squirmed yet beamed. "Well. I want to feel useful."

Petra nodded. "You're doing great things. Thank both of you guys for taking care of Sig all this time."

Sig stuck his cold nose into the thin skin of Petra's neck, and she yelped.

"Your bath is ready," Maria said.

Petra sighed in happiness. She hadn't had a bath since she left for treatment. Just showers in the communal shower on the hospital floor. She gratefully followed Maria down the short hall to the bath.

Maria had drawn the curtains, and the bathroom was in shadow. It smelled amazing, like rosemary and peppermint. Water steamed in the tub, a cheesecloth bag of herbs floating on the surface, slowly tinting the water the color of tea.

"Fresh towels," Maria said, pointing to a stack on the countertop, beside a lit candle. "And a robe." A plush violet velveteen robe hung on a hook. Maria's handiwork, no doubt.

"Ahhh. Thank you," Petra said, but Maria was already gone, having shut the door behind her.

Petra stripped down, avoiding her reflection in the mirror over the sink. She sank up to her neck in the hot water, hissing as it came into contact with the spot on the inside of her elbow where she'd ripped out her IV. There must have been salt somewhere in the water; she could feel it crunching underneath her skin. It was a good pain, though—a pain that felt like healing after so much pain that was just, well, pain.

She breathed deeply, feeling the humidity and fragrance dripping into her lungs. In her scientist's mind, she knew that there was nothing that the herbs, salt, and candlelight could do for her condition. She was beyond any magic Gabe had been able to access, and was beyond any touch of Maria's kitchen witchery. But it was still soothing. It would still fortify her psychologically for the fight ahead, she reasoned. And she needed whatever edge she could take.

She remained in the bath until it cooled, then scrubbed herself thoroughly with the soap Maria had left in the soap dish. It looked like it had bits of oats in it, and it felt soft and soothing against her skin. It made her smell like an oatmeal cookie as she scrubbed the blue and red marks that spidered across her body. She took a handful of Maria's rosemary-scented shampoo that she kept in a wine bottle and scrubbed it through what was left of her hair, feeling the tingling lather penetrate her scalp. Finally, she peeled herself out of the lukewarm water, toweled off, and stood before Maria's mirror.

She looked gaunt, fragile—a paper doll of her former self. She grimaced and reached for the robe, not wanting to look at her body. She tried to wrap a towel around her head, but her hair seemed to cling to the towel. She glanced back at the bathtub, seeing long strings of her hair collecting near the drain. She pulled them out and dumped them in the trash, not wanting Maria's sympathy or to clog her drain.

She took a breath. She wasn't a vain woman, but she

had to deal with the hair. She opened Maria's drawers, searching through the combs and brushes until she found a pair of scissors. Feeling like a small, rebellious child, she began to pull out sections of her hair and cut them. She'd never really paid much attention to the skill of haircutting. Instead, she'd usually left hers long enough to pull back in a ponytail, ignoring it except to pop into a walk-in haircutting place maybe twice a year, when it got to a length that it annoyed her or if it got something sticky in it that she couldn't remove.

It seemed to her that it wasn't supposed to go like this, pulling out sections and cutting them randomly. But she needed to do something with it. No point shedding all over Maria's house.

"Petra." There was a knock at the door.

"Yeah?" Petra's eyebrows worked up.

The door opened a crack, and Maria rolled her eyes. "Oh, good grief."

"What?"

"Get over here." Maria hauled Petra out of the bathroom and to the kitchen. She parked Petra in a kitchen chair, throwing a towel over her shoulders. She stomped back to the bathroom.

Nine popped her head into the kitchen. "Nice haircut," she said before ducking out again.

In the reflection of the toaster, she could see that half of it was at her ear, and the rest was a freshly toweled rat's nest. She shrugged. "It could be worse."

"No. It couldn't." Maria reappeared with a comb and took the scissors from her. Petra felt like she was eight years old and her mother was cutting her hair. Honestly, there were a lot worse ways to feel. Maria combed out Petra's thin locks, muttering to herself, and began to snip at what remained with precision. To her credit, she didn't ask the question Petra's mother asked when she was eight: "Whatever possessed you to cut your own hair?"

Nine wandered back into the kitchen to take the teakettle off the stove. She poured boiled water into three mismatched mugs, where tea already waited. She carefully handed Petra a mug and slurped noisily at her own. Petra drank deeply. It tasted of mint— several kinds—a bit of chocolate, and something else she couldn't identify. Something earthy and bitter. At her feet, Sig chased around bits of her hair clippings, batting them to and from Pearl. The cat carefully selected the largest chunk of hair, delicately took it in her mouth, and vanished down the hall with it. Petra had long suspected that Pearl had built a secret nest somewhere in the house, decorated with ribbons, string, and other such fascinating findings.

"There." Maria pulled the towel from her shoulders.

Petra reached up. It felt short, around her jaw and ears. She slipped back to the bathroom to peer at it.

"It's cute, thanks." And it really was. Maria had taken what was left of her hair and trimmed it into a long shag. Pieces drifted around her face. Petra ran her fingers through it, and it fell in feathered wisps. She hadn't had hair this short since she was a girl. She looked different with it. Pixieish. Not like herself. But then again, she wasn't really herself—her body wasn't hers, anymore. So no use hanging on to the hair. At least now she felt she could go out in public without a hat on.

"You're welcome." Maria grinned at her, picking stray bits of hair from her shoulder.

Petra took a deep breath. She was about to ask for a notebook, to start planning. And to charge her phone, so she could call Mike and see if he'd run down any leads. Perhaps he'd found some way to execute a bullshit warrant on the Rutherford ranch, to search Sheriff Owen's house. If not, maybe he had some idea when Owen wasn't home, if . . .

Maria took her hand and led her to Maria's bedroom. The bed was made with layers of quilts and chenille coverlets.

"Maria. It's only afternoon. I need to—" But she could feel drowsiness overtaking her. Maria had put something in the tea.

"You tricky . . ."

Maria shoveled her into bed and tucked her in, pulling the covers up over her ears. The last thing Petra heard before she drifted off was her command "Sleep."

And she did, falling down the dark spiral of memory and sadness.

THE HOURS OF strongest magic had always been midnight and noon. That had been true since the very beginning of time. Ancient peoples clutched their amulets close at these hours, convinced that evil spirits could wander close to earth at these times, that the movements of the sun and moon opened doorways for chaos to slip in. Vestiges of this knowledge still slipped down in stories of coaches turning into pumpkins at midnight and witches drawing down the moon, images of gunslingers facing off in the street at noon.

Lev was far removed from these things, from the fear of noon demons combing fields for peasants to cull. But he respected those hours on a marrow-deep level. He was never *not* in bed by midnight, and was always awake before noon. Even in the modern world, there was no reason not to be vigilant. Lev spread rosemary oil on the lintel of the door to the bar. It smelled sharp and crisp, a blessing in plant form. He smeared the oil over the elaborately carved door that had once belonged to a church. In fact, the whole bar, now called the Compostela, had been a church in a former life. There were no religious services held here, just beers served by the only remaining confessor, Lev. Any oaths sworn at the bar were easily broken. As the owner and the bartender, he'd seen and heard enough in the small town of Temperance to make him cautious. And as he had for many years, he rubbed the oil deep into the wood with a clean white cloth and his callused hands. The oil had given the wood a sheen and a scent that even managed to temporarily overpower the smell of spilled liquor. There was something meditative about this, the washing of the door every day at noon.

And the ghosts knew, they always knew it was noon. It was like a bell was rung in the spirit world, and they stirred, turning their faces to the sun.

A woman in a Victorian-era dress perched on a bar stool. Her Gibson-girl hair had gone slightly askew, and her dress was unbuttoned a bit lower than it should have been. She smoked a cigarette in a holder, and the smell of smoke drifted from her. Wilma. Wilma was a ghost. She'd come with the bar. She preferred the term "adventuress" to "prostitute." He wasn't about to argue with a dead woman.

She closed her eyes, as if listening to that invisible bell. *"Another day, another fucking dollar,"* she muttered.

Father Caleb stood beside her, his hands folded in prayer. He visibly winced at Wilma's swearing. Light glinted off his round, 1930s-era glasses. Father Caleb had also come with the bar. He prayed each noon and midnight.

"You know, He ain't listening to your pathetic ass," Wilma told him, tapping out spectral ash on the bar.

Caleb opened one eye.

"Your God. He's not listening. Never fucking did, even when you scream."

"He hears all of us."

"And doesn't do a damn thing."

"It's not up to us to question His motives or His love, Wilma."

"Eh. If He's up there, He enjoys our suffering. Maybe He gets off on it."

Lev let them bicker. They'd been doing it forever.

Lev thought that arguing was why they stuck around and hadn't moved on. That, and the fact that the both of them had been murdered here. By the same man, oddly enough, who was later run over by a train. Apparently, that hadn't been enough to appease their restless spirits. Some days, though, Lev thought they stuck around because they were really in love with each other, and if they moved on, they'd be moving on to separate places. So they stayed here, just to bicker like an old married couple and annoy Lev as much as he would let them.

Lev pressed his hands to the closed door. The wood was warm from sunshine on the other side. This place had a soul of its own, a soul that he respected and nurtured, despite the quirks that it housed. It had stood for more than a century and a half, and Lev thought of it as rooted in this place. Though Lev had only been here for a few decades, he knew each creak of the floorboards and sigh of the rafters by heart. He knew the exact count of glasses behind the bar and the thickness of the plaster. He knew everything under its vaulted roof, natural and supernatural.

It was familiar. It was home.

He stepped away from the door, the ritual complete. He took two steps back and had turned to tell Wilma and Caleb to shut up . . .

. . . when the door flew open, slamming against the interior wall. A wind rushed in, rattling the lights above the bar in the apse.

Lev stood his ground. The wind pushed in dust

and litter as it swept in, curling around cut-up pews that served as patron seating. The gust smelled like stagnant water and black rot and whipped Lev's pony-tail against his jaw.

The wind seemed to sigh, and then dissipated.

The ghosts were frozen at the bar. Wilma was still perched on a stool, sunlight shining through her translucent skirts. Caleb had stopped wagging a finger in her face, his glasses half-slid down his nose. He dropped his rosary beads.

"What the hell was that?" Wilma finally squeaked, breaking the silence. She patted her hair.

Caleb crossed himself.

The ghosts were used to being the primary supernatural forces around the Compostela. When any mischief happened that they didn't cause, all spectral eyes turned to Lev for explanation.

Lev walked calmly to the door. There was no one there. He looked up and down the empty street.

He carefully closed the door, making sure that it still fit properly in its antique frame, and locked it. He ran his fingers over the wood, examining it for splits, and inspected the hinges for warping.

"What the hell was it?" Wilma demanded again.

Lev thought a moment. "It's a sign. An omen."

"An omen? What's it saying?"

"That something dead is coming."

He reached for a broom to sweep the dirt from the floor.

CHAPTER 3

Waiting and Other Exquisite Tortures

She waited in the cold and the darkness, her fingers wound in soft silt. Her breath was slow and shallow, drawing in frigid water that passed over her gills and into her lungs. It was like being in a trance, this waiting, locked in weightlessness. Though a distant warm spring fed these waters and kept them from freezing in winter, it was cool enough for her heartbeat to slow to only a few beats per minute. There was no light, no sound, only the churn of her memories and plans moving behind her eyes. In this darkness, she saw much. It granted her patience. It granted her strength.

Muirenn was very good at waiting.

Eventually, as she knew it would, a light pierced the darkness. Distant, like a star, it moved above her.

She sensed this slight disruption in pressure, her black eyes dilating even farther as her eyelids rushed open. Rain at the surface of the water had shifted a bit, an air current interrupted.

She watched the star as it moved in the black, reducing some of it to tatters of rotten grey.

She pushed up from the bottom of the river, skimming close to the shore. Looking up, she could see the beam of a flashlight soaring above her, shattered into bits by the incessant rain in this place. She took it in, and she stilled for some minutes, not wanting to seem too eager.

"Hello?" a muffled voice sunk into the depths of the water.

Muirenn lifted her head, and the misty air felt sharp on her brow and cheeks. Rain peppered them. She looked up at the man on the riverbank. She swallowed a mouthful of water before she spoke. When she did, it was with a chiming lilt, like the tremor of copper wind chimes. She intended to sound that way: "You came."

"Yeah. How could I not?" The man stood on the bank, but out of immediate reach. He was wary. Muirenn didn't blame him. Eel-like, she paddled a bit farther away to put him at ease. "I don't understand any of this."

"You will." She lifted her chin and smiled with her mouth closed. "You are the king of all this. The inheritor."

His eyes tightened at that. "Sounds like a hell of a set of shoes to fill."

A laugh burbled behind her tongue. "Many wonders await you." She flicked her fingers through the water, fast as minnows. Her skin had gone green over time, the color of sea glass and nearly as translucent. Her fingers sketched out a bit of mist above the water. It resolved into shapes, shapes from the man's imagining and her own nudging: vast fields under a sun that never set, a skeleton made of gold, dusty tomes with disintegrating paper.

The man leaned closer, peering. He was fascinated. Good. She swam closer to him.

"It's all yours now, Owen."

He glanced down at her. "Things like that look like they have a high price."

"One that you've already paid. Many times over. This is your reward." She lifted her cupped hands up, slowly, and offered their contents to him: pearls, dozens of them. The smallest was the size of a pea, the largest, the size of her eyeball. She carefully poured them into Owen's outstretched hands. He gaped at the dripping mass of them, rain dribbling down his face.

Pearls were easy enough. They took some time, but all she had was time. She stretched her shoulders back. A delicate chain mail of smaller pearls covered her chest, lacy and thick with nacre.

"Wow," Owen blurted. "Thank you."

"An offering. To the new king." Muirenn nodded. "And did you bring what I asked you to?"

"Yeah. Yeah." Owen dug into his jacket pocket and

came up with a set of tarnished metal keys on a brass ring. "It was right where you said it would be, buried under the stone shaped like a head in the west field, wrapped in oilcloth. Took some doing to get it out, but . . . this is it."

"Very good, Owen." Muirenn peered at the keys as he extended the brass ring. "Very good, indeed."

She scooted into the shallows and lifted her tail out of the water. Where her ankles once were, ragged fins blossomed. Above that joint, a heavy manacle was fastened, with a chain leading away into the dark. The chain was very long—she had measured it, link by link, many times, as she searched for a weakness. One mile exactly. Generous enough to allow her movement, just enough to show her that she was truly trapped. Her scales were red and infected above and below the manacle. It had been forged for her by the Hanged Men, and every cell in her body had tried to reject it. Many years ago, she had tried to cut off the fins with a sharp rock to release herself, but had been unsuccessful.

"If you would, please. The key is the iron one, third from the left."

Owen paused. His fingers worked the keys, selected the rustiest one. He gingerly approached her and placed the key in the lock. Muirenn remained still as stone as he worked the key into the lock and the manacle opened an inch. He pulled back the key. "I don't know if that . . ."

"Thank you." She reached for the manacle, peeling it from her flesh with a wince. Scales clung to the metal as she worked it free. Finally, it came loose, and she was able to put that heavy thing in the sand.

She slid slowly into the water, hissing as it made contact with the open wound. Painful as it was, it felt nothing short of exhilarating to be free of the shackle.

"Now, please follow me."

She swam along the edge of the shore, slow enough that he could follow on foot. Owen shuffled along, his hands jammed in his pockets and his shoulders hunched about his ears.

"Why does it always rain in here? How?" he asked.

Muirenn looked up at the roof of the cavern canopy of the underwater river, where rain clouds gathered in a soft grey fuzz. "It always has. Ever since I came here. I think it's an excess of water elemental power concentrated in this place. Soon, that too will be under your control."

"Heh. That would be helpful for my tomato garden," he joked.

Muirenn made a polite giggle she didn't remotely mean and swam evenly down the river. They continued for more than a mile, until the darkness lightened a bit. The river flowed into a grate that stretched to the roof of the cavern. Muirenn knew from experience that it extended deeply into the bottom of the riverbed, beyond any efforts to dig beneath it. The grate was clogged with bits of dried grasses and old leaves, but water still sluiced through it. Beyond it was the softer darkness of dawn, pink and gold. Grasses crowded the riverbank, and there was a purple swipe of mountain beyond.

"What's this?" Owen asked as he examined it.

"It's the gate to your dominion over this land," Muirenn said. "Open it, with the silver key."

Owen shone his light on the brass ring and fumbled with the keys. Muirenn stayed still as he plucked one out of the clutch that was tarnished badly. He found the lock on the gate, cleared it of sludge, and turned the key.

The gate groaned as he pushed it open. The current caught at the sludge and took it from his hand, pushing the gate all the way open, ripping the bottom hinge away with a metallic shriek.

"Thank you, Owen," Muirenn said. Laughter bubbled up behind her teeth.

She dove deep in the water, flipping her fish-like tail. Her tail slapped the keys from Owen's hand, sending them flying into the water. She made it look like an excited twitch, like an accident. But it was on purpose. No one would ever have the means to lock her up again. She plunged down the river, beyond the gate, and to freedom.

Beyond the shadow of the cavern, the water had warmed in the sun. It had the unmistakable tang of algae and living things about it, unlike the clear cold water of the underwater river. She breathed deeply, and it chased the ice water from her lungs. Her blood moved as she swam, warming, strengthening muscles that moved under scales and fin. The river narrowed to a creek, crowded by cattails and the chirping of spring frogs. Wind pulled through trees and pale green grasses. It had been so long since she had seen these things. Her vision was bright and blurry even before the sun had climbed very high; it would take her eyes time to adjust.

She smiled.

At last.

Free.

She swam until the creek made a lazy turn. She stopped, hearing whistling. Peering through the cattails, she saw a man with a fishing pole, standing on an outcropping. He seemed alone, caught in a bit of reverie, gazing at his bobber skipping among the cattails.

She dipped below the surface of the water, toward the shiver of the fishing line. With green-spotted fingers, she lifted the struggling fish from the hook. The line jerked away.

The man swore.

Muirenn lifted her head above the water.

"Holy shit." The man stumbled backward. "I didn't realize you were swimming there . . . I . . ."

His expression changed from embarrassment to curiosity as he looked at her. The pupils of his eyes dilated. "Who . . . are you?"

Muirenn gripped the fish close to her chest, giving a small smile.

The fisherman crouched on the rock, setting his pole beside him. "Wow. You're uh . . . green? Is that real?"

Muirenn cocked her head and slipped forward a bit in the water. The edge of her tail skimmed above the surface.

"Is that like . . . one of those tails that the girls have at that park in Florida? For a movie or something?" His suntanned brow wrinkled. "No. That's real," he decided. "You, um . . . want the fish? You can have it."

She was within arm's length of him. She released the squirming fish into the water.

"You wanted to let it go? Look, I . . ."

The man talked too much. She swam closer, tentatively.

The fisherman looked at her, at her dappled skin and the dark rust hair spreading into the water. She wouldn't ordinarily have been so bold. The weight off her tail was going to her head. She let him take in the black of her eyes, the gills on her throat. He gazed in wonder, and his fingers twitched to a small square piece of plastic on top of his tackle box.

"Can I take your picture? What . . . are you?"

A smile played across her lips, and she spoke to him in a silvery voice. "I'm the Mermaid."

"Wow. I . . . wow. I'm, uh, Norm. Do I, like, make a wish or something?"

"You can, if you want. I'll listen."

She reached up with delicate fingers to touch him. Her fingers brushed the pockets of his fishing vest, playing with wonder over the bits and baubles there meant to lure the attention of fish. The man forgot about his camera and stared, transfixed.

Muirenn reached up for his collar . . .

. . . and dragged him down into the water.

He splashed and flailed. She brought him down—down to the bottom of the creek. It wasn't so far, but it was far enough for a land dweller. He couldn't fight her for long. He thrashed until his lungs grew heavy with creek water. He convulsed as the lack of oxygen reached his heart and filtered up to his brain. And then he stopped.

Muirenn grinned, showing row upon row of shark-like teeth. She ripped off his arm and began to chew. It had been so long since she'd had anything but the errant fish that wandered into her realm . . . this was a meal worth waiting for.

The creek ran red.

Red as the idle red-and-white bobber drifting on the surface of the water.

PETRA AWOKE WRAPPED in darkness.

Or maybe it was just a tangle of quilts.

The sunlight had drained out of the day. She pressed her hand to her head. She felt dizzy. Not the nausea she was used to, but a disconnectedness. She glanced to the other side of the bed. Maria was asleep, motionless, her head crowned by a tight ball of grey and white cat fur.

She glanced at the foot of the bed. Sig sat upright, as if he'd been watching her sleep, afraid that she might vanish if his back was turned.

That's not in the slightest bit creepy, she wanted to tell him, but didn't want to risk waking Maria. Slipping out from under the covers, she got off the bed and padded, barefoot, across the rugs. Sig hopped down and followed. The hallway was illuminated by the yellow light from the kitchen range hood. She stepped out into its soothing light.

A figure sat on the living-room couch, in shadow. Petra caught the shadow out of the corner of her eye.

"Jesus, Nine," she whispered. "You almost gave me a heart attack."

"Sorry." Nine shrugged.

"What are you doing . . . sitting here in the dark?"

"Couldn't sleep. Was gonna go out for a walk." She pointed to her boots. "Want to come?"

She looked down at Sig, who thumped his tail on the floor. "Yeah. A walk sounds good." Maybe stretching her legs would help her feel a bit more grounded, less like she was walking around in a daze.

She peeked into the hallway laundry hamper. "Nine, do you know where my clothes are?"

"I burned them."

She blinked. "You what?"

She shrugged, and she said matter-of-factly, as if it were reason enough: "They smelled like death. Maria left some things for you." She gestured to a laundry basket beside the couch.

Petra bit back a retort. Her phone and keys and wallet were on the coffee table. It didn't seem like Nine burned anything important. And her clothes didn't fit anymore, anyway. She rummaged through the basket and came up with a pair of leggings, a tunic top, socks, and underwear. Everything was black, and it struck her as a little morbidly funny.

She dressed quickly in the bathroom. She thought she'd feel sort of naked in anything but cargo pants and a T-shirt, but these clothes molded around her body like a second skin. Surprisingly comfy, she thought. When she came out to the living room, Nine had her coat on and handed a black sherpa coat and boots to Petra.

"Where are we going?" Petra asked as she laced the boots. They fit perfectly, and Maria had great taste in boots. They were suede and lined with what felt like fur from a skinned Muppet.

"Out there," Nine said laconically.

Sig lunged out of the door as soon as Nine opened it. Petra slipped outside behind them, into the black-and-white landscape of night.

It smelled as spring always did to her: like mud and flowers. Nine wound through the yard, around the garden. A thin moon illuminated the field beyond. Stars swept in a curtain across the sky. Dew had begun to congeal on the grasses, dampening Petra's leggings as they walked a well-worn track in the shadow of the mountain. Sig bobbed and wove through the field, disappearing and reappearing as he hunted shadows.

"You come out here all the time," Petra said softly in realization. "Every night."

"Yes. Sometimes, Sig comes with me. Most of the time, I go by myself."

They walked to a black mirror in the field, a perfectly still pool of water ringed by large chunks of sandstone.

"The Eye of the World," Petra breathed. "Does it show you anything?" She sure as hell wanted it to show something to her. She'd tried, time and time again, before she went into the hospital, to get the oracle to offer up a path to the spirit world, to give her a clue about where to find Gabe. She'd gained nothing, however, not so much as a whisper, even when she screamed and yelled and threw rocks into her reflection in the water. It was a gate to the spirit world, but capricious as hell in who and what it let in.

"Sometimes," Nine admitted, kneeling before the black edge. "It shows me the rest of the pack." She frowned, and a heavy curtain of shimmering grey hair fell over her face. Her sorrow at being separated from them was palpable in the line of her spine.

Petra put her hand on Nine's shoulder. "I'm sorry."

Nine didn't respond. She reached into her coat pocket for the lid of a Thermos. She dipped it into the water and offered to Petra. "There's no harm in trying again," Nine said.

Petra sat beside her and took the battered metal cup in her hands. Her father made her promise not to try to go to the spirit world while she was undergoing treatment. Technically, she was no longer undergoing treatment . . . so what did it matter? The moon was reflected in the black water of the cup, like a nail cutting on dark carpet. She lifted it to her lips and drank it down, every drop.

In the past, when she'd taken the water, it had tasted a bit sweet, like diluted tea. Now, it tasted sharp and metallic, like water that had been standing in a rusty can.

She handed the cup back to Nine, who dipped out a portion of the black water and drank. By this time, Sig had reemerged, covered in burrs, and began to slurp noisily from the pool. He plopped down beside Petra and began to chew the burrs from between his paws.

Petra idly plucked bits of the burrs from his coat. "When you see the pack, are they well?"

Nine nodded, gazing across the water. Her reflected silhouette was a dark, inscrutable silhouette in the water. It could have been wolf or woman in this dimness. "Last year's pups are grown and strong. Starling is going to have more pups any time now. They are . . . happy."

There was no mention of whether or not they missed her. Petra didn't pick at that scab of memory. She looked down at her own hands, pale as bones strewed in her lap. She didn't know what to say. Her hands became blurry, and her eyelids felt heavy.

She blinked.

When she opened her eyes, she was no longer beside the spring. She sat on a hard, cold floor that stretched onward into darkness. It was dirt, but it looked as if it had been hand-worked, pressed into a floor after decades of hammering. In the background somewhere, water dripped. Petra looked down at herself. The handful of times she'd managed to cross into the spirit world, she had physically changed.

This time was no exception. She was still dressed in black. But her skin had bleached out to a near-translucence. She could see the blue of blood vessels moving underneath, the shadow of bones. She looked away. Something wobbled on her head. She reached up for it. A hat—a black cowboy hat.

She snorted. The spirit world had a sense of humor. She turned it over in her hands, considering. Gabriel had owned a hat like this, once upon a time. But she found no evidence of him on it—no notes or coins or playing cards tucked into the brim. Not so much as a stray hair.

She scanned her surroundings. It was dangerous to be distracted in this place. Sig stood beside her, ears pressed forward, alert. Sig always was himself in the spirit world, unchanging. His attention was fixed on the darkness beyond the small, perfectly circular pool of light in which they sat. His eyes narrowed.

They weren't alone. Petra climbed to her feet, but had only gotten to a half crouch before a wolf appeared in the darkness. The wolf gazed upon them with liquid gold eyes. Its coat was soft and silvery, familiar . . .

"Nine?" Petra asked. "Is that you?" She'd seen people take the shape of animals here; and Nine was, after all, a wolf underneath her human skin.

The wolf cocked its head. "Yes." Nine's tail wagged, and her mouth opened in a canine grin.

"Are you always a wolf here?"

"Yes." Sig offered her a nose-snoot, and Nine dipped her head to let him get a whiff. "But this is not the place I usually arrive at. I usually come to the forest. This is . . ." Her nose wrinkled, and her lips drew back in a grimace. "This is underground."

Petra stood, gazing up, her fingers gnawing on the brim of the hat. "It has to be a clue. About Gabriel. Maybe he's underground. Maybe . . ."

The light that shone from above wasn't the moon. It was too yellow, too artificial. As she squinted and reached up, her fingers came into contact with a hot light bulb, suspended from a wire. She hissed, snatching her scalded parchment-pale fingers away from the surface.

"What the hell? The spirit world has electricity?"

"The spirit world has everything the middle world has." Nine pressed her nose to the floor. "Just in more symbolic language."

"Gabe has to be here, somewhere, then," Petra decided. She struck off into the darkness, her heart hammering.

"Be careful." Nine and Sig loped after her. "You can't see in the dark."

"It doesn't matter," she whispered. Dark was coming for her, no matter what she did.

As she strode away from the light, Nine and Sig pressed against her right and left sides. She could feel the warmth of their fur brushing against her legs. They could see much better than she could, and they herded her. Petra steadied herself by tracing her fingers along Nine's ruff and trying to peer into the blackness. She thought she could make out shapes, walls and edges, but that might have been her imagination playing tricks on her. The floor underneath her boots remained the same: hard-packed earth, uneven in spots, but consistent in its stability.

She heard her soft footsteps echoing around her, as if she walked in some large, vaulted cathedral. It smelled of earth, and Petra tried to square it with what she knew of the underground tunnels beneath the Rutherford ranch. Perhaps Gabe was there. If she could just find a landmark, some way to orient herself . . .

Sig chuffed at her side, and she slowed. She thought she could see something, like smoke, unspinning. She sucked in her breath and held it. A twist of vapor wearing the suggestion of a human face moved past, as if pushed by an unseen breeze.

Once it was gone, Petra hissed at Nine: "What was that?"

A trace of a whine echoed in Nine's voice. "I think . . . it was a ghost. We might be . . . in the land of ghosts."

CHAPTER 4

The Ghost Land and Ever After

What the hell is that?"

"It's the in-between for the fresh dead, a place where people forget who they were in life. They become trapped, like flies in honey. My father spoke of it, but I never thought . . ."

More of the wispy creatures began to form. Nine pushed her to a wall, next to Sig, who panted against her calf.

"Don't let them touch you!" Nine whispered. "They'll steal the life from you."

A veil of white mist, like rotted linen on a clothesline, dropped from the ceiling. Petra recoiled, bending down to shield the canines. The edge of the ghost brushed Petra's sleeve, and her arm went instantly numb.

The ghost turned. There were no eyes in its face, just caverns of black. It seemed to glow brighter, more solidly than before, reaching back for Petra with fingers that looked like broken shards of chalk.

"Run!" Nine barked.

Petra lurched forward. The other ghosts turned, alerted either by the sound or the brighter glow of the ghost. Petra heard the skitter of claws on the hard ground ahead of her . . .

. . . and a growl behind her. Sig. She would recognize that growl anywhere. She stopped. "Sig!"

She would never leave him behind.

But he had no intention of retreating. He snarled and barked at the ghosts. Petra automatically reached at her waist for a gun with her arm that wasn't numb, but she had no gun, no knife . . . nothing to defend them with.

The ghosts . . . well, the ghosts were plenty impressed with Sig. They seemed to drift back, like dandelion seed in a stiff breeze. And Sig himself was a bit different, too, it seemed; he was outlined in a dim pale-green glow, like foxfire.

"Sig!" She knelt and threw her arms around him, trying to drag him away, even as the ghosts seemed to cower before the coyote.

Something flew overhead, and she ducked, covering her head with her good arm. When she looked over her elbow, she saw it, and her breath caught in her throat.

A white eagle. It glowed with a curiously incomplete

light, not translucent like the ghosts, but not entirely corporeal. It streaked over her head and slammed into a wall.

Petra knew it instinctively. It was trying to escape. She stripped out of her coat and tried to throw it over the eagle, to try to trap it. The coat got only partway over it, and she fumbled with her dead arm. The eagle's talons were fierce, tearing into her chest and arm. She could hear her blood striking the floor in a rattle.

"Gabriel!" she shouted at it. Surely, there was some piece of him in there, some piece that might know her . . .

A golden, inhuman eye rolled back at her, and the eagle screamed in panic.

It split apart in her arms into a dozen screaming ravens. They sluiced through her arms and fingers with razor-sharp feathers and pitiless caws, smacking her head and face before they dissolved into the dark.

SHE BLINKED, AND it was still dark.

Just less so. Petra's chin jerked up, and her eyes fluttered open to see the star-spangled sky above the Eye of the World. The Milky Way stretched in all its glory from horizon to horizon. Sig snored with his head in her lap, moving his paws. She squeezed her eyes shut, trying to return to the vision. But it was no use; a cool wind scoured the sandstone sentries around the Eye of the World.

"Damn it," she muttered, blinking up to the sky.

"You saw?" Nine had curled into the shadow of a rock and crept into view on all fours. Her long hair was mussed, flipped awkwardly over her shoulder and tangled in her hood.

Sig yawned and stuck his cold nose in Petra's armpit. Petra moved to rub his forehead and found a black feather stuck to her collar, brushing her face. She plucked it from her coat—a broken pinfeather.

"Yes." She glanced back at the water that was suddenly blurry.

"What did it mean?"

"It means . . . Gabe is alive. Somewhere underground."

Nine was still, her head tipped in the attitude of a canine with a flipped-over ear. "You know where?"

"Rutherford Ranch. Has to be."

Nine said nothing. She waited for Petra to shift Sig to the ground and climb to her feet. Sig yawned wide enough to twitch his ears and plodded forward on the path back to the house.

As they walked, Petra gestured over her shoulder to the Eye. "It let me go to the spirit world that time. Not any of the times I tried before. Why?" It seemed as if Nine had more answers that she was giving up.

Nine shrugged. "It opens for me, though I don't go that deep. I just stay on this plane of the living, watching the pack. I think . . . that the barriers between this world and the next are thinner for you. You can slip back and forth more easily than you could before."

Petra made a face. Time was running out, and that

was just more proof. "Then I'd best begin looking for Gabe . . ." Her fingers clasped around the car keys in her pocket, and they jingled.

"Get some sleep. There's no use searching for the Raven King in the dark, especially without a plan."

"Or without guns," she murmured.

They didn't speak further on the way back to the house. Nine didn't even turn the lights on when they arrived. Petra's eyes had adjusted so well outside that the dim light above the stove seemed bright as noonday sun. She left her coat on the couch and navigated to the bedroom by Sig's claws clicking on the hardwood. She heard him jump up into bed, and she climbed in beside him. Maria and Pearl hadn't moved.

Petra stared at the ceiling. The Eye of the World had opened to her . . . and it shook her. She hadn't given much thought to what was going to happen to herself afterward, after she was gone. She had deliberately decided not to think about what might happen to her soul, since she guessed she possessed one. She'd actually thrown the hospital chaplain out of her room after he had wanted to get into an inventory of her sins. But having seen what could be, she sure as hell hoped that however lengthy the list of her sins was, she wouldn't be trapped in the land of ghosts.

SHE CONTEMPLATED STRIKING out and never returning.

Once she'd felt the sun on her body and the taste

of blood again, it was a tempting thought. Returning to that dark den where she'd spent the last 150 years was a thought that filled her with visceral dread and hate.

But there were things that Muirenn wanted. She had not yet had time to scout the new world beyond her lair. Things had clearly changed; she could hear it in the distant rumbling of machines and taste it in the tang of the fisherman's blood. She saw it as she rifled through his box and his shiny belongings that chirped and beeped until she drowned them in the water. She knew it as the creek formed unfamiliar bends and odd flows that she suspected were manipulated by men through earthworks she couldn't fully imagine.

All around her was change, and she needed to soak it all in. Good thing that she was, above all, patient.

She returned after night fell to the gate to the underground river, which remained jammed open. She rolled her shoulders, feeling the memory of sunshine leaving her as she dove into the black water and swam slowly upstream to her old prison and the keyless warden.

She lurked in the darkness of the deep water, listening before she broke the surface.

Owen's voice was clear, echoing in the space in a one-sided conversation:

"You said to trust her. I trusted her. And now she's gone. She might not ever be coming back.

"Yeah. Yeah, I know. But how do you know that?

"I can't. No. I don't have what I need from him, yet. He knows too much. No. No, I can't just set him loose.

"Well, there's such a thing as being in too deep. And I deserve some answers."

She waited until he had lapsed into silence before she lifted her head above the surface. She spied Owen, sitting on the bottom step of a narrow flight of stone stairs that led to the tunnels above. An electric lantern sat beside him, illuminating the cavern in a blue-white brightness. Not as bright as outdoors, but perhaps bright enough. Drizzle made it shimmer in a pale fashion. After seeing outside, it seemed very artificial to her.

He jolted to his feet. "You came back."

"Of course." She paddled close to the shore. "I would never leave you, Owen."

He gazed at her with narrowed eyes. "You didn't tell me you'd take off."

"Owen, I've been imprisoned for many, many years. You can't imagine how badly I wanted to feel sunshine on my face." She lifted her speckled hand to her face and smiled.

Owen's resolve to chastise her visibly faltered. "Well. I'm glad you're back."

"I have many gifts to give you. Many things that can be yours."

"Like the pearls?"

"The pearls are small things. I can give you so much more."

"How about you start telling me about why you're

down here? Someone clearly put you here. And I'm thinking that I just pissed off whoever your jailer is. Was."

Muirenn shrugged. "I was captured by an alchemist, many years ago. He enslaved me, made me conjure things for him." She gave a shudder. "He wasn't as kind as you were."

Owen's mouth twisted. "How long ago?"

"So long. I've forgotten." She started to sink below the surface of the water.

"Wait."

She paused, just her black eyes above the surface.

"I'm not him. Not that . . . alchemist."

She lifted up her chin. "I know. Which is why I am pleased to serve you. There are many things I can do for you."

"You keep saying that. But what exactly do you mean?"

The water greyed and became fuzzy. It showed Owen's reflection as he stood, with one difference: the silhouette showed him complete, with two hands and all his fingers. He gazed into the reflection, unconsciously flexing his right hand missing two fingers.

"Given time, and the proper resources, I believe that it would be possible to restore your hand."

Owen looked down at his mutilated hand. "Really?"

"It can be done. And I can free you of that ghost that haunts you."

Owen stilled. "The ghost. You can see her?"

She nodded. "She has been with you a long time."

He scrubbed his hand over his forehead. "Yeah. For years. Since I couldn't solve her murder . . ." He paced and turned back to face her, babbling. "But Anna's just a little girl. She deserves better. Can you send her on? To heaven, I mean, not leave her here or send her to hell? Because that's just not right. She needs to go to some bright white light somewhere."

"I can send her to the light. It will take time, though, to prepare the magic that can do it," Muirenn said soothingly. "Just not tonight—I am exhausted from my brief journey outside. We should speak of this more in the days to come."

Owen nodded. "That's fair."

She inclined her head. "I look forward to serving you, my king."

She sank beneath the water, to the darkest black of the river, where she couldn't be heard.

And she laughed.

"Good morning."

Sunshine filtered through Maria's lace curtains, forming soft shapes on the walls and bed. Petra dragged herself to a sitting position under a mountain of bedclothes. She smelled bacon.

Maria sat on the edge of the bed, wiping her hands on a dish towel. "Would you like some breakfast?"

"Yeah. Thanks." Petra pulled aside the blankets to put her feet on the floor, and noticed that she was wearing the plush robe she'd gone to bed in—not the black clothes she'd worn the night before. Had she dreamed the whole thing? Her brow wrinkled, and she glanced at Sig. His nose was working, and he clambered out of bed, more interested in investigating breakfast than ruminating the nature of Petra's reality.

"You okay?" Maria reached out to press her hand to Petra's forehead, as if checking for a fever.

"I think so? I can't remember if . . . I went for a walk last night or if I had a dream."

"Either way, you're here now." Maria's cool palm remained on her forehead.

Petra sighed. Maybe it didn't matter. Maybe she had the information, and how she came by it was irrelevant. If it wasn't some stupid hallucination, like she'd had at the hospital. She'd had a vivid dream there that she couldn't find the light switch and had woken up to find herself pressed against the wall like a spider, searching for it, while her IV pole bleeped its electronic brains out.

Maybe this was the business of dying. Maybe the line between reality and Other blurred until there was no differentiating the two, and one slipped away into Other. The hair on the back of her neck stood up at that realization, the truth of that sliding over her skin.

"Come have something to eat," Maria said, ever the pragmatic one.

Petra obligingly followed her out to the kitchen, awash in sunlight. Nine was seated at the table, eating bacon with her fingers. Sig was slobbering all over a plate on the floor that was now empty, while Pearl looked onward from her perch on top of the refrigerator, washing her face. Petra was betting that the small bowl beside her had also been full of bacon.

A man with a buzz cut in a park ranger's uniform sat at the table, and he stood when the women came down the hallway.

"Hey, Petra," he said quietly and gave her an awkward hug. It seemed that he was afraid of crushing her.

"Mike. It's good to see you." She hadn't seen her friend and coworker for a couple of weeks . . . had it been that long? Longer? She couldn't remember. He'd definitely come to see her in the hospital. She just didn't remember when.

"Like the new hairdo." He glanced at her hair, as if he was afraid to comment on the rest of her.

"I owe it to Maria's fine knowledge of a pair of scissors."

"Yeah. Well, she's always been good with sharp things. Scissors, knives . . ."

Maria jabbed him in the ribs with an elbow.

"Elbows."

"Don't get me started," Maria said, waving a spatula at him. He held his hands up in mock surrender.

Smiling, Petra sat down at the table before platters dauntingly filled with toast, scrambled eggs, and bacon. Maria put a cup of tea down before her. "Drink this first."

Petra did as she was bid and grimaced at the bitterness. "Any news on Gabe?" she asked, choking down the tea and reaching for a piece of toast to quell the taste.

Mike frowned. "I put out an APB for him. Didn't get any leads in Yellowstone. But the highway patrol found the truck he was driving."

Her heart jumped. "Where?"

"At a bus station near the state line. A city policeman slapped three tickets on it before it was towed as an abandoned vehicle."

Petra leaned forward on her elbows. "Was he in it?"

"No. It was empty."

Of course it was.

"I called in a favor and asked to look it over myself," Mike continued. "No blood inside, no damage to the truck. Change was left in the console, and it was locked up tight."

"Who left it?"

"It's not like there was surveillance footage to show who left it there," he said gently. "I did a quick dust for prints—mind you, I'm not an expert. But I didn't find anything besides the ones I found on the kitchen table of your trailer. If I was a betting man, I'd say that somebody planted it there to make it look like he was on the lam." Mike drained his coffee. "It's just too convenient."

Petra's shoulder slumped. "Dammit."

"Look. Nothing ever disappears without a trace. There has to be evidence out there," Mike affirmed, nodding reassuringly.

Petra offered him a thin smile over her teacup. She didn't know how much of this was to soothe her, and how much he really believed as the World's Biggest Boy Scout.

"You just gotta concentrate on getting better," Mike said.

Petra nodded. "I will."

He didn't look as if he believed her. One eyebrow quirked up a bit, and she knew that to be his trademark sign of skepticism.

"I'm in the best possible hands," she protested innocently.

"Yeah. I know." He glanced at his watch. "I gotta head in to work. I just wanted to check in with a report before I went. And snag some breakfast, of course."

"Thanks. I appreciate that."

He stood, put on his jacket and boots. Maria gave him a peck on the cheek, and he waved as he headed out.

Maria waited until the sound of his engine receded, then turned to Petra. "Would it be too much to hope that you'd stay here and let Mike track down Gabriel?"

"Yep." Petra scooped a spoonful of eggs on her plate.

Maria sat in Mike's chair at the table. "What does that mean?"

Petra murmured around a mouthful of eggs, "It means that I'm going to war."

"I'd guessed as much."

Nine plucked a piece of bacon from the tray, broke it in two. She gave half to Sig and crunched on the other. "I'm going with her."

"As if there was any question about her going anywhere to look for him alone. But you've got to be properly armed." Maria went to the stove, where she lifted the lid off a pot. A jumble of herbal fragrances and the sharpness of alcohol flashed over the smell of breakfast. Maria stood a battered Thermos beside the pot and perched a strainer on top of it. With expert care, she poured the brown contents of the pot into the Thermos. When it was full, she screwed on the lid and parked it on the table in front of Petra.

"What's that?"

"A tonic for strength. Drink a cup every four hours."

"Thanks."

"I wouldn't thank me—it's going to taste terrible. But it *will* help. And follow the instructions in here." She placed a lunch box beside the Thermos, a grey metal thing that probably dated from the 1940s. "There are some smudge bundles, tea, and oils in here."

"Will do." Petra knew that there was no arguing with Maria.

"And you'll need some guns."

"Guns would be really nice. I mean, I bought a couple of my own, but if you're offering . . ." Petra hadn't been able to bring her six-shooters to the hospital. She'd left them at her trailer.

Maria crossed to the living room and pulled a

quilt off the top of a trunk serving as a coffee table.
Petra followed her, slurping on her tea, and almost
dropped her cup.

"Wow. You're like the Fairy Godmother of Fire-
arms."

"Eh," Maria said noncommittally. "Clutter accu-
mulates."

The chest was full of ammo boxes, sawed-off shotguns, a rifle, and an assortment of handguns. Petra
reached in for one of the shotguns. "Not exactly legal,
is this stuff?"

"Mike's gone. There's no paper on any of it. So.
You do what you have to do." Maria shrugged. "Just
don't get caught."

CHAPTER 5

The Door

The gate to the underworld wasn't like Rodin pictured it. There was no grand carved door adorned with foreboding friezes of angels and demons warring. No nude figures writhed in bronze agony, thought really hard in hunched postures of contemplation, or plotted in cabals at the lintel. There wasn't even a door knocker. No decoration to show outsiders where it was. The real door to the underworld was hidden, anonymous.

But Petra knew this place by heart.

She thought about waiting until dark to return to it. She didn't put it past Owen to have put up all manner of cameras, surveillance equipment, and even booby traps to guard it. He knew it was there. And he knew she knew, too. But what she was counting on was that he didn't think she'd be brazen enough to walk through the front door to hell in broad daylight.

"Where are we going?" Nine asked.

Petra's old Bronco bounced over the ruts in the field of the Rutherford Ranch's back forty. The fields were beginning to green, and cows spotted the distance. There was still snow on the mountains, but enough had run off to make the ground soggy in the lowlands. The Bronco's tires kept wanting to get caught in mud and spin. Petra picked a longer route than she might have otherwise, sticking with higher ground. To foil any attempts that Owen might have made installing remote surveillance, Petra even cut through a couple of barbed-wire fences and peeled them back, like scabs on fresh skin.

"We're going to the Tree of Life," Petra said. "What Gabe called the Lunaria." She sucked on an ice chip as she spoke to ease her flopping stomach. "It's hard to explain, but there used to be a lot of men like Gabe. They were more than human. More raven than man, actually. And they could split up parts of themselves into ravens. Weird supernatural stuff. And they were bulletproof."

It sounded nuts, her saying it like this, but she went on, anyway: "They were immortal. The Lunaria gave them that. But they had to return to the tree . . . underneath it, every night. They slept, rotted, regenerated . . . it was bizarre."

"Sounds romantic," Maria muttered from the passenger seat, where she fed shells into a shotgun.

"Yeah, well. It's not like I was sleeping with him then."

"Since he is immortal . . . why does he bother with all this?" Nine's gesture encompassed the world beyond the Bronco. Beside her in the back seat, Sig yawned.

"Because he's not. Not anymore. Sal Rutherford—the asshole who owned this ranch before he willed it to his cousin, Sheriff Owen—burned the tree. Without the Lunaria, their power was gone. And they—" Petra hesitated, but decided that the time was too short for secrets "—they killed Sal."

Maria paused in fiddling with the shells, but didn't remark at first. Petra knew she suspected, but she'd never said it aloud before.

"Sal was a man who needed killing," Maria said quietly.

Nine seemed undisturbed by the discussion of killing and revenge. Instead, she asked, "And these men . . . where are they? Why aren't they helping to find the Raven King?"

Petra swallowed. "They died. All but Gabe. He was stripped of his powers, though. And now he's gone."

"If he's here, we'll find him," Maria said reassuringly.

But Petra wasn't so sure. The Rutherford Ranch was vast topside, extending from a state road on one horizon to the mountains on the other. What spread out underground might be an even larger empire of

byzantine tunnels, hidden chambers, and bizarre secrets. All she could do was hope.

Petra glanced down at her GPS. "We're almost
there."

She slowed as they tooled through a green field,
coasted to a stop in the center. This was where the
gate to the underworld lay.

"Oh, no," Petra said. "Oh, no. No."

She popped the door and jumped out, sinking to
her ankles in the cold mud.

Underneath a leadening sky, huge piles of fresh
earth had been turned. It was as if a mole the size
of a Greyhound bus had been tunneling through the
once-placid field.

Where the tree had once been was now a giant
bank of earth, piled taller than her head.

"No," she whispered. "The door was here."

She jammed her fists into the mud and climbed up,
smearing mud on her black leggings and coat. The
freshly turned earth slid under her, but she was determined. She scaled it, clawing into the earth with
fingers and heels, dragging herself up over the crest
of the hillock. Sig scrambled up beside her, with more
grace than she could muster, even on a good day.

"That fucker." Owen had been busy.

Dirt had been piled up in a circle, surrounding a
small flat space. At the center of the flat space was
a withered sapling tree. Beyond this man-made hill
was another one, a straight one, fifty feet beyond.

She slipped down the mud to the sapling. This was

all that remained of the Tree of Life—this sapling, struggling from the burned roots of the original tree. It was in much worse shape than the last time she'd seen it. Back then, she'd had hope that the tree had life to it, that it would survive. But now, the green leaf buds that extended from its brittle branches were a sickly shade of chartreuse, unfurled and warped.

All that despite the fact that someone had been caring for it. She knelt at it, touching the small trunk. There were fresh tree fertilizer stakes here. Her fingers brushed three of them, pounded into the soft earth. And the earth had been dressed with a fresh layer of bitter-smelling compost.

Owen. He knew what it was. If he was trying to save it . . . it was for his own power, his own purposes.

Sig trotted over to the Tree of Life and pissed on it.

"Yeah," Petra said, her vision blurry. "That's what I think, too."

"I don't see a door," Maria called down from below.

Petra stood with her back to the tree and counted off nine paces. The third pace landed her knee-deep in mud, and the ninth almost at the crest of the hillock of dirt.

"It was here," Petra said with narrowed eyes, pointing down at her feet. "It was a door in the earth, here . . . about six feet under. That rat bastard buried it."

Maria lifted her chin, hands on her hips, and looked up at her.

"It's only six feet. Six feet is just the depth of a man's grave."

As a geologist, Petra always had shovels in the back of the truck. And she was committed enough to dig down to the door with a toothpick and her bare hands. But there were faster ways to get to the bottom of this earthwork.

Petra rooted around in the back of the Bronco and came up with twenty-five feet of half-rusted chain and a tarp. She chucked them on the ground and stared at them.

"What are you thinking?" Maria asked.

Petra squinted and pointed to a spot a hundred feet away, where a pile of rusted metal leaned against a fence post and ruined section of barbed wire. "I'm thinking I want that torn-up section of cattle gate."

"Done."

Petra grabbed a pickax from the back of the truck and walked to the cattle gate. It wouldn't deter much cattle-wandering, now. The tubular steel was bent on one corner and torn from one post, likely by a pissed-off cow. The thing was ancient and dissolving in rust.

But it was exactly what she needed. Maria tried to take the pickax from her, but Petra shook her head. She really wanted to destroy something. With two satisfyingly quick strikes of the pickax, she'd severed the last two hinges holding the gate to the remaining rotted post. Nine and Maria caught the gate, and the three of them carried it back to the Bronco.

Petra directed them to put it behind the wall of

dirt, on the tree side, about halfway down the soft yellow clay. Petra threw the blue tarp over it, roughly tying the edges to the gate frame so dirt wouldn't slip out behind it.

"Okay," she said. Her heart hammered, and she felt a little light-headed. This was more activity than she'd had in weeks. And it felt really good, oddly enough. "Small amount of digging."

Using the pickax, shovel, and a metal pan that Petra had in the truck, the women dug two narrow trenches perpendicular to the edges of the bank. Sig, ever thrilled to have the chance to dig, threw himself into a trench so deeply that only his tail appeared above the surface.

"Now what?" Nine asked, surveying the odd arrangement. All of them were covered in mud up to their necks.

"Now we attach the chain."

Maria hopped into the Bronco, started it up, and turned it around so that its back end faced the hill. Petra hooked one end of the chain around the trailer hitch and ran the other end through one trench, wove it into the metal cattle gate, drew it back through the second trench and to the trailer hitch.

Petra nodded. "Yeah. The ground is soft enough that we should be able to scrape it right away. It may take a couple of passes, but the clay should stick to the tarp on the gate."

Nine glanced at her, stepping away from the jerry-rigged contraption. "You think?"

"Well . . . I hope." Petra grabbed Sig and moved clear with the wriggling coyote in her arms. He was slippery, and it was like holding an unhappy pig—he wanted to get back to the business of digging, his favorite pastime. She gave the signal for Maria to hit the gas.

The Bronco's engine grunted, and the chain snapped taut with a rusty ringing sound, bringing the gate tight to the back of the dirt pile. The truck groaned, then howled, the front passenger tire spinning in the dirt.

Slowly, with a sucking sound, the dirt began to move. The top three feet of the hill came down in a mudslide, dislodging the gate. The gate banged into the back of the Bronco, and the truck lurched forward twenty feet, dragging empty chain and the gate behind it.

Petra gave a whoop of joy. The top of the hill had been smeared off, like cow shit from a shoe. Just a few feet to go.

Maria backed up, and Nine and Petra arranged the gate behind the last bit of the hill, mashing the chain deep inside the mud. That run was less successful, unevenly scraping off a couple more feet before a chain snapped, nearly hitting Nine in the face and ringing against the brown hide of the Bronco with a sound like a cathedral bell.

Petra waded into the slop with a shovel. It had been enough.

At a feverish pace, she worked at scraping the mud

away until she could see brown, ruined grass. This was the spot. She knew it.

She dropped to her knees, combing her fingers through the grass. There was a brass ring here, hidden, that would open the hatch to the underworld. After some minutes of searching, she found it. Her slippery fingers curled around it, and she pulled.

Nothing happened.

She pulled as hard as she could, but her fingers slipped off, and she landed on her ass in the mud.

"Dammit," she breathed. She'd grown weaker than she imagined in the hospital, and it made her angry. She crawled back to the door on all fours and wedged the shovel under the edge of the door as a lever. She leaned on it as hard as she could. It didn't budge.

"Let us try," Nine said, and all three women pushed on the shovel handle. The blade of the shovel worked open a square seam in the earth, but the door would not move.

"Oh, hell," Petra said. She was cold, wet, and filthy before, but now she was truly pissed. She scrambled back for her pickax and whaled away at the door. It didn't matter if she broke it; Owen would know someone had been here one way or the other, and he would guess it was her. So she might as well get out some frustration in the meantime.

Chunks of turf split away, and Petra slung them over her shoulder. She would hit the dead, black air of the chamber beneath any moment. She could anticipate dropping into that space beneath the tree where the Hanged Men slept, finally getting this mission underway . . .

"What the hell!" she exclaimed, then sat back on her heels, rubbing her brow.

The turf door had come up in pieces. But what lay below it . . . tree roots tangled into a thick mat. They laced in and back on each other, roots as thick as her wrist, forming an impenetrable basket-weave of wood.

Sig sat down beside Petra's feet and whimpered.

"What is that?" Maria whispered.

Petra looked back at the sapling. "The tree," she said, stunned realization falling over her. "The tree . . . has sealed itself off."

"You mean . . . the tree has volition?"

"Of a sort, yes. And . . . it's not letting us into the underworld."

"What does that mean?"

Nine stood quietly beside the sapling, regarding it. When she spoke, it was with a hollow voice. "It means that we're in even more hostile territory than we thought."

Petra stood up. She swung the pickax, once, twice, contemplating breaking into the roots. Maybe she could do it, maybe she could break through that fortress of wood into the chamber she knew had to exist below . . .

Nine's cool hands were on her wrists. "You'll kill the tree. Just so you know."

Petra paused, her heart thundering and her breath

scraping her throat. If Gabe was alive, somehow, he might need that tree. She blinked back tears as rain began to speckle her face.

Sig clambered to the topmost part of the hill. His ears were pressed forward, and he began to bark so loudly his collar jangled around his neck.

"Let's get out of here," Maria said. "A truck turned down that road—maybe two miles away."

Petra grabbed her tools and clambered through the mud. The women chucked the tools in the back of the truck and unhooked the ruined chain. They piled into the Bronco, and Petra cranked the engine. Sig stood with his feet on the dashboard and peered into the gloom, his nose smearing the windshield.

Choking back the bitter bile of anger, Petra put the truck into gear and hit the gas. The vehicle jounced over the ruts of the field, and she deliberately headed in the opposite direction of the nearest truck, heading for a parallel road that ran north of the ranch.

The gate to hell might be closed, but this sure wasn't going to be the end of things.

Or her.

"TELL ME ABOUT how this all began."

Gabe looked up from the battered writing desk. His pencil stilled.

Owen stood underneath the naked light bulb of the basement, pacing. He'd been gone for a long time. Long enough for Gabe to investigate the exact nature

of his restraint. The chain was heavy iron, forged
a long time ago, but all the links were strong and
firm. He'd wandered around the full circumference
allowed by his leash, and found little within reach
that might assist in his escape: a handful of lint, two
crusty dead spiders, and a nail he'd dug out of one
of the ceiling joists by standing on the desk. The nail
held the most promise, but he'd bent it badly scratching at the lock on the shackle around his ankle. He
hoped it wouldn't break. At the very least, he might
be able to use it as a weapon if Owen got close.

But he never did. Owen seemed to have measured
off exactly what Gabe's reach was, and stayed beyond
it. When he came to collect the pages Gabe scribbled,
Owen would have Gabe push them across the floor
to him. On another day, Gabe might have found
those kinds of precautions to be flattering. Today, he
was just tired. Tired of sleeping on the floor, eating
peanut butter sandwiches, and pissing into a bucket.

And wary of spewing forth the ranch's secrets.
Gabe had served many masters as a Hanged Man.
Some had been better than Owen, some worse. For
all that time, he had served unquestioningly, offering
up to the ruler of this realm whatever he asked.

But now . . . now, he was no longer a Hanged Man.
His loyalty had shifted. The Lunaria was gone. The
rest of the Hanged Men were gone. Maybe it was time
that the enchantment of the ranch died with them.

He had begun writing the story of Sal's death. That
much, Owen already knew. He had taken his time

writing and handed the pages to Owen as he filled them:

There was once a tree.

And a man who owned the land on which the tree grew. But he didn't really own the tree. No one did. The tree had been there for hundreds of years, far beyond the memory of white men who came to Temperance.

The men who lived there before told a tale of the tree, which had been told to them by a tribe of Sioux who had traveled through the area. They said that they had camped here for a fortnight, looking for good hunting. One of their young men was nearly seduced by a sorceress, and the despairing young man lay on the earth. An oak tree grew through his body and reached to the sky. The man was one with the tree, tangled in its roots, pinned to the earth. The tribe's medicine men and women tried to extract him, but to no avail.

In desperation, the young man's sister cried out to the Great Spirit in the sky, promising marriage to anyone who could rescue her brother.

A storm swept in, and a tall man arrived, striding across the plain. This man was surrounded by a peculiar glow. The stranger announced that he was Thunder and Lightning. He had struck down the sorceress on his way to the camp. When he arrived at the camp, he threw a lightning bolt at the tree, releasing the young man. The young woman was brought up to the sky in a clap of thunder.

The tree didn't die, though. It survived. It grew out of ash, growing larger and stronger. In later centuries, it was used as a hangman's tree. And then it came to the attention of the alchemist who founded Temperance in the 1850s. Lascaris believed it to be the Tree of Life, and the men he hanged from it were granted eternal life . . . of a sort. They were doomed to rot beneath the tree at night and roam about during the day. They could transmute their bodies into murders of ravens, and were able to recover from all harm except that inflicted upon them by wood. And they were loyal to him.

These Hanged Men served Lascaris from that time, until the Alchemist's untimely death. The landowners, the Rutherfords, inherited the Hanged Men. They then served generations of Rutherfords.

Until Sal Rutherford. The last ruler of the realm. He punished the Hanged Men for rebelling against him by burning the tree. I watched the men hang Sal from the last ruined branch. I did nothing to stop them. He deserved it.

The Hanged Men went under the Lunaria for the last time. None of them woke up, except for me. I don't know entirely why—perhaps it's because I was made first. I was the oldest, and I had more of its power than the others.

What I do know is that they are gone now. And Sal is gone.

And the tree is gone.

Gabe put the pencil down and scrutinized Owen. The sheriff was rubbing the stubble on his cheek. He'd muttered to himself as he came down the stairs, talking to his "ghost," Anna. Gabe knew that Anna was nothing more than the reflection of his own madness. Gabe was still working on a way to use that, to determine if Anna was perhaps a reflection of Owen's ego or his stilted conscience.

If "Anna" could help free him.

"The Mermaid," Owen said. "What is she?"

"Leave her alone, Owen. She's not what you think she is."

"Then tell me what she is."

"Well, for starters, she's not human. Though she once was." Gabe leaned back in his chair, and the chain around his ankle squeaked. "She's very old."

"How old?"

"As old as I am."

"So. She was created by the alchemist of Temperance, Lascaris."

"Yes. She was actually one of the glittering people at Lascaris's parties. To the townsfolk, Muirenn was a wonderful singer, a woman with the voice of an angel. Behind closed doors, however, she was a witch, interested in learning from Lascaris.

"Initially, Lascaris was pleased to have the help. I wasn't sure if she seduced him, or if he seduced her. But the two of them were a force to be reckoned with. She knew the mechanisms of ceremonial magic, and he had a library of alchemical tomes to work from.

"They achieved a number of interesting things, complex operations that Lascaris. would not have been able to carry out on his own. When Lascaris discovered that I was a Pinkerton agent sent to investigate him, he had me hanged from the Lunaria.

"Muirenn watched. I still remember those cold dead eyes as she sang me to sleep in the tree."

Gabe lapsed into silence. It had been eerie, hearing her song over the cartilage in his neck breaking. Like a lullaby from another world, while he flopped and choked like a fish on a line.

"When did she become what she is now?" Owen demanded.

"Like most things, the relationship between Lascaris and Muirenn didn't last. She had no tolerance for Lascaris's other dalliances. In a fit of rage, she tried to kill him. She would have been smarter to work behind the scenes, to cast a curse that would drain him slowly, but that wasn't her style.

"No, Muirenn had a flair for the dramatic. She tried to confront Lascaris in a battle of magic. And truth is, she nearly succeeded in killing him . . . she chased him deep into the backcountry, had followed him on horseback as if he were a fox for three days and nights around Heart Lake.

"But she grew careless. She had him cornered one night at what is now Witch Creek—had run him beneath the horse's hooves. She could have trampled him, but she decided she wanted the satisfaction of seeing death on his face, close-up.

"Lascaris was strong in his desperation. He pulled her from the stirrup and drowned her. For a week afterward, the creek ran red. He wasn't finished, though. He took her body back to his laboratory and worked a conjunction process on her with the fish bones and shark teeth he had on hand."

"A conjunction process?"

Gabe explained patiently. "There are seven stages in classical alchemy—calcination, dissolution, separation, conjunction, fermentation, distillation, and coagulation. The fourth process, conjunction, is the fusing of the sacred feminine and sacred masculine, a rectification of spirit and soul."

Owen's eyes glazed, and it was clear he didn't get it. He tried a different tack anyway. "How did she wind up under the ranch?"

"Lascaris had the Hanged Men build a prison for her. That underground river is restrained by gates to the east and west. Her domain is only a couple of miles of river. When we brought her there, she was furious. She vowed revenge on all of us, especially Lascaris."

"Well, that explains why she seems to have it in for you."

"She told you to break our bargain. To bring me here." Gabe said it without rancor, just seeking a confirmation of the fact.

Owen looked away and wouldn't answer, which was answer enough for Gabe.

Gabe frowned. "She's still harmful, imprisoned. When she died, she laid a curse on Lascaris, one that he was never able to escape."

"What curse?" Owen's eyes narrowed.

"She swore that he would die at the mercy of the elements. And his house burned down. You do the math." Gabe shrugged.

Owen rubbed the back of his neck. "Do you think that . . . people . . . change over a couple centuries?"

Gabe considered this. "Yes. And no."

"What does that mean?"

"We are all our base elements at the core. If we allow ourselves to work the psychological stages of transformation . . . yes. We can change. If not . . . one can become trapped in a stage, stagnant. I have no idea if the Mermaid remains in the conjunction stage, or if she has moved on." Gabe leaned forward. "She was dangerous then. If she has amassed more power, she could be unstoppable. Be very careful with her, Owen. Whatever you do, whatever she tells you, keep her in her cell."

Owen pinched the bridge of his nose. "Well . . ."

Damn him. Gabe closed his eyes. "Then your fate is sealed. And mine. And so many more."

CHAPTER 6

Letters from the Past

Home was a tin can on wheels. But it sure beat being imprisoned in a hospital cell.

Petra rolled up to her Airstream trailer when sunset was bleeding across the horizon. Sig bounced beside her on the passenger seat of the Bronco, excited to be home, a sentiment Petra agreed with wholeheartedly. His fur was still wet from the bath he'd been given at Maria's house, further dampening the seats that had been hastily hosed off in the yard. Sig smelled like rosemary. The truck, however, did not. The floor mats were still squishy on the floorboards. She'd leave the windows down, and it would dry out in a couple days. Hopefully. At least it didn't look like the Swamp Thing had rolled around on her upholstery anymore.

Gabe's truck was parked in front of the Airstream. For a moment, her heart leaped, and she thought that he might have come home . . . then, she remembered that Mike had said that the truck had been found at the bus station. Likely, Mike had it towed here after he'd finished with it. She'd owe him a beer.

She popped the door on the Bronco and climbed down.

"Home sweet home." Despite her depression at what they hadn't found at the Rutherford Ranch, Petra was cheered a bit by the prospect of being able to sleep in her own bed, humble as the futon inside was.

Sig clambered up the steps to the trailer and smeared his nose on the screen door.

"Hold your horses," Petra muttered. She hauled her bags out of the back seat, full of Maria's potions and hand-me-down clothes that smelled like lavender. Hoisting a bag on each shoulder, she shuffled to the mailbox.

The mailbox was crammed full of several weeks' accumulated mail. She jammed the bundle of paper under her arm, nudged past Sig, and unlocked the front door. She flipped on the kitchen light.

Sig bounded into the trailer with a yodel of glee. He launched himself across the linoleum floor of the kitchen and flopped onto the futon bed. He rolled blissfully in the unmade covers, making *hrrmphs* of delight. Petra snorted. Little dude acted as if he hadn't been allowed to sleep in beds at Maria's house.

Parking the mail on the kitchen table, Petra wrinkled her nose. It smelled funny in here. Not bad, just . . . weird. Not like home.

She circled the trailer, opening windows to the oncoming spring night. Everything looked as she'd left it, her sparse belongings taking up little room. She unpacked her bags full of Maria's clothes, more dark tunics and leggings, and put them in the dresser drawers. She shoved to the side her usual T-shirts and cargo pants, then changed her mind and jammed them all in the bottom drawer, out of sight and mind. She had to deal with her body as it was now, not how it had been, or how she wished it to be.

She lined up Maria's potion bottles on the kitchen counter. Maria's flowery handwriting spelled out instructions on a piece of legal paper, and she anchored that page of paper on the counter under a dark blue glass bottle. The bottles were pretty, bits of plant matter swimming like shadows underneath the caps. Whether or not they made her physically feel better, they made Petra feel cared for. And that was something.

She peered in the fridge and made a face. Just a few ketchup packets, a couple of beers, and a jar of pickles. Her stomach growled.

Those pickles were probably no good. And the beer was probably the last thing her fading body really needed. She opened a cabinet and pulled down a box of crackers. She slathered some peanut butter on them and crunched quietly, looking through the window over the sink.

The field spread out in growing darkness beyond the window. She remembered Gabe standing there, months before, trying to court ravens with bottle caps and cat food. Her stomach knotted. She would find him. Somehow. The Lunaria knew more than it was telling. It was protecting something, or working at the behest of someone. Sal had ruled the ranch from a position of bullish ignorance. She knew that Owen had more of a taste for the hidden side of life. Had he discovered enough secrets to get the magic of the place to do his bidding? Or was there enough life left in the tree that it was running its own pissed-off agenda?

Trailing cracker crumbs across the linoleum, she fingered through the mail. Lots of advertisements for stores at the county seat, a good hour away from Temperance. Sales on linens, furniture, cars, tans, and tires. Most of them had expired. If she was into long-range planning at this point in her life, she would have given consideration to the tire ad, but she chucked it into the trash can with the others.

Her fingers paused on a plain white business envelope. No return address. The postmark was two weeks ago. Her name and address were written on the front in a familiar copperplate hand—Gabe's.

She ripped it open and unfolded a letter written on plain lined paper:

Dear Petra:

I wish I could ask you to come with me, but I have to leave. I'm sorry.

Gabe

"What the hell?"

Rage boiled up in her throat. To get dumped in her dying hours . . . and by letter? Three freaking lines?

She wadded up the paper, took a deep breath.

From his perch on the bed, Sig whined.

This wasn't Gabe. She spread out the paper again on the kitchen table, smoothing the wrinkles. He wouldn't have written to her like that. For all his faults, he was an honorable man. He would not have left her voluntarily. And even if he had, he would have had the spine to tell her in person. Not in some half-assed note. He would not have copped out in order to save himself discomfort.

She crossed her arms, staring out the front window at Gabe's pickup truck. Maybe Mike was right. Maybe the truck had been staged, and the letter was part of it. With a note on record, the cops could close the books and say definitively that he'd gone away of his own volition, that he hadn't been abducted. They could wash their hands and say, "Oh, well. Sorry for your luck."

Someone was playing a game. They wanted Gabe never to be found.

And the setup was smelling like the player knew the game well. In her gut, Petra felt it was Sheriff Owen. But was he acting alone, or did he have help?

Petra headed to the bedroom to a loose piece of faux-wood paneling on the wall above her bed. She peeled it back, revealing a void in the wall where she kept all her valuables. She pulled out a wad of cash and set it on the bed, a gun belt with two antique pistols, and then a golden pendant. The pendant had been given to her by her father. It was an alchemical symbol: a lion devouring the sun. She'd been told that the green lion devouring the sun was the key to all alchemical secrets. She set it on top of the money. She had worn it every day before going into treatment, and it had felt a part of her then.

She experimentally put it on around her neck. It felt heavy, foreign. It had been weeks since she'd worn it. She took it off and put it on top of the money.

She returned her attention to the makeshift safe. After some digging into the hole, she came up with a golden compass-shaped object, engraved with alchemical symbols. The Locus.

Sig whined.

"Hey," she said. "*You* found it." Sig had found the Locus, digging in Petra's backyard, the first night she'd come to Temperance. Over time, she'd discovered that the Locus was a magic locator—it could detect the presence of the supernatural. Unfortunately, it hadn't been of any use to her so far in finding Gabe—as a mortal man, Gabe had nothing of the supernatural about him now. But if Owen was playing games, perhaps he had supernatural help. It would be good to know for certain, to apprehend how big and dangerous the problem she faced could be.

Only problem was, the Locus ran on blood, and it wasn't like she was a paragon of health at the moment. There was nothing to be done for it, though—she had to *try*.

Petra stuffed the cash and pendant back into the void and buttoned it up. She muttered to herself as she headed to the kitchen, digging a paring knife out of a drawer. She poked at her fingers, but her chemo-addled blood was determined not to flow. She finally picked at the scab of the blown-out IV line inside her elbow, and that dripped freely. She dropped a few runnels of blood into a groove circumscribing the outside of the Locus before trying to stanch the flow with a paper towel.

She held her hand to her shoulder, pressing the paper towel tight in the crevice of her elbow, and held her breath. For all she knew, the Locus might reject her blood as too inferior to run, if it recognized it as blood at all. There were, after all, such arcane poisons as arsenic in her chemotherapy lines.

The Locus seemed to take its own sweet time thinking about it, tasting the blood. The blood seeped around the groove, looking for all the world like a cranberry juice ring from a juice glass on a coffee table.

Finally, the blood sluggishly began to turn, a small bubble.

"Aha," she breathed. Carefully cupping the Locus in her hands, she carried it outside to the Bronco.

In the dimming red light of sunset, the Locus seemed to take strength. The blood swished around the circle, and a runnel of it dripped off the rim in the direction of Gabe's pickup.

She knew that Mike had already searched the truck for earthly evidence. Maybe there was something he missed. Maybe some residue of magic . . .

Magic had been there. Petra's mouth tightened. She approached the pickup and opened the door. Mike had left a file folder of paperwork for her about the tow on the passenger seat. She brushed it aside and placed the Locus on the seat. The blood churned lazily, indecisive.

Petra tore into the glove box. She flipped through registration and repair records, jabbing herself on a piece of loose bailing wire in the process. Under the passenger's seat, she found a dead flashlight. She shoved the seat back to find a dry canteen. She peered inside it to be certain before chucking it aside.

There needed to be something here, aside from crusty mud and loose change. As she ran her fingers underneath the driver's seat, she thought she felt something wedged between the seat frame and the well of the console. She dug around until her knuckles bled, unearthing two stale french fries, a wad of calcified gum, and a copper penny before she got the object loose.

"Oh," she said, blinking at the thing in her bloody palm.

It was a pearl. Looked like one, anyway, though it had a soft blue sheen that made her think it could be fake. There were no drill marks, nothing to indicate that it had come from a setting. She rubbed it against her front tooth, and it felt gritty. Likely real, then.

As she turned it around in her hands to examine under the dome light, the Locus burped a burble of blood.

Magic. It was magic. Now, to figure out where it had come from.

She had some suspicions. Months ago, she'd been pursuing a ghost in the Yellowstone backcountry with Gabe. Owen had chased them down, and he'd spent a good deal of time babbling about the supernatural shit he'd stirred up on the Rutherford Ranch: about the Hanged Men, ghosts . . . and a *mermaid*. Her brow wrinkled. She knew that Gabe had told him to leave the Mermaid alone. Had Owen listened? Or was he mixed up in something even stranger, now that he had full run of the ranch and a questionable grip on sanity?

Petra knew that all information in Temperance passed through the town bar. Maybe if she made the right inquiries, something would shake loose. If no one had seen Gabe, that was one thing. But maybe someone could speak to this mysterious pearl.

Petra locked up the truck and headed back to the

trailer. She hid the Locus away and bound up her arm properly. She grabbed her jacket and stuffed her wallet into the coat pocket. She was increasingly annoyed that the women's clothes that Maria had given her—soft black velvet leggings, knee-high boots, and a black sweater—had no fucking pockets.

"You hold down the fort, Sig," Petra said to the coyote, who had wormed his way underneath his favorite blanket. Only his tail showed. He slapped it against the mattress. "I'm going to the Compostela."

The coyote huffed and burrowed farther underneath the blanket, disappearing.

Petra locked the door behind her and moved carefully down the steps. Night had fallen swiftly, bringing with it a violet sky with pinpricks of stars. In the distance, frogs had begun to chirp. A stiff breeze swept in from the mountains, stirring the new grasses sprouting in the field surrounding the trailer.

Once upon a time, this had been where the first alchemist of Temperance had lived. The town founder, Lascaris, had built a house upon this land. It had burned to nothing and sunk into history. Though Lascaris was long gone, his power was still felt. The Locus had been one of his creations. As were the Hanged Men. Petra wondered if anyone who came here ever escaped his influence.

She set forth on the gravel road toward lights in the distance. The town of Temperance was only a short hike away; she could see the red glow of its single stoplight, always set on flashing red, from here.

On an ordinary day, a spring-night walk might have felt invigorating.

But she felt tired. Tired, angry, and completely ineffectual. She thought about turning around and joining Sig in bed. But it was a Friday night; there was no time like the present to pump the locals for information.

She plodded to the main street in Temperance. Across the street from Bear's Gas 'n Go, the only convenience store in town, sat the Compostela.

Petra shoved the door open and slipped inside, feeling like an eavesdropping shadow. Voices swirled and beer bottles clinked around her. Card games went on around tables scattered across the floor. Cue balls cracked in the back. Petra headed toward the bar.

The bar was hewn of a single, massive tree, set in what was once the apse. The tree had been varnished and lacquered dozens of times, and its glasslike surface reflected tin star lights dangling above. Petra slipped into an empty stool at the far end of the bar, her eyes roving over the patrons. Maybe she could find someone who knew someone. But the best place to start was with the bartender.

He was pouring rum from a cut-glass bottle, silent as a ghost. Even the liquid he poured made no sound. Petra had spoken with him a handful of times, and she realized that she didn't know his name. He seemed the enigmatic sort: a man dressed in black, a good twenty years older than Petra, though his exact age was hard to place. Long blond hair was caught in a ponytail behind his head. It was difficult, in this light, to pick out how much of it was grey.

He finished pouring and drifted down the bar toward Petra. He gazed at her with pale eyes. "Didn't expect to see you here."

"No?"

"You look like death. No offense. But Death comes by here often, and you have that way about you." He poured her a Coke and put a cherry in it, without asking, as if she was a small child who was not allowed to have alcohol.

She chuckled. It was somewhat refreshing to discuss death with someone who had no emotional investment, with someone whose emotional reactions she didn't have to manage. "Well, I may be short-timing it, but there are a few things I want to do before I go."

"Oh? Last time I heard that from a fellow, he robbed two banks before he got caught. Nobody ever found the money, so I guess he took it to the grave with him."

Petra smiled and shook her head. "Bank robbery isn't on my bucket list. But finding my errant husband is. Wondered if you'd heard anything about him."

"Ah. I heard you and Gabriel got hitched." His mouth turned up. "That surprised me. Gabriel didn't seem like the marrying kind. Or any other kind, really."

"There's not much you don't hear."

The bartender shrugged. "People talk in bars. I hear what the walls hear."

Petra stirred the ice in her drink with the straw. Talking to the bartender was like working a riddle; one had to play the game. "Did the walls hear anything about where he might have vanished to?"

The bartender looked down at a glass he cleaned, peered at the bottom of it, as if it were some kind of oracle. "A man like Gabriel plays the long game. Seemed to be committed. I doubt he would have left you if he had anything to say about it."

"That's what I kind of figured. I have the feeling that someone's trying to make it look like he walked away."

"Like he rode off into the sunset?" The bartender flicked his gaze up to the tiny television bolted in a corner of the bar. The local news was playing above, a news reporter sitting before a green-screen image of a man in his sixties. ". . . Norman Ashland, age sixty-eight, was last seen in the vicinity of Witch Creek in Yellowstone National Park. He suffers from early-stage Alzheimer's. If you have seen this man, please contact the Yellowstone National Park Police . . ."

Petra turned her gaze away. Not her problem, though she felt a flash of empathy for the wife he likely left behind, looking for him. "Right. And once I'm gone . . . who will look for him?" Petra swallowed a mouthful of sugary liquid around the lump in her throat. There sure was no chance of getting Gabriel's picture on the news. She was the only person who cared about him enough to miss him.

The bartender glanced back at Petra. "A man like

Gabriel can look after himself, and I'd advise you to let him get out of his own jams. You should go home and prepare yourself for a good death."

"He is not who he once was. And I'm not leaving until I find him." She lifted her chin stubbornly. She reached into her pocket and put the pearl on the bar top with a *click*. It rolled toward the bartender.

He caught it and stared at it. "Where'd you find this?"

"In his truck. I think whoever took him dropped it."

The bartender put it between his hands on the bar top, keeping it from rolling by boxing it in with his thumbs. "You don't want to mess with that. Pearls are bad luck."

"Why? What does it mean?" she demanded.

He rolled the pearl back across the bar to her. "It's a sign. It's a sign that your husband is well and truly lost."

LEV HATED TO say it to her. He really did.

Petra Dee wasn't long for this world. He could see it in her aura, the way it had thinned and paled. In a matter of a few weeks, she'd slip away from her body entirely, leaving behind that worn-out shell that burned hot with fever and black marrow.

He hated the idea of not being able to give her any hope. The dead should pass on, happily, if they could. But she didn't have an easy death in front of her, and chasing after the ghost that was Gabriel Manget would do neither one of them any favors.

"What do you know?" she growled back at him.

"Just a gut feeling," he said. He usually spoke the truth. Usually. That was an understatement he gave her.

"Does Sheriff Owen have anything to do with it?" She pushed again.

"Leave it be. For the good of everyone."

And he moved away, back down the bar, feeling her glare drilling a hole in his back. He didn't turn around until he felt her gaze fall and move away. When he glanced to the door, she was walking through it. It occurred to Lev that he was unlikely to see her again alive.

He sighed. He might see her again, dead. Maybe then she would understand. But she'd be stuck here, then, holding on to a man who wasn't.

But such was the way of things. People moved into life, they moved out of it. Sometimes they lingered on, and sometimes they left. If they were lucky. Getting too involved in other people's problems was never a good idea. He liked his life problem-free. Picking up problems from others were unnecessary attachments, things that caused trouble.

"You gonna go to her funeral?" Wilma perched on a bar stool and watched the woman go.

Lev shook his head, refusing to talk to ghosts in the presence of paying patrons. People depended on a bartender to make decent drinks and exact change. And they tended to like them sane.

"Why not?" Father Caleb sat beside her, resting his face in his palm, his elbow on the bar.

"I dunno. She doesn't seem like the type of gal who'd go for a full-in funeral," Wilma said, squinting at the door.

"Everyone deserves a funeral. A chance to say goodbye."

"Your funeral was quite nice. But you never really did say goodbye, you good-for-nothing chalice-licker." Wilma shot Caleb a dirty look. She'd had the place to herself for only a decade before he moved in.

"I'm needed here," he said quite haughtily.

"And exactly how many souls have you saved among these dumb shit barflies since your expiration date on the earthly plane? I mean, it's not like you're a paragon of effectiveness. They can't even hear you."

"Wilma! Don't swear." Caleb's mouth puckered into an expression that bore a remarkable resemblance to a cat butt.

"Yeah. Thought so." She blew cigarette smoke in his face, in a perfect ring.

She turned to Lev. *"You gonna go to her funeral?"*

He didn't answer, bending down to kick one of the kegs beneath the bar. Almost time to refill . . .

"Uh. Lev?"

Lev's head snapped up. It had been at least a decade since anyone living had uttered his name.

A young man in his late teens or early twenties climbed up onto a bar stool. He was a lanky guy, with short-shorn blond hair, an aquiline nose, and eyes the color of winter. He was wearing a navy-blue wind-breaker.

Lev's eyes narrowed. "Who's asking?"

"My name is Archer. I, uh . . ." He fished in his pocket and pulled out a wrinkled photograph. "Wow. This is awkward. I think you knew my mother. Bridget Harker?"

He pushed the photo across the bar. Lev didn't take it. He squinted at it. There was a dark-haired woman in the photo, wearing a flower-print dress and holding a floppy straw hat on her head.

"She came through here, about twenty years ago. She said she knew you."

Lev touched the corner of the photo, dredged his memory. "Bridget. I remember." He remembered that she had a smile like summer. She had stayed for a week at the end of August one year, like a shimmering heat. She arrived, and then she was gone, blew out of town with a kiss and a laugh.

A low wolf whistle emanated from Wilma. *"Bridget was a nice piece of ass."*

Lev ignored her, but the young man stared at her. "Bridget's my mom."

"Sorry, kid."

Lev's head snapped up. "Who are you talking to?"

The young man hooked a thumb at a bar stool that was now empty. "I, uh, thought there was a woman sitting there." He looked confused and shook his head as if to clear it. "Uh. Anyway. There's not a good way to say this, so . . . I think you might be my dad."

Lev rocked back on his heels. "That's not possible," he said.

The young man winced and glanced around at the busy bar. "I, look, I know that this is outta left field."

Lev was speechless.

The young man nodded to himself. "Yeah. Awkward. My number's on the back of that picture. I'll, uh, come back tomorrow, when you're not busy."

Without waiting for a response, the young man slid off the bar stool and headed out the door.

Father Caleb levitated behind the bar, his glasses round moons in the dim light. *"Nice-seeming kid. Congrats."*

Lev watched Archer leave. There was an unmistakable resemblance, sure. And he and Bridget had been lovers. In ordinary terms, it was possible. A man could definitely have children. A family.

But Lev had never been a man—not a human one, anyway—and this was not possible.

CHAPTER 7

Below

That bartender knew more than he was saying.

Petra lay awake, staring at the ceiling, contemplating how to wring it from him.

Sig snuggled in her armpit on the futon, snoring, with a paw across her belly. The window above the futon was cracked open, letting in a slowly warming spring breeze. It was perfectly silent here, so much more so than the hospital. She should have been able to sleep; she'd even taken one of Maria's sleeping drafts.

But she couldn't. She watched the dim light of night move the stripes from the blinds across the wall and up the ceiling. There was no way that she could think of that would get the information from the bartender without threatening him. Not that she'd ruled that out; she'd just have to figure out how to get the jump on him. She'd never seen him anyplace except the bar, and always with too many people around. Figuring this out would bear further thought, but with her head swirling, it was just one of many concerns.

Another was the spirit world. Her gut churned with the memory of being down there. Of what she'd seen. And she knew Gabe had been underground, but now the Tree of Life had blocked off the door to hell.

Yet, she also knew there was another way to the underworld. A riskier way in. But maybe the only way . . .

After a couple of hours of tossing and turning, she hauled herself out of bed. She took a small handful of ibuprofen and one of Maria's invigorating tonics that smelled of ginseng. She dressed in the dark clothes that were now her new shadow to wrap around her thin, pale frame.

Sig yawned with a squeak and jumped down from the futon. He trotted to her side, claws clicking on the linoleum. He gazed up at her as she fastened her gun belt around her waist. The belt fit much more loosely than it had before. She tightened it to its farthest punch hole, and it still hung around her hip bones. She clipped a flashlight on the back and shrugged into a jacket. She dropped the Locus and her cell phone into the pockets.

"You up for a late night field trip, Sig?"

Sig *harrumphed* and followed her as she locked up and headed out across the gravel parking area to the

Bronco. It was a new moon night—dark and soft and dewy. She wouldn't have much deeper darkness to work in for another month. Who knew if she'd still be vertical then, or drooling into her oatmeal?

Or six feet under for good?

"Carpe noctem," she muttered, repeating a slogan she'd seen on a T-shirt decades ago.

She and Sig piled into the Bronco. She started it up, flipped on the lights, and headed down the road, through town. She cast a dark look at the fully lit Compostela, still haunted by a few late-night denizens.

For another time, she thought.

She turned east, heading to the Rutherford Ranch.

She knew that she was driving, but she didn't remember the trip. She wanted to chalk it up to road hypnotism, to being tired. But she realized that she had made it nearly to the Rutherford Ranch without remembering driving there. To be honest with herself, that spooked her. She bit her tongue, hard, to keep herself awake and focused.

About a mile from the ranch house, she pulled off the main two-lane road into a ditch. She shut off the engine and listened to it ping in the darkness. She wasn't sure that she could run a full mile with Owen chasing her without collapsing, but hopefully she wouldn't have to.

She reached under the seat for a couple of tools to fill her pockets. She popped the door, jumped out, and Sig followed. She locked up and crossed the road. The Bronco's location wasn't very obvious to a casual observer at night. It would be found the next day, though, when the sun rose and drove away the ditch shadows. With any luck, she'd be long gone by then.

If not, she'd get caught by Owen. And if she didn't find Gabe on her own, confronting Owen was the number two item on her list anyway.

In the distance, she could see the ranch house, a modern log chalet perched on the top of a hill. There were no lights on inside—a good sign. Especially because she wasn't heading for the house. Instead, she walked down the hill, keeping to the weeds near the drive. She made for the barn, where the second door to the underworld lay.

The barn was still and silent, surrounded by trucks and farm equipment. It was buttoned up tight, the sliding doors secured with a padlock. But Petra had anticipated that Owen would be stricter about security than Sal—Sal believed himself so invincible he left everything open.

Petra pulled a cable saw from her pocket. It took a few minutes for the diamond-coated cable to chew through the hardened steel of the hasp, especially as she was going a bit slower to reduce the sound. Eventually, the lock broke away, and she pitched it into the field. Perhaps Owen would believe that a field hand simply forgot to lock up and was walking around with it forgotten in a pocket.

Honestly, she didn't really care.

She opened the door just a foot and a half and slipped inside, Sig underfoot and his ears pressed forward. She pulled the door shut and clicked on her flashlight.

Shadows of farm machinery moved under her light beam, around a harvester and a grinder-mixer. She swept the light before her, around bales of hay, tools, and bags of fertilizer. She moved to the back corner of the barn, around the blades of tillers and a rusted tractor.

The back corner was littered with straw and debris. She shoved it aside with her boot, moving her light back and forth.

There. A wooden door in the floor of the barn, exactly as she remembered. She had not been here in many months, but her memory hadn't failed her. This door led to another part of the underworld of the Rutherford Ranch. And likely Owen didn't yet know it was here, or he'd have fortified it as well as he had the opening near the Lunaria.

She pulled the door of the hatch open and shone her light into the tunnel. Dirt formed a steep incline, rolling away into black. That was the problem with this door: it was a one-way ticket. The incline was too steep for her to climb up, even at her healthiest. This spot was like a whirlpool—things went in, but they couldn't get out.

She grimaced into the dark and glanced at Sig.

"You don't have to come."

Sig snorted. He was coming.

She was relieved.

Petra wrapped her arms around him. She put the

flashlight in her teeth and sat on the edge of the entrance. Taking a deep breath, she looked down into the darkness one more time . . . and jumped.

The impact of the landing jarred her body, from her ankles to the crown of her head. She fell on her right hip and skidded, finally resting in soft dirt. She might have chipped a tooth on the flashlight, and she gasped.

Sig squirmed out of her arms. He whined and licked her face.

Petra groaned and pulled the flashlight from her mouth, rubbing her jaw. She tasted the coppery tang of blood. She'd already lost one back tooth in chemo; another was no major loss. She winced and pulled herself to a seated position. She glanced up at the door in the ceiling . . .

. . . but it had banged shut.

"Well, we're here," she muttered to Sig. She shone the light around the tunnel.

The air was cool, the earth still holding some of the touch of winter. She crawled forward on her hands and knees until her back stopped spasming enough for her to climb to her feet.

The last time she'd been here, she'd found her way to the Tree of Life. She was pretty sure that had been as much luck as anything—the tunnels beneath the ranch were vast. And while she'd walked many miles of them before, that had usually been with Gabe. He knew this rabbit warren; she didn't.

Which meant she had only one tool that might lead her through this labyrinth: the Locus.

She fished it out of her pocket and shone her light on it. Not really loving the idea of having to pick at her scab again for blood, she chewed her lip . . . and it came to her. She spat into the device, and blood gracelessly dribbled over her lip into the groove on the compass. She was certain that this was not how high ceremonial magic worked, but it would have to do.

The Locus churned to life. Her spittle-flecked blood slid around the groove and clotted in the western direction.

"Okay," she breathed. "We go west."

She plodded along the dark tunnel. As she remembered, the tunnels weren't uniform. They were narrow in places, with ceilings low enough that she had to stoop and feel the roots of plants comb her hair. In other places, two people could easily walk abreast, and the ceilings seemed to be that of a vaulted cathedral. It seemed organic in many places, as if it was a gap created between sliding faults. In others, the walls were smooth and round as termite tunnels. In more, the roof was held up by rotting pieces of wood, drizzling water. It was both familiar and foreign to Petra. Yes, she had been here before; it just hadn't seemed to be exactly this way. Underfoot were bits of slate that she would surely have remembered. Sharp pieces of sandstone jutted out of walls, as if the tunnels were being closed by small earthquakes. But there had been no significant seismic activity in this area.

Sig rubbed up against her, and she welcomed something wholly familiar.

Petra trailed her fingers around the crisp edges of newly broken sandstone. Gabe had once intimated that his world had the ability to change. She assumed that applied only to the chamber beneath the tree, that the tree roots moved and were able to alter their immediate environment, according to the Lunaria's influence. It would be impossible for the other tunnels to shift without there being some evidence of the movement reflected in the ground above—upheavals, sinkholes . . . or was it? Her rational mind tried to puzzle it out. Were these passages deep enough that small shifts and slips could occur without being obvious on the surface? Or was this, far more likely, a psychological trick meant to discourage intruders? One tunnel branched and melded into the next . . . In the darkness, it felt claustrophobic, and it was hard not to feel a sense of panic sinking in. Petra was reminded of a television show she'd seen about the tunnels surrounding the cave of an ancient sybil—they were designed to create awe, disorientation, and, in the presence of noxious gases, hallucinations.

Maybe that's what this place was. A hallucination.

It occurred to her to strike a match, to test the volatility of the air. But her hand stilled, hovering over her pocket. Too much of her life was bleeding off into hallucinations and the spirit world. It didn't matter, now, how real or unreal this place was, as long as it led her to Gabriel.

She walked on, sweeping her light before her. She took a sharp corner and found herself in a tangle of roots. The twisted shadows bounced off the walls of a chamber, seeming to seethe in that trick of the light. The roots were blackened, curled.

Petra knew instantly where she was: beneath the Lunaria.

But it was much different than the last time she'd been here. Then, the roots had extended into a spacious chamber, where the Hanged Men dangled, like rotting fruit. Despite the smell of decay, the place had exuded life—artificial sunshine had pulsed in the tendrils of the roots, and the tree reacted to intruders, sensing the presence of life other than itself. It had been warm and womb-like, living and still at the same time.

It was nothing like that now. The chamber was a tangle of blackened, rope-like roots, twisted in a frozen moment of writhing agony. The roots pressed up against the ceiling of the chamber, like smoke, as if they'd tried to flee from the fire. More spilled out limply along the floor, where they had begun to decay. The whole of it smelled like bitter smoke.

Tears stung Petra's eyes. The tree had been magnificent in life. In death, it was heartbreaking.

But some part of it still lived, surely. Aboveground, the sapling had sprouted from the blackened earth.

She shone her light up into the chandelier of tangled roots. Some of them were greenish and brown at the uppermost levels, bearing feathery tendrils cradled in structures that look liked eagles' nests. It *did* live.

She squinted up and peered at the area where the door was. New brown roots covered it—that must have happened after the fire. She was right—there had been some desire for the tree to shield itself from outsiders, from further pain. Maybe . . .

Sig growled beside her, a deep vibration against the side of her leg.

She turned, a squeak escaping her lips.

Roots had unwound themselves from the nest-like tangle and reached toward her. Sig barked and snarled. Petra dodged and made a run for the entrance.

But a tendril caught her, snatching up her wrist with speed like a striking snake. She wrenched against it, splintering off green wood, yet another root slipped around her ankle, and she stumbled. Appendages as thick as her arm wrapped around her waist and throat, lifting her from the floor. Above Sig's frantic barking, blood pounded in her ears as her fingers dug into the root curling around her neck.

No good. She felt the blood draining from her head, and she reached for a gun at her waist. Her jacket was bound up in the tree root, and she struggled to get it free. Fingers of roots dug into her ribs, and she gasped.

Her fingers working frantically, she finally got a gun free and fired blind, up and away from Sig. The report was deafening in this small space, and her

ears rang. That's about all the gun did, though—it
didn't deter the tree, its roots continuing to dig into
her throat and ribs. She hissed as they tore open the
flesh of her torso, feeling the heat of blood soaking
through her shirt and down her belt.

The fucking tree . . . maybe it was like the Locus,
craving blood, she dimly thought. *And I served mine
up to it on a silver platter—*

Abruptly, the tree loosened its grip and dropped
her to the ground like a used tissue. Petra clambered
to her feet, clutching a gun and flashlight.

The thick root that had chewed into her ribs was
stained red. The root flicked itself, like a dog that had
gotten into something disgusting, trying to shake off
the red. It clearly wasn't the nourishment it expected.

"Oh," Petra breathed, scowling, as she pressed her
gun arm around her waist to stanch the bleeding.
"Chemo blood doesn't taste good? Maybe it's the arsenic. Or the cancer."

The roots retreated with a rustle and a wooden
groan.

Whatever the tree thought, Petra wasn't sticking
around. Sig barked at her to follow him down another
dark tunnel, away from the suddenly carnivorous tree.

Once she'd fled beyond the reach of the tree, Petra
dropped to one knee. She shone the light at her dam-
aged skin, peeling back her shirt, which was stuck to
it. Not as bad as she thought—the injury was pretty
superficial. It might ideally need a couple of stitches,
but nothing major had been torn. Still, the blood loss

made her vision narrow a bit, and she still wasn't used to this kind of exertion. She pressed her jacket against the worst of it, and the flow slowed.

Sig leaned in over her knee and slurped soothingly at her side.

"Not you, too," she muttered. Everyone wanted her blood.

She climbed to her feet and trudged down the tunnel. She squinted up ahead, and it seemed that there was a bit of light.

Her heart rose in her throat. Perhaps this way led to Gabe.

The passage narrowed, and the ceiling lowered to the point where she had to stoop. She followed it until she wound up on all fours behind Sig, her back scraping against the roof. She had the feeling of crawling into some creature's den that would corner her.

But she focused on that tiny patch of light, that bit of dark that was greyer than the surrounding black.

She wound up on her elbows, prone, crawling forward while her ribs ached. Sig had gone ahead of her, and she had a prime view of the coyote's ass. Here and there, he'd stop to dig, kicking clods of dirt back in her teeth. She had to wriggle and suck in her breath to proceed, and she began to despair—this passage was clearly too small for Gabe to get through. In her emaciated state, *she* barely fit, and there wasn't enough room for even the coyote to stand upright. She couldn't even back up—dirt rained down on the backs of her knees.

This was a mistake.

A cold puddle soaked her knees and elbows. She made a valiant effort to push forward, following the coyote's wiggling ass . . .

. . . and got stuck. Her hips jammed in the passage. She tried to pull herself forward with her fingers and push herself with her toes. No good—she was wedged tight.

"Sig!" she rasped, and the undulating coyote ass before her stopped. A nose and amber eyes turned back. "I'm stuck."

Panic rose in her. Of all the ways she'd contemplated dying lately—in a hospital, at home in a bed, in a firefight with Gabe's abductors—this was the absolute worst. She'd likely die of dehydration, maybe exposure.

Maybe stupidity.

Fuck, fuck, *fuck*. A veil of claustrophobia fell over her.

Sig slapped her in the face with his tail, and she blinked.

"You're right," she said to the coyote. She wasn't going to die here.

She squirmed right and left, turning her hips. Her gun belt slipped. She sucked in her breath and pulled. At the same time, Sig leaned in and grasped her jacket lapel between his teeth and pulled as hard as he could.

The gun belt shifted, then slipped over her hip bones. Petra flopped forward in the mud, face-first in a puddle. She was filthy, and now she was cold. But she was free.

"Good boy, Sig," she breathed.

She wriggled forward, managing to hook the loop of the gun belt around her ankle as she progressed.

The light . . . it was close. She could see bits of it around Sig's backside.

She closed her eyes and lurched forward with the last bit of strength she had.

Panting, she splashed forward, feeling cool air around her face. She lifted herself to a push-up position, up to her wrists in cold water.

She was outdoors. In a culvert. Frogs sang around her, and she saw the blacktop of road just above her. She turned her head, and she could see the hiding place of the Bronco about a quarter-mile down the road.

"Fuck," she said.

Sig sat down beside the puddle and gave a yip in agreement.

CHAPTER 8

Above

What the hell did you do?"

Petra sat in a hospital bed, squinting at the bright fluorescent light. She'd fallen asleep, somehow. She remembered driving to the ER just to get some stitches. Somehow, she'd sprouted a line to an IV bag on her left arm and had grown a calico hospital gown over her chest.

Maria stood over her on one side, arms crossed, glowering. Mike stood on the other, with the same expression. Petra had the same feeling she'd had as a little girl when she'd gotten into trouble with her parents.

"Ugh." She rubbed her face. "I don't remember." She said that for Mike's benefit.

"You don't get to go anywhere until you start

remembering," Mike said. She mentally appended "young lady" to the end of it, in her father's voice.

"Huh. You're not actually my supervisor, Mike."

"Well, Maria and I are apparently your emergency contacts. And the ER won't let you go without someone to take you. So maybe a little less sass, okay?"

She made a face. She doubted that. "Look. I just came in for a couple of stitches." She lifted up the edge of her hospital gown to show a handful of neat black stitches tracking across her midsection. The skin was puckered and blue where it was held together. "No big deal."

"They said you were dehydrated," Maria said. "Your electrolytes are shot, and your white cell count is low enough that they're really worried about infection."

"Yes—it's called having cancer, Maria."

Her friend glared at her.

"I'm sorry. Look, I promise to drink some water. They can give me some antibiotics, and I can go." Petra leaned back to search for the nurse call button.

"What were you doing?" Mike demanded.

"I was looking for Gabe, okay?" she spat. She was aware that she sounded like a teenage girl. What the hell.

"God, Petra. Look at yourself. You can't go it alone right now, all right?"

"All right," she said, blowing out her breath. "Will you sign me out?"

Maria and Mike traded glances. "Okay. But no more wandering around without supervision, okay?"

"Fine. Can I go home now?"

"We'll talk about it."

Eventually, the doctor on rounds came by and agreed to let Petra go. Petra went through the motions mostly out of politeness. She knew that they couldn't keep her here against her will. But she didn't look forward to yanking out her own IV and doing a dramatic stomp. Her shirt had been ruined. Her black jacket might be salvageable after a trip through the washer. They were both rolled up in a paper bag for her. A nurse had given Petra an additional hospital gown, and she layered it over her existing one, in the reverse direction for modesty.

Petra returned with Mike to the Bronco, while Maria cranked up the ignition on her Explorer. Petra climbed up into the passenger seat of the Bronco and closed her eyes. She was tired, even if she didn't want to admit it.

A cold nose pressed against her neck, and she reached up to pet Sig.

Mike started the engine. "I think you should go see your dad," he said quietly.

Petra opened one eye. She glanced at her reflection in the side mirror. She looked like hell. "I will," she said.

"You haven't seen him since you started chemo."

"Yeah. Well." She turned away. "I've called. A lot." And she had. She'd called her father nearly every day at the hospital. They were both stuck in institutions with nothing much to do except bitch about the food and reminisce about times past. She privately thought it was a good thing he was in a nursing home; if he wasn't, she was certain he would have been hovering over her bedside, chattering at her when she craved nothing more than silence. She knew she needed to let her mother know, too . . . but it seemed just too big a thing to do right now. Like it was admitting defeat.

"That's not the same."

"I will," she said, putting him off. She didn't want her father to see her this way. Who would want that?

She leaned back and closed her eyes. Parents expected their child to outlive them. Her dad wasn't taking this well. And she honestly didn't have the emotional bandwidth to deal with his feelings bombs right now.

But she knew she'd have to. To say goodbye, just once. Maybe that would be enough.

FATHERHOOD WAS NOT anything Lev had ever contemplated. Not seriously.

But he was contemplating it now, in the cold light of morning.

He was washing down the bar in the silence of midmorning. He enjoyed working at this time of day more than any other. Light poured in from the stained-glass windows, making bright patterns on the floors. In warm weather, he'd prop open the front and back doors, letting a cross breeze in to sweep away the smell of cigarette smoke and spilled beer.

He'd swept the floors earlier, and a bundle of sage was burning in an ashtray. A bucket of lavender floor wash was steeping in the corner. These were his rituals; the clearing out of the old and stale things that could cling to a building. Lev knew about these things, perhaps more than he knew anything else.

"You'd make a great dad," Wilma said. Her cigarette smoke snaked over the lavender and sage. *"I'm not shitting you. You'd be good at it. Better than my fucking shitheel father, anyway. Obviously."*

"Wilma. The swearing." Father Caleb groaned.

Wilma shrugged. *"Sorry that I offend your tender fucking ears, Father. But I was here first. My house, my rules."*

Caleb began, *"It's still God's house . . ."*

"Not anymore," Lev growled. "It's mine."

"Well, regardless of who owns the property, you'd best be stepping up to fatherhood now."

Father Caleb was looking at Lev with as much sternness as his round face could muster, as if he could force Lev into saying Hail Marys by sheer force of will.

"I don't even know for sure he is my son," Lev said.

"He looks like you. And he saw Wilma."

Wilma smiled and puckered up her face in a kiss. *"That's because my irresistibility extends beyond the ether."*

"Guys. Leave it alone, okay? I don't know what he's doing here, and I just need to think."

Both ghosts appeared to sulk. Wilma crossed her arms and Father Caleb's frown deepened into his jowls. Lev continued scrubbing the bar, ignoring them, until the ghosts moved away into the back, cackling at each other like magpies.

A thin shadow appeared at the door. "Lev?"

He looked up. Today, he'd contemplated keeping the door locked. But the young man had said he'd come back. Lev had seen in him much of the same quiet determination Lev had at that age; he was pretty sure that if he locked the door, the fellow would keep coming back anyway.

The young man, Archer, entered the bar.

"Could you close the door behind you?" Lev asked. If they were to talk, what Lev had to say wasn't meant for human ears.

The young man obeyed, then walked to the bar, his hands in his pockets and looking up at the windows. "This is some place. How long have you been here?"

"A very long time." Lev figured that he'd probably best ease into this. There was no point in burdening him with too much information, particularly if Lev determined that Archer was not his son.

Archer climbed onto a bar stool. He smelled a bit like leaf mold, as if he'd been camping. His boots left a fine crust of mud on the floor, but Lev didn't say anything. Instead, he poured him a ginger ale.

Archer smiled and cupped the glass between his hands. "Ginger ale. My favorite. How did you know?"

"It's a gift. I've been bartending for a very long time."

"I wasn't sure if you would still be here," Archer

admitted. "It doesn't seem like people really stay in the same place for very long. I'm glad you are."

Lev nodded. "What makes you think . . ." He tried again. "What did Bridget say?"

"About my father? She said that she'd met a man, here, in Temperance. You," he amended, twiddling this thumbs against the glass. "She said she'd spent the summer here, before leaving for graduate school in California in the fall."

Lev's brow wrinkled, plumbing the depths of his memory. "Art? Art history?"

"Yeah. She was a painter."

"She was quite good."

"Yeah. She painted everything she saw. There was even a portrait of you that she did from memory, I guess. It hung in my bedroom. She said . . . she wanted me to know that my dad was watching over me."

"I didn't know she had a child."

"She said she asked you to come with her, when she went to grad school. She said . . . you were rooted in place, somehow. That that's just the way you were. That it was nobody's fault. She said . . . some people are rocks, and some are wind. She said you were a rock."

Lev stifled a snort. That sounded like Bridget.

"She was never angry with you. Not a bit. I think she always loved you, and that you not being there with us was just . . . a fact of life. Nothing to resent or rail against, you know?"

"And you? Were you angry?"

Archer shook his head. "Why would I be? I mean, without you, I wouldn't be here, right?"

Lev's guts softened a touch. The young man had a good soul. So did his mother, never having poisoned him against Lev. This was not a disaster.

"Is your mom doing well?"

"Yeah. She teaches art at a high school now, and has her paintings in shows every so often. She really likes what she does. I mean, we moved around a lot, but I got to see a lot of cool places. Albuquerque, Vashon Island, Denver. I think she always liked it best where there was a cool arts community, you know?"

"What made her tell you now . . . where I was?" Lev still had a tickle of skepticism in his mind. "And what made you start looking?"

Archer stared into his drink. That was the great thing about bars—they gave people scrying mirrors to peer into, in their glasses. It was difficult to lie under the influence of those liquid oracles. "Weird stuff started happening."

"Weird like . . . how?"

Archer rubbed his temple. "Look. I'm not crazy, okay?"

"Never said you were."

"I started hearing voices a couple years ago." Archer looked away. "I looked it up on the internet. I guess it's a classic sign of schizophrenia. But it's not like that. It's not. I'm not talking to myself . . . it's other people."

Lev waited for him to continue, but his knuckles were white behind the bar.

"I hid it for a long time, but . . . my mom heard me talking to this old man that lived in our apartment. Sometimes I even saw him. She took me to a shrink. I got doped up on all kinds of meds . . . but I still heard them. The voices. The—"

"—ghosts," Lev finished for him. "You kept hearing the ghosts that no one else could hear."

"Yeah." The young man's face relaxed in relief. "Exactly. They're everywhere . . . on the street, in my apartment, at school . . . most of the time, they go away after a few days."

Lev nodded. "Human souls that are ready to progress to the next level leave Earth after three days. Unless there's a problem and they get held back. Then, they can become hauntings, plugged into the energy of people or places. They have to be sent on, pulled out of the fabric of reality . . . kind of like a nettle on your jacket." He reached out to Archer's coat, pulled out a nettle, and cast it out on the floor.

"So you believe me?"

"I do."

"Can . . . can you hear them, too?"

"I can." Lev took a deep breath. There was no running away from this. Archer was his son. "But there are some things you need to know."

He pulled a bottle out from beneath the bar, pouring himself a glass of vodka. It tasted like winter, bright and clear. He never drank on the clock, but this was beyond such mundane concerns.

"You can control it," he began. "You can shut them up . . . shut them out." He decided to take the easiest road first. Ease the young man into the strangeness he'd inherited.

"Show me," Archer demanded. "Please."

Lev took a breath and dropped his shoulders. He shut his eyes and gestured for the young man to do the same.

"What do you hear?" he asked.

"I hear . . . tapping. Whispers. Singing. Faint. Like . . . Ick."

Lev heard Wilma giggle. He opened one eye. Wilma was trying to kiss the young man on the cheek, while Father Caleb was pulling her back. Archer still had his eyes closed, but he was rubbing the side of his face.

Lev pointed with two fingers at the ghosts, then upstairs to the attic. Wilma rolled her eyes, and Caleb stuck his lower lip out. But they vanished.

Lev cleared his throat. "Good. Those are the ghosts of the Compostela. There are a couple still here, as this place is very old."

Wilma giggled from upstairs and there was a thump.

"For Christ's sake, woman! Let them talk."

Lev continued. "The ones still here are mostly harmless. Think of them like squirrels in the attic."

"Okay. Squirrels. Making noises."

"Good. Take a deep breath and drop your awareness into your chest. Are you there?"

"I think so."

"It's dark and quiet here. You don't have to perceive
everything through your head, your ears and your
eyes. Now imagine that . . . you are surrounded in a
suit of armor made of lead. And there's a helmet for
that armor. It's impermeable. Nothing gets through it
unless you allow it. It feels heavy, and still. And safe.
A vault."

He heard Archer's breath echoing shallowly, then
it slowed, softened.

"Do you still hear them?"

"No . . . not nearly as loud as before. They're very
distant."

"Good. It will get better, but that will come with
practice. You can open your eyes." Lev looked at the
young man. "After practice, you won't be able to hear
them at all. Or see them. Or even smell them."

"Wow." The young man nodded. "I mean, I tried
meditation and things . . . but all that stuff seemed
to really focus on opening up my chakras and stuff.
And thinking about clouds."

Lev snorted. "The last thing you need is to open
up your chakras. Or whatever they call your ethereal
body these days." He dug into his pocket for a jagged
black stone. "Here." He extended a piece of obsidian
to his son in his open palm. *His son*. It still felt odd to
contemplate.

Archer took it. "What is it?"

"Obsidian. To help you visualize it, at least until it becomes second nature."

"Will you teach me?" Archer's hand closed around the sharp stone.

"I have to," Lev said quietly. "Or else you'll be bat-shit by the time you're thirty."

The young man looked crestfallen.

"And I want to," Lev amended. "It's just . . . I hadn't expected this to happen. I didn't think I could have children." That was true. An over-simplification, but true.

Archer seemed to relax a bit at that admission. "I know that you didn't know."

Lev stared at his reflection in the bar top. "And there's a whole lot that you don't know. That you may not want to. You'll have to decide how much you want to know . . . how far down the rabbit hole you want to go. I can teach you some tricks about how to shut up the dead, and you can lead a pretty normal life."

Archer looked him square in the eye. His eyes were like Lev's, only with a dark rim of grey around the irises, like Bridget's. "I want to know it. I want to know it all. Like . . . when you said that the ghosts could be gotten rid of"—he glanced down at where the nettle had been plucked from his shoulder—"why don't you kick them out of here, go all *Ghostbusters* on that shit?"

"Because these ghosts mean no one any harm. They're on their own trajectory toward the light, in their own time. It's not worth wasting the magic it would take to speed that up." He gazed upstairs, at the attic. He knew they were listening. One of them huffed.

The pair of them materialized, sitting on a rafter in the open part of the ceiling, like birds. Wilma held her finger to her lips, as if she was promising to be quiet.

"Magic? There's magic? What about magic?" Archer was unaware of them.

"In time. For now . . ." Lev came out from behind the bar and pulled up a stool. "Tell me about your life."

The young man began to speak, haltingly at first, then more rapidly. He spoke of mundane things, of school and his childhood. He had a dog named Sydney growing up. He talked about Christmas trees and seeing his grandparents on the East Coast and learning to play guitar. He talked about his love of the outdoors and how he thought he would want to go to school to be a park ranger. He'd broken up with his first girlfriend just a few months ago, without acrimony, since she was going to college in Europe. He hoped they could still stay friends. He had just learned to drive a stick shift, and was kind of curious about restoring classic cars. There was a garage down the street from his mom's place that did that, and he was thinking about applying for a summer job there, taking a gap year.

They talked until the sun moved from the stained glass and the light grew dim.

Lev listened to him and not the ghosts in the rafters, and it was perhaps the best conversation he'd
had in twenty years.

No ONE REALLY wanted to see their father in the
nursing home.

It wasn't to say that Petra wasn't used to it. In the
time she'd moved to Temperance and found her father, she'd gone weekly to see him. He had his good
days and his bad days. On his good days, he was very
much like the man she remembered from her early
childhood: quick, fun, with an easy laugh and still
trying to pull quarters from behind her ears. He liked
to play chess and checkers and make fun of daytime
television. On his bad days, though, he was a stranger:
a raving alchemist, lost in his own delusions. He'd go
wandering somewhere in his own head or the spirit
world, and forget to come back for dinner. He'd mut-
ter about lead and mercury and bitch about where
he'd left his crucible, which more often than not
wound up just being a foam cup on his bedside full
of green peas that he'd left there to rot.

She hadn't seen her father in weeks. Mike had
been right; she needed to see him. She just didn't
know which father she'd get today. More than anything, she hoped that it was the father she remembered from her childhood. She wasn't sure she could
deal with Alchemist Dad in her current state.

She had let Maria fuss over her, letting the other

woman dress her again: dark leggings, tall boots, and a tunic. Thankfully, the tunic was soft on her seeping stitches. She'd even let Maria fluff a bit of rouge on her face, to make her look a bit more lifelike. Petra couldn't care less for artifice at this time, but she admitted that she didn't want her father to worry any more than he had to. And he was going to.

Like Maria was. Maria had driven her to the nursing home. "You don't get to run," she said.

Petra rolled her eyes.

"I'll wait in the lobby," Maria said.

Petra waited until Maria's skirts had swished around the corner. She moved down the hall and paused before her father's door. She knocked, a soft, reluctant rap.

Her father was sitting in his wheelchair, working what looked like a child's cardboard puzzle. Her heart sank. She wouldn't be getting her favorite father today.

But he looked up at the door, squinted at her.

"I can almost see through you," he said.

She came to him and bent to give him a hug, mindful to keep her sore side out of his reach. She sat in the visitor chair, opposite him.

"How are you doing, Dad?"

Her father's fingers stilled on the puzzle pieces. He lifted one liver-spotted hand and pointed at her. "You look like hell."

"Yeah. I know, Dad. I stopped the chemo. I'm just gonna . . . wait." There. That sounded softer, somehow.

"No." He almost lurched out of his chair, and she rushed to catch him. "You can't do that."

She poured his liver-spotted hide back into his chair and tucked his blanket around his spindly legs. "Dad. It's okay."

"No, it's not." His lower lip quivered. "You have to fight."

"I'm fighting another fight," she said, grasping at straws. "I'm looking for Gabe. Have you seen him . . . in the spirit world?"

His eyes were glazed. Whether it was from dementia or drugs, she couldn't tell. "There are too many eagles out there."

"Where have you seen the eagle?" she demanded.

He made a dismissive gesture. "Flying around light bulbs like moths. They keep smacking themselves to pieces, burning themselves. Don't concern yourself with birds."

She reached out to take his hand. "Dad. Where are the birds?"

Gabe had told her that the eagle was a symbol of renewal, of released spirit. He'd now taken that shape in the spirit world. She suspected that he had evolved beyond the raven, was moving into another form beyond her reach. Now, she wasn't so certain.

He shifted away from her. "Leave the birds alone. Go back to the hospital." His jaw was set, and he would say no more.

She sat with him for an hour, in stubborn silence.

At the end of visiting hours, she stood and kissed him on his balding forehead.

"I love you, Dad. Bye."

But he would not say goodbye to her, just stared at her with palpable fury as she left. She felt his gaze heavy on her back.

But she was past expectation, past his anger.

She met Maria in the lobby. Her friend was flipping through a six-month-old magazine on sailboats.

"Did it go okay?" she asked, brow creasing.

"No. But that's all right."

She had the sneaking feeling that things were never going to be okay, that she'd never get closure, that she'd step off this mortal coil like a ball of loose yarn and no anchor, just rolling off the table and bouncing to the dark floor beyond.

She was losing.

CHAPTER 9

The Shallows

The feel of sun on her face was glorious.

Muirenn drifted in the shallows among the cattails, letting the sun warm her speckled face. She noticed that it had been driving some of the green tint from her skin, and it was pinking a bit underneath. Muirenn dimly recalled what it was like to have a sunburn. Judging by the position of the sun, she guessed that it was months past the spring equinox now, likely late June. Her fingers twisted in the reeds, stroking the long fronds. It had been such a long time since she'd been near anything that really lived, beyond the unlucky fish that had wandered in her domain.

She was truly sick of eating fish. She'd had 150 years of eating those pale, eel-like creatures that meandered into her dark current. As she reveled in the sun, she licked pollen that was just beginning to form on the cattails and scooped bits of algae around the rocks. She caught a frog and devoured it in two bites, savoring the twitching as it came down her throat. It tasted like sun and life. She hadn't realized how malnourished she'd been, just lurking in the dark, trying to survive on cold water and frightened fish. She'd grown weak. Her fingers traced the spaces between her ribs, lingered over her plumping belly. She wanted to eat everything she saw, but she had to be careful not to be seen. Some things, like frogs and cattails and grass, were the same as she remembered. The rest of the world had moved forward without her, and she knew little about it. What place might she have in it? She didn't know yet. All she knew was that she had to gather her strength. Eat. Think. Digest. Then act.

She ventured farther downstream than she had before. Meadows surrounded the creek, as the water deepened. Elk and bison dotted the fields. At least that was the same. But strange things flew overhead. She watched them, how their wings didn't move. They left behind white streaks of clouds, like chalk on the deep blue sky.

Something shiny caught her attention downstream: a glint, like a mirror. She slid below the water and approached it from below, allowing the shape to blot out the sun. A boat. Not like the wooden boats she recalled from her time as a woman, but one made of metal. She pressed her hand to its cool hull. She felt vibration in it, the scrape of movement. Something was in it.

Food. Food was in it.

She floated in the water below the boat, listening with her palms pressed against its cool skin. Her hands followed the shuffle of movement, the scraping of a box, muttering. There was one person in this boat, she decided. That was an acceptable risk.

She waited until the person above kicked around a bit and cast a fishing line into the water. She gazed dispassionately at the hook and shiny lure falling past her shoulder. She had no more interest in fish. She wanted to eat something warm-blooded that would warm her own blood and belly.

The man above—she was convinced by the slosh of water against the small boat that it had to be a man—stretched out. The boat creaked and shifted, and she had a sense of the weight redistributing. She waited until he was still. It may have taken minutes, or an hour. She'd lost track of the ability to tell time well, deprived by the sun and stars for as long as she had been.

She slowly pushed water from her lungs and pulled herself to the surface. She peered over the prow of the boat.

She was right: a man lay in the boat, a hat pressed over his face to protect him from the sun. His hands were clasped over his belly, and he snored softly against the brim of the hat, gently moving the edge of it. He was a middle-aged man, a little soft around the gut, but the muscles of his arms were likely well-marbled. They were covered with symbols and letters, like drawings on paper. She squinted at them, trying to decide if these decorations meant that the man wasn't good to eat, if the ink was permanent and had seeped into his flesh. She remembered that she once had eaten a trout that was sick. She'd had nothing else to eat and had risked it. The fish had made her vomit for days, until she was certain she would die. From that time on, she vowed that she would rather starve than eat poison.

While she was contemplating the man's edibility, he snorted against the hat, waking himself up. He shifted to adjust the hat.

"Oh, shit!" he exclaimed, spying Muirenn. He flopped against the far side of the boat, rocking it and splashing.

Instinct kicked in. Muirenn lunged for him, grasping his shirt. He tried to beat her back, and he was strong. He'd dragged Muirenn half into the boat, swinging one arm like a windmill and bellowing. Blows landed against Muirenn's side and face. It hurt, but it also made her feel alive. A smile crept over her face as she took everything in. It didn't take long before she knew what she had to do.

Air was his element. So she leaned sharply back, capsizing the small rowboat. She and the man spilled into the water. He made to swim away, flailing in the clumsy way that people did. She let him for a little bit . . . just because.

Then Muirenn slithered to the bottom of the creek, came up from beneath him, and grabbed his boot. He struggled against the anchor, but that only made things easier as she pulled him down. Muirenn guessed that he might be just a bit stronger than her in the air, but even then, not by much. Besides, she was growing stronger with good nourishment, and in the water, he didn't stand a chance.

His fingers could just reach into the air and stirred it, but his head was beneath the waterline. He shouted, thrashing and spewing bubbles. Muirenn held his boot close to her chest, cradling it as if she were a still stone.

Eventually, he convulsed, and stopped. Muirenn waited until he was well and truly still, though. She shook him a couple of times to test if he were playing opossum, but his arms just floated above him, limp and lifeless.

Grinning wildly now, she pulled him down to the bottom. She began to take him apart. The flesh separated easily, bones popping out. Through the red haze, she could see that most of the flesh was pink and healthy-looking. It smelled fresh, too. She tasted a bit of rib meat, and it was savory and soft with fat. It was good, and she didn't think it would make her sick.

But the arms . . . she wasn't sure of those. Too big a risk. She ripped them off and thought of casting them away. Perhaps someone would find them and come looking for her. She grimaced a bit at that.

She hunted around, waiting for the water to rinse the body clean. She found a heavy rock in the middle of the creek, at least forty pounds. She jammed the ink-poisoned arms underneath the rock. A snapping turtle ambled forward, his interest piqued. He began to nibble on a finger, severing the digit neatly. A plump trout flashed by and took a bite of shredded flesh.

Muirenn contemplated the turtle. The turtle might be delicious, but it would be a waste of energy to clean the meat out of that shell. As for the trout . . . she hadn't been kidding: she'd had more than enough of fish.

She let the scavengers be and grasped the body of the man by an exposed collarbone. She towed him back upstream, going slowly and carefully. Even waterlogged, the body still tried to float, and she wanted to attract no more attention than the trout and the turtle.

She hauled it back, miles, to the broken gate at the Rutherford Ranch. She slipped into those cold, dark waters. This food would last a long time here, in the chill.

Swimming until she found the formation of rocks that she'd used as her pathetic pantry over the years, Muirenn pushed a stone aside. The remains of two broken trout were there, and she shoved them to the back. Humming to herself, she tried to jam the body into the little cave. She had to do some creative folding—and break the body at the knees—but she was able to accomplish it. As a treat, she took a foot and chewed the sinew away from the toes. The nails were cartilaginous junk that she spat out; she reminded herself that she no longer had to eat offal.

A ripple formed in the water above her, a splash and then a plunk.

Muirenn put the foot back in the pantry. Still chewing, she slipped up to the surface to see.

Owen stood on the bank, casting pebbles into the water. One skipped past her, and she flinched.

"Oh. Sorry," he said. "I don't know how else to . . . summon you."

Muirenn swallowed her food and swam to the bank. "Is all well in your kingdom?"

She noticed that he stood farther back from the water than usual, well out of her reach. His posture was wary.

"I spoke to Gabriel about you."

Muirenn nodded. "I expected that you would. A wise king would always collect information from many sources."

"He said you nearly killed Lascaris. That you betrayed him. That you were once human, and that he changed you to . . . what you are now."

"That is true," she said. "I hunted Lascaris down and had almost killed him. I had been his confidante, a fellow sorcerer. I learned many of his secrets."

Owen was a skeptical man. She knew that in order to gain his trust, what she told him would have to be very close to the truth.

"Like what?"

His avarice might outstrip his skepticism. She stirred her fingers in the silt beneath her and pulled up a pearl. "I learned how to transmute a great many elements. How to turn sand and water and moonlight into pearls. You have seen this."

"True. But why try to kill him?"

"Lascaris had crossed a line. When I met him, he was conjuring gold from rocks, supporting the economy of Temperance. He was a man who loved luxury, who imported fine silks, perfumes, and beautiful works of art." She made a self-deprecating shrug. "I was guilty of shallowness. I let myself be seduced by the beautiful things he gave me. I was the most finely dressed woman for hundreds of miles. I ate with real silverware from bone china plates. As a poor woman who had once been in an unhappy marriage in Ireland, I felt like a queen. Unlike the husband I fled, Lascaris seemed to have the power and wealth to protect me."

"You were seduced by pretty things and not by the power?"

"The power, too. He had a fine laboratory, and created many innovative things in his glass apparatuses and crucibles. I saw him crush diamonds in his hands, create fire that never needed fuel. If he had the proper influence, Lascaris was a man who could have changed the world for the better.

"But Lascaris had a cruel streak. He thought his power was license to do what he pleased. He began to experiment on humans, collecting people who would not be missed . . . prostitutes, itinerant workers. He would offer bounties for healthy men and women. Even children. What he would do to them . . ." She closed her eyes. "Most did not survive."

"And this offended you? Gabriel tells me you sang at his . . . uh, funeral."

"I sang. I was powerless to stop it. I sang him a lullaby. I sang for all the Hanged Men. It was the only small kindness I could offer them. That distraction, as Lascaris strung them up in the Tree of Life and broke their necks." She lifted her chin. "You do not understand Lascaris's power.

"I watched. I waited. I waited for six full moons, to gather the power to challenge him. I laid a trap, tried to separate him from his alchemical tools. But I failed to realize that he was beyond the need for tools to do the alchemical work. He fled. I chased him for three days. I chased him around Heart Lake, and he figured out how to walk on water. I almost had him, nearly ran him under the hooves of my horse at Witch Creek . . . but he got the better of me. He drowned me." She lifted her fingers to her gills. "And I became his experiment, like all the others. I awoke in a glass tank in his basement. Like a fish. I was bloody and beaten, bits of fish parts sewn onto my body. My legs had been ripped away. He broke all the teeth from my mouth, replaced them with the teeth of . . . of a shark." Her fingers pressed her mouth.

"He didn't feed me. For his own enjoyment, he made me eat what remained of my legs."

Owen rocked back on his heels. "Jesus. I'm sorry."

She looked up at him. "He became bored of me. He fed me bits and pieces of his enemies, when he remembered. He eventually gave me over to the Hanged Men. He told them to lock me away in case he thought of any better use for me. Gabriel and the Hanged Men built this prison for me." She gestured to the roof of the cave. "They chained me up and left me. Never offered me a scrap of food. They left me to starve." She sank up to her nose in the water.

"I'm sorry," Owen said again. She had struck a chord of sympathy in him. She could see it in the way his eyes dilated. "What can I do? Can I bring you anything . . . like, uh, steak? Something?"

"You have given me freedom."

"But . . . can I bring you something? I have no idea what you need, or . . ."

"Yes," she said, gesturing him nearer. "There is one small thing that you can do for me. And I will serve you well for it."

Owen leaned close to the water to listen.

"You aren't allowed to be alone. Not anymore. We can't trust you not to do colossally stupid shit."

Maria paced behind Petra in her kitchen. Petra sat on the couch like a chastened child. Sig had stretched out in her lap, and Pearl was purring behind her neck, on the back of the couch. Nine sat on the floor before Petra, watching Maria and Petra argue, still as a stone.

Petra idly wondered if this had been her response to the inevitable turf wars in the wolf pack—to sit and wait for the drama to shake out before wading through the shitty aftermath.

"What were you thinking . . . skulking around Owen's ranch? You were lucky that all that you encountered was a tree."

"It's not like there's a whole lot left for me to lose," Petra said quietly. Her side ached from the stitches, and she really wanted to ask Maria for a soothing cup of chamomile tea, but she'd be damned if she'd ask in the middle of an argument.

"And there could have been a whole lot less!"

Fair enough.

Maria continued, softer now. "We can help you . . . but you can't just go running off half-cocked like that. You can't help him if you get yourself killed."

At this, though, Petra threw up her hands. "I've done everything else! I've gone through all the proper channels. I've filed missing persons reports. I've asked Mike to run down any leads. I've asked everyone around town if they've seen him. You've asked folks on the reservation to look for him. I am out of legit ideas and almost out of time. So crazy is all I have left."

Maria leaned over the back of the couch, on her elbows. "You need to give yourself the gift of a good death. You need to be ready to go . . ." She looked away, blinking away tears.

Everyone kept saying that, this thing about a "good death." Petra had no idea what it really meant.

Did it just mean stopping, letting death catch up with her? And what about Gabe? What did he deserve? But it hurt so much to see how Maria was taking all this. She reached up to give her friend a half hug and sniffed. "I know. I just . . ."

And then they were bawling like little girls. Nine crawled up and pressed her cheek against Petra's knees. Pearl's purring against the back of Petra's neck intensified, and Sig burrowed farther into her side.

Surrounded by so much love, it was hard not to at least *imagine* what a "good death" would be like.

She just wasn't ready for that quite yet.

After the sobbing subsided, Nine said, "Don't worry. I will stay with her. I promise."

The young woman sat upright and alert at Petra's feet, chewing at a hangnail on her right thumb.

"You're going to be my guard?" Petra said.

Nine nodded solemnly. "I've been a guard dog before. I can do it."

"Okay," Petra agreed. "I won't go out of Nine's sight. Unless it's to go to the bathroom. I can go pee by myself, right?"

Maria was mollified. "Okay."

She was appeased enough to make chamomile tea and peanut butter sandwiches, without asking. Petra devoured a sandwich and downed two cups of tea.

"About that good death thing . . ." Maria began. "You should call your mother."

Petra groaned inwardly. Definitely not what she imagined. "You know, this good death business is a lot of really painful bullshit." And she was back to not entirely buying into the concept of a good death. It was one thing to be with the people you loved and who loved you back. But a lot of it sounded like varying degrees of shitty.

Nine poked at the tea bag in her cup. "There are two kinds of wolves. Death sorts them out. There's the kind of wolf, when dying, who wants to be surrounded and soothed by the rest of the pack, who wants to feel their warmth around them. And then there's the kind of wolf who walks out of the den to die on her own. I think you're the latter."

Petra made a face. "You mean that crawling off into my cave is not an option?"

"No," Maria confirmed. "But once you get through the obligations, you can go soak in a bubble bath."

She went out on Maria's porch to get some privacy, making a point to leave the keys to the truck behind on the kitchen counter, just so that Maria didn't think she'd take off. She punched the last contact number she had for her mother into her cell phone. Last time she'd talked to her, her mother had been in Turkey on an archaeological dig.

She waited for her cell phone to make a connection. It seemed to take forever, but the phone didn't click over to voice mail. Finally, a sleepy female voice answered.

"Hello?"

"Hey. Mom. It's Petra."

"It's the middle of the night. What . . . um. Let me find my glasses. Okay."

"Sorry." Petra winced. "Where are you?"

"Malangangerr."

"Australia?"

"Yes! Found some ax heads that are really interesting . . ." Her mom went on for a few minutes, obviously forgetting she'd just been woken up in the wee hours. Her mother had become an amateur archaeologist when Petra had gone to college. When Petra had left home, it had been as if her mother had been a balloon with her strings cut suddenly. She had sold their house and lived out of a suitcase for the next fifteen years.

"So how's it going with you?" her mom finally asked. Petra knew that her mom was a little sore about not being invited to her wedding. She thought they were past it. Her mom had sent her a lovely Turkish wooden bowl as a wedding present when she'd found out. But maybe not.

"Well . . . I didn't really want to tell you, because I thought I'd, uh, get over it. But I have leukemia."

There was a silence. Then, "Oh, honey."

"Yeah. It's not going really well. I just wanted to call and . . . well. Say it, I guess."

"Why didn't you tell me before? How long have you known?

"Um . . . months."

"Honey!"

"I know. I guess I thought that treatment would be successful."

"What are you doing? Chemo? Surgery?" Questions tumbled out, one after the other. Petra sat down on Maria's porch swing and fielded them as best she could. No surgery. Too far along. Chemo and radiation were possibilities. She'd had enough chemo.

"Well, it'll get better. Everyone says it makes them sick, but—"

"I quit it, Mom. My numbers weren't getting any better, and the side effects were miserable."

"You have to go back in and do it." The brittle edge of control was crackling all over her mom's voice. Petra's mom freaked when stuff happened that she couldn't control. Or strangle. Which played no small part in why her marriage to Petra's father failed. Petra's dad needed a lot of strangling, and he just up and vanished one day. Petra had spent no small amount of time contemplating the correlation between those two things. Her parents had been equally difficult, just in different ways. Some days, she felt a pang of sympathy for her father for getting a wild hair up his ass to pursue an alchemical quest.

This was one of those days.

"No. I'm not going back to that, Mom. I'm just . . . making peace with things."

"That's frankly ridiculous. Let me talk to your husband."

"Gabe's not here."

"What do you mean, 'not here'?"

Petra rubbed her eyebrow. "Something happened to him. He's disappeared."

"What! Just like your good-for-nothing father." Petra heard huffing on the other end, and pictured her mother's hands knotting together, as if they could choke the life out of him.

"No. It's not like that." Petra held her head in her hand. "He was kidnapped."

"Kidnapped? What the hell was he involved in? Drugs? Guns? You had an uncle who did gunrunning for the IRA in the 1980s. Was it like that?"

"No drugs, Mom. No guns. It's complicated."

"So you're all by yourself?"

"No. I have people taking care of me. I just . . ." *I just wanted to have a human conversation with you. To have a connection and feel acceptance.*

"I'm heading back," her mother decided. "I can get to Queensland in maybe a week and get the next flight to the US from Brisbane."

"No. Mom. No."

"You need someone to talk some sense into you. You're not thinking right. Cancer does that to your brain. Remember your cousin Sandy with breast cancer? She got so out of her mind on her meds that she was walking the dog naked at noon."

"Mom. I have that covered. I just want to talk with you right now, okay?"

Her mom fell silent. That never happened.

"Okay," she said. "What would you like to talk about?"

Petra looked up at the sky. "Do you remember when I was seven and you got me that giant doll-house from that garage sale? That was the best doll-house ever." It had been a 1970s-vintage structure of plastic and cardboard with orange plastic columns and psychedelic polka-dotted plastic inflatable furniture. Even then, her mother had been excavating in flea markets and garage sales. There hadn't been a lot of money then, but her mom always made it work. She could conjure treasure from dust.

"Yes. It was, wasn't it? You put Wonder Woman up on the balcony and told Ken that he wasn't allowed in. Buck Rogers was allowed, though."

"Yeah. I was thinking about that the other day. I never saw another one like it."

"Neither did I. I think it was just meant to be yours."

They chatted for a while longer, about the maple tree in the backyard and the chemistry set that Petra had in the basement that evaporated away. They talked about the road trip they'd taken to a *Star Trek* convention because Petra had wanted to meet Mr. Spock.

"We did have a good time, didn't we?" Petra's mom said.

"Yeah. We did," Petra agreed.

"Sweetie. Hang in there. I'll be there as soon as I can." Static was beginning to creep into the connection.

"Okay, Mom," Petra said. "I love you."

"I love you, too."

Petra ended the call and stared at the phone in her lap. She thought she'd be gone before her mother arrived, and she honestly cringed at the thought of having to manage her mother's emotional reactions on top of her own.

Yet, she really wanted to have her mom's arms wrapped around her, too.

"I guess I'd better figure out how I want to do this dying business," she said to Sig, who had sneaked out and lay at her feet. He looked up at her, his canine eyebrows working.

There were things to consider: How to make sure Sig was cared for. Burial or cremation. What to do with her stuff, what little she had. She supposed she'd have to go download some forms from the internet. What did she need? Living will? Trust? DNR order? About all she had organized was Maria's promise to care for Sig and the organ donor symbol on her driver's license. Not that anyone would want her diseased organs. Gah. Thinking about it, she decided that what she had should go to Maria for Nine's care and to the nursing home for her father. She had a life insurance policy that was in Gabe's name. If Gabe never returned, then . . .

Maria stepped out on the porch, holding her briefcase. She was dressed in work clothes—a voluminous skirt, a blouse with a cardigan—and had her hair neatly gathered on her nape. "I got called in to work. Shockingly, there are folks in bigger trouble than you."

"Go social work 'em over," Petra said. "Nine won't let me out of her sight."

"Good."

"When you get back, can we do some paperwork?" Maria would know how to handle this. She was a social worker, already initiated into the arcane arts of paperwork.

Maria nodded. "Yes. That would be a load off your mind, I'm sure."

"Thank you."

Maria headed out to her green Explorer, cranked the engine, and backed out the gravel drive, past the Bronco, to the road. Petra waved cheerfully. She figured that Maria had hidden her keys or taken them with her.

Good thing she had an extra set.

Petra stepped back into the house. Nine was sitting on the couch with Sig, and it seemed that they were deep in conversation.

Nine looked up. "How is your mother?"

"Preparing to descend upon me with both feet." Petra grimaced and flopped down on the couch. "I'll have to get some paperwork together to get my shit in order before she gets here and goes all control-freaky over stuff. I guess that's included in everyone's idea of a 'good death.'" Petra made air quotes around the words. "I think that Maria wants me to meditate and achieve some enlightenment before I take a dirt nap." Petra sure didn't feel enlightened or ready for anything. She sank back into the velvet couch.

Nine shrugged. "A good death is different for the wolves who want to be surrounded by the pack. When a social wolf is ill, the other wolves surround it. They try to care for it as best they can. The wolf's mate and children all come and sleep around the sick wolf to try to draw off the sickness. We also eat a lot of grass."

"Yeah. I can sure eat grass. But my mate isn't coming back." There. She said it. It felt hopeless and summoned tears to her eyes. She was feeling sorry for herself and was tempted to wallow in grief. "I guess I'd better get started on that solitary wolf business of finding a cave to die in."

Nine turned to face her. "No. You need your mate to be with you to have a good death. You do whatever you need to do to find him. Only then can you have a good death."

Petra looked at her, surprised. "Are you with me for some batshit crazy stuff, Nine?"

She sighed. "I am with you for the batshit crazy stuff. As long as we follow Maria's rule, and you stay within my sight."

"I'm counting on it."

CHAPTER 10

Stupid Oaths and Other Dumb Ideas

Walking up to Owen's front door might not have been the brightest idea on the best of days.

But these were not the best of days, Petra reminded herself. These were the last of hers, and she was going to use them to make war on Owen.

At least it wasn't broad daylight, she consoled herself. She'd waited until the sun had set, and she expected Owen to be home, doing whatever corrupt lawmen did in their spare time at home . . . reading *The Art of War*? Smoking cigars? Clipping the tags from a collection of worthless Beanie Babies?

She stormed up Owen's front steps, the hand-hewn logs of the front porch planed and polished smooth under her feet. She planted the butt of her pistol into the doorbell with a video camera embedded inside, shattering the expensive plastic. It didn't matter if Owen saw her. Having a record of Nine would be more problematic, even if she was out of his jurisdictional reach on the reservation. Nine had no fingerprints on file, no driver's license or identification, but it still couldn't be that hard to find a young woman with a head full of silvery hair on the reservation.

Nine slid from behind Petra, and the women kicked the door in unison. Once, twice . . . three times. The antique door cracked open. The expensive lockset remained in place, the panels splintered around it.

Petra stepped over the mess into Owen's entryway, pistols lifted. Nine and Sig slipped in behind her, fanning out to her right and left. No alarms echoed. Petra scanned the slate entryway and the staircase of logs winding up to an antler chandelier.

"*Owen*," she shouted. "*Get down here.*"

There was no answer.

Her eyes narrowed. He should be home. His vehicles were here. Most likely, he was holed up in a back room with a gun, waiting for her to come to him. Maybe he'd even had enough time to barricade himself into a safe room and was summoning his deputies. By her estimation, the deputies were at least a half hour away.

That was fine with her.

She and Nine swept the first floor—the kitchen, the living room, a bathroom, the study. The whole place was decorated in over-the-top faux rustic stuff.

The only real things were the log walls that Petra guessed were original to the house and the trophies of elk, bear, and bison that gazed down on them from the walls. Even the books in the study were fake, fancy stamped wallpaper.

She caught Nine's eye across the living room. Nine shook her head. Petra gestured with her gun up the stairs.

Petra went first. The log steps were creaky, and she winced at that. After the first step, she moved closer to the wall, Sig on her heels.

She kicked in the doors to the bedrooms upstairs and the bathrooms. No one was there. She even looked in the closets. In the master bedroom, Owen's bed was unmade and rumpled. His walk-in closet was full of his uniforms, a gun safe bolted to the floor. For grins, Petra tugged on the handle. Locked. She wondered what the hell he kept in there.

She scanned the bedroom once more and paused. In a tray on his bedside table sat coins, keys, rings, and other glittery odds and ends. And among them . . . a pearl.

Petra picked it up. It was like the pearl she'd found in the truck—that curious blue sheen. Her eyes narrowed. The pearl meant something . . . just what, she wasn't certain. But she'd find out, even if she had to lie in wait for Owen to return and get it at the business end of a pistol.

Nine popped her head into the room. She gestured for Petra to follow. Petra dropped the pearl back into the tray and stepped noiselessly over the carpeted floor, down the steps to the first floor.

Sig was clawing at a door that Petra assumed led to the kitchen pantry, but there was a lock on it. Nine pulled Sig aside. Petra shielded her face and shot at it.

The bullet bounced against the lockset and the fancy marble floor of the kitchen, fracturing a tile. The lockset broke, and luckily none of them were hit with the ricochet or shrapnel.

Never does that in the movies, Petra thought.

Ears ringing, she opened the door.

This definitely wasn't a pantry. It was a set of stairs, going down to a basement. She felt around for a light switch. She flipped it, and plain wooden stairs were illuminated below . . . by a naked bulb at the bottom of the stairs.

Like the light in the spirit world. Her heart thumped hard behind her ribs. This was the place where Gabe was. She knew it.

She plunged down the stairs, guns extended before her. Sig clambered down behind her.

"Gabe?" she whispered. "Are you here?"

This place was more a cellar than a basement. It had been clearly dug out beneath the original house, centuries ago. The ceiling was low, and rickety wooden shelves lined the sandstone walls. The floor was plain dirt, pounded to a smooth sheen over time under the tracks of the owners.

As she turned a corner, Petra spotted a battered, unoccupied desk. Sig went immediately to it, his nose pressed to the floor, and whined. Petra stepped over a chain snaking across the floor. One end was buried in a floor drain. The other end was an open shackle.

Papers were stacked on the desk. Petra immediately recognized Gabe's handwriting, scrawled across dozens and dozens of pages. There were scribblings of maps, sketches of people . . . all on the same notebook paper used for the curt letter she'd found in her mailbox. She skimmed them. It was a history.

A history of the magic of Temperance.

"Shit," she breathed. Gabe had been here, and he was alive. At least he had been recently. Disappointment and hope warred within her.

She scooped up all the papers and jammed them into her jacket pockets.

She whistled softly for Sig and rushed up the stairs.

Owen was responsible—she now had proof. And she would wring the truth out of him, even if it killed one of them. If she was lucky, maybe it would be both.

That might fit the definition of a "good death."

"Where are we going?"

Gabe already knew the answer. He just wanted to force Owen to acknowledge it. A man like Owen wanted to believe that he was on the side of the angels, serving truth and justice. He'd do anything to turn away from any information to the contrary, to preserve his own image. And with no other options in terms of resistance, Gabe had no choice other than picking at the scabs in Owen's self-concept.

Owen was silent for a moment. He'd been chatty on the way down, but not with Gabe. He'd been carrying on conversations with himself, with the ghost he imagined, muttering about black water and the afterlife. The way down had been foreign to Gabe. He had known many of the rabbit holes that led to the underground of the property, but Owen had marched him to a broken-down grain crib on the north side of the ranch that hadn't been used in many years. Gabe had actually needed to dig deep into his memory to even come up with the last time he'd been here—it had been decades. Those years showed in the dilapidated state of the structure. The concrete floor had ruptured, opening a seam into the earth that was full of mud and gravel. This must have been a place that the Mermaid told Owen about.

Owen marched Gabe ahead of him, and it was almost impossible not to feel the gun aimed at the back of his head, even though he couldn't see it. And despite the fact that Gabe's hands were bound, he would ordinarily have made an attempt to fight and run, gun or not. But the implicit threat wasn't the gun— not to Gabe, that was. After all this time, he just didn't fear death. No, the threat that hung over him wasn't his own mortality, but the knowledge that if he didn't cooperate, he had no illusions about Owen going after Petra. Then again, he might, anyway. The calculus of resisting lay heavily on him.

"The Mermaid wants to see you," Owen answered him, finally.

"The Mermaid wants to kill me." Gabe wanted Owen to face it, to own it.

"She says she just wants to talk."

"And you believed her."

"She hasn't given me any reason not to."

Gabe shook his head. "You're on a slippery slope, Owen. Once she has you, she won't let you go."

Owen said nothing, just shoved him forward, down the dark passageway.

It had been many, many years since Gabe had been in the Mermaid's domain. To be honest, he had hoped that she'd simply wasted away. There certainly wasn't much to sustain her in her prison. But deep down, he knew better. So he'd avoided the tunnels that he knew led to her realm. Sometimes, he had heard the echoes of her singing, and as he thought about it now, he suspected that there was some hypnotic magic in her voice, and that the more Owen listened to her, the more entranced he became. The Hanged Men called her the Mermaid, but she was just as easily the Siren. No matter what she was called, she was dangerous. Gabe knew that. Even weakened, she was formidable. And more than that, she was patient. She had overcome the impulsivity that had caused her to run afoul of Lascaris in life, and an opponent capable of evolution was the most dangerous kind.

Gabe descended the steps to meet his fate. Grey

mist made the treads damp and slippery. Despite his lame leg and impaired vision, Gabe knew these steps better than Owen did—he and the Hanged Men had hewn them out of sandstone and set them. They'd settled over the years, but their contours were still familiar. He could smell the black river from here.

Behind him, he heard Owen stumble. He sensed the opportunity, spun back, and rammed the man with his shoulder. He connected, and Owen's flashlight bounced away. A shot rang out, and the muzzle-flash glittered in the darkness, enough to show Owen sliding down the steps past him. Gabe kicked him the rest of the way down and turned to ascend to freedom.

A hand clasped around his boot, tripping him. Gabe landed with his chin on a step, tasting blood. He felt himself being pulled down, and rather than letting Owen control this struggle, he kicked out into the black even as they tumbled down the steps. He landed in the soft crunch of pea gravel, rolling in the dark to his side. He got his cuffed hands below his ass and flopped and folded his body until he got the cuffs behind his knees. He wriggled the cuffs behind his legs and cleared his boots. At least with the cuffs in front of him, he could swing properly . . .

There was a splash behind him, and a cold hand grabbed his shirt, hauling him back. He swung, connecting with flesh and scale. He knew he was a goner in the water, knew that he was as good as dead. And that meant Petra . . .

Sinewy arms tangled in his handcuffs and yanked him down into the shallows. He dug in his heels, staggering, but she was too strong. A muscular tail slashed at his good knee, and he fell in the water. Before he could take a good, deep breath, he was towed into the cool blackness of the water. It lapped over his cheek, and he gurgled for air. He swallowed a mixture of air and water, fighting to keep his head above the surface.

Owen must have regained his posture and his flashlight. A silhouette on the bank stood in a blue-white halogen glow.

"I've done as you asked," Owen panted. "I brought him to you."

Cold fingers slipped over Gabe's cheek, and a musical chuckle rained down his cold spine. "You have. You brought me the last of my enemies. Such a shame that there is only this one left."

"What are you going to do with him?"

The fingers traced his temple. "Gabriel and I are going to talk. We have much to discuss." The arm around his neck pulled him into deeper water.

He grimaced as the water closed over his head.

The water was cold, but not enough to induce hypothermia. That was the least of his concerns, though, and he fought to push his head above water—fought against being pulled down by that fearsome undertow. His head broke the surface, and he gasped. Mist and rain swirled around him. Fragmented images surfaced in the dark: the Lunaria, the shadows of the

Hanged Men. Whether these were from his memory or Muirenn's, he didn't know. He closed his eyes against them to focus on fighting back.

The Mermaid had hold of his handcuffs and was towing him with his arms over his head. She moved with the speed and ferocity of a shark, pulling him away from Owen's light and into the black downstream. She hummed softly to herself; Gabe thought he detected some fragments of the melody of the lullaby she'd sung to the Hanged Men when they were killed.

"I have waited a long time for this," she said.

She crushed him up against a stand of rocks. She worked loose a rusted chain, one that Gabe recognized. This was the one the Hanged Men had used to bind her here, a century and a half before. He could still see the arcane symbols that Lascaris had required them to etch into it, even as rusted as they were now.

"You know this, don't you?" she demanded, hissing, the chain rattling in front of his face. "This was my leash. You bound me here with this, while you built the gates to keep others from finding me."

"You always had a sense of poetic irony," Gabe murmured dryly. He wouldn't give her the satisfaction of showing any fear. "Actually, Lascaris had ordered that the chain be only fifty feet. It wasn't as if we had no sympathy for you."

"Screw your sympathy!" she snarled at him. She threaded the chain through his handcuffs, tied them to a bracket on a rock that Gabe remembered. That chain had been enchanted by Lascaris, long ago. It could only be unlocked by the will of the landowner, the ruler of the Rutherford Ranch. Gabe was pretty sure Owen wasn't going to be inclined to help him.

He turned his head. He smelled something, like rotting meat.

Muirenn chuckled. Of course she could see in the dark—she'd had many decades of practice. "You kept me from food for many years, Gabriel. I will never, never be without it again. When we last met, I promised you that I would see you dead. Do you remember?"

He remembered. He said nothing.

The water churned, resolving into shapes and forms. An image came into focus. It was the Hanged Men, hauling Muirenn down the steps to her prison. She fought and gnashed her teeth, but the men carried her, above their heads, gripping her writhing form as if she were no more than troublesome cattle.

"Lascaris!" the shadow-Mermaid bellowed. "You can't even bother to do your dirty work yourself!"

The image of Gabriel had hauled the chain out of the water, where it was anchored deeply in bedrock—anchored exactly where he was now. Another Hanged Man had to sit on her tail while he'd fitted the manacle at the joint above the fin. He remembered.

She snarled at him. "I will see you dead."

Gabriel, in those days, was convinced he had seen everything, and that there were no greater horrors than those that he had already wrought or had been visited on him. He told her, sadly, "Of this, I have no doubt."

He picked her up, spitting, and carried her into the water.

The image faded, and Gabe had the feeling that he had foretold his own demise.

"Get it over with, then," Gabe finally muttered through gritted teeth. "Have your dinner and your freedom." He couldn't grudge her this revenge. She had seen him hanged. He had imprisoned her. And she was pissed. It was a never-ending cycle of hate. One or the other of them had to be the victor.

A blinding pain dug into his shoulder. Teeth. Gabe gasped as a chunk of flesh was ripped from his shoulder. Hot blood flowed down, over his chest.

This was going to be a very bad way to die, taken apart, piece by piece, he realized. But even pain like this would not last forever. He steeled himself for the inevitable.

There was a hissing, and then a spitting sound as Muirenn spat the chunk of flesh out against his face.

"*Gah*," she growled.

A splash rattled against his body, and the currents slowly stilled. The underground river lapped up against Gabe's throat. Instinctively, he pushed his ear to his wounded shoulder, trying to staunch the flow of blood.

Muirenn might not want to eat him quickly, he thought. But she would surely find a worse way to kill him. Perhaps it would be bite by bite, over days or weeks. Or she'd just tear him to pieces and gobble him up in one sitting.

Gabe leaned his head back against the stone and stared up at his chains. He tested them, scraping them against the soft sandstone. Grit rained into his eyes. They were just as strong as they had been when they were wrought.

He swore under his breath. There had to be a way out that didn't end in the Mermaid's belly, but he couldn't see it.

He gazed morosely into the dark. He could let himself bleed to death. That might keep him from experiencing an unpleasant end as Muirenn's chew toy. As far as deaths went, bleeding out was not the worst one imaginable. He would have made a choice, owned it, and thwarted the Mermaid's plans. Objectively, this was not a bad deal and a relatively good death, given the options available to him. There was something to be said for dying on one's own terms, regardless of how limited those terms were.

But there was Petra.

He knew that she was above, somewhere. She had to be searching for him, turning up every rock between here and Yellowstone. If there was even a slim chance that she could find him, or that he could escape, he owed it to her to hang on . . . even if it meant enduring whatever torture Muirenn had in store. He'd had one bad death before, when he was hanged from the Lunaria . . . How much more terrible could a second one be?

He pressed his shoulder tightly to his ear, feeling the bleeding slow.

Before him, the blackness of the water burbled and squirmed, revealing a new image: the Lunaria, in all its former glory.

Gabe stared hard at it. This image was likely not of Muirenn's doing, if she had already retreated. Maybe the water in this place was truly enchanted. He had suspected that there was something odd about it when he and the Hanged Men built this place. Lascaris had given them tools, to be certain—axes and shovels that cut through stone like butter. But it had always seemed to Gabe that the water came up from someplace unusual that he could not follow. He had tried, but the source slipped underneath a granite shelf that he was in no hurry to excavate. Part of him wondered if it originated from somewhere even deeper and more dangerous.

Lascaris had warned them never to drink the water. Not that Gabe had any desire to do so. When he and the Hanged Men labored to create this magnificent prison, it had taken much work, even with Lacaris's magical tools. Stone still had to be carted away. Even then, Gabe had been convinced that there were other monsters in the depths. As they dug, they found bones of large, fantastical creatures. They couldn't bring those topside; they just cast them on the cavern's beach. But there had been the rattling skeletons of wings, skulls with great smiling teeth, and tusks as tall as his waist.

All those years ago, Gabe thought he saw things stirring in the water. But nothing had tried to take a bite out of him, or the other men, so he had warily worked to complete his task. Today, however, he couldn't help that his mind's eye still imagined the great beasts that had worked those skeletons, the shapes of things that no man had ever seen.

The water did not show him bones and beasts and the building of the prison. Instead, the Lunaria stood before him now in that black mirror, the image of the tree spreading out its glowing canopy in the water. Tears sprung to his eyes. He missed it, the warmth, the life. Now, he was forever parted from it.

His chest ached, seeing the tree. It ached as if a splinter of wood still remained at his core. He closed his eyes. And it was then that he could feel it, behind his lungs, stirring.

A splinter . . . or a seed.

MUIRENN RINSED HER mouth out with water. The Hanged Man, she'd been told, was an ordinary man now. Human. But he tasted inedible—like sour magic fermenting in the back of a pit. She could not risk eating him, and her hands balled into fists at the disappointment. That only lasted a moment, though—she would just have to find another way to deal with him. And in the meantime, he would be her prisoner while she decided. Perhaps she would be indecisive for a long time, and he could feel what she had felt, just a taste of it, over time. It might take her years. Decades to decide, and she could force some of that sympathy upon him. That, and minnows.

Her disappointment was rapidly diminishing.

Owen was waiting for her at the riverbank near the steps, haloed in shivering blue-white light. He sat on the bottom step, head in his hands.

"What have I done?" he whispered. Likely, he was talking to his ghost, the hallucination that he'd given thought and form.

"No," he said, shaking his head vigorously. "She said she wanted to talk.

"I have to trust her. She came back all the other times."

Muirenn made a deliberate splash, and Owen's head snapped up. He rose to his feet and approached the water's edge.

"Where's Gabriel?" he asked.

"Downstream," she said. "He and I have much to discuss."

Owen's eyes narrowed. "You aren't going to kill him, are you?"

Not at the moment, so she could truthfully answer: "No." Muirenn beckoned to Owen. "Let me see your hand."

Owen didn't move.

"I want to try to heal it," she said. "As a gesture of goodwill. You have given me much, and I should return some of what has been given."

Owen crouched at the edge of the water. He stripped

off his leather glove and extended his right hand, palm down, over the water.

Muirenn approached his hand, craning her neck to look at it from every angle. The ring and little finger were missing. "What happened to it?" She expected to hear a story about how he'd shot them off or some such stupidity. Drinking games. A jealous woman. Something idiotic.

Owen flinched a little. "A . . . creature. Ate it. For the ring I had on it. It was gold."

Less inane than she'd thought. Muirenn nodded sagely. She reached for his hand.

Owen jerked back.

"You have to trust me. Please—let me help."

Owen took a deep breath and reextended his hand to her. She took it in both of hers. The blood flow was good; she could feel his pulse, warm and strong. She began to sing, a distant, distracted tune that pulled power from the unseen moon and from the current of the water and from the sand. It also pulled some of Owen's hectic thoughts away, soothing him.

If . . . when . . . she decided to take Owen's ghost away from him, it would be an easy thing to do. A bit of hypnotic suggestion. Much easier than the work she was doing to make him trust her. Owen was a guarded man. Wrapping him around her finger took a great deal of energy, and there was only a small amount that she wished to spend on him today. She'd give him the fingers that he lost, and then he would be hers. Her puppet. She knew that she couldn't escape this form, that the world was larger than the underground river and the surface waters. She would need Owen, happily serving her, in the world of earth.

She reached down to the bottom, for river silt. She coated his hand in it, smearing it in layers. The silt was thick and chalky. She worked it around his hand, slowly sculpting fingers in the shape of a hand around his. As she worked it, it dried, hardening, a pearly sheen beginning to glow underneath the sand. It was soft nacre, vulnerable, and new.

"Give me a piece of cloth," she said.

Owen fumbled in his pocket for a handkerchief and handed it to her. She tenderly bound up his hand tightly.

"Do not unwrap it. Do not wash or disturb it for three days," she instructed. "On the third, wash it in salt water."

Owen stared at his bundled right hand. "It tingles. What did you do to it?"

"I kept my promise, Owen. I always keep my promises. All of them."

She smiled, sinking below the surface of the water.

CHAPTER 11

The Ancestral Tree

"So, do you like, own this place?"

Archer sat opposite Lev on a threadbare couch in the attic of the Compostela. Lev hadn't realized how shabby it had gotten over the years, but he'd grown used to it. When he'd led Archer here, it hadn't occurred to him how others might see it.

Well, he had Wilma's and Caleb's considered opinions, formed by time and leaving the television turned on to HGTV for their viewing pleasure—at least until Wilma had figured out how to change it to HBO. But he disregarded them, as he did much of what the two of them had to say. Amazingly, tonight the ghosts had done him the rare courtesy of haunting the downstairs, where they were banging about and playing a game of turn-the-lights-above-the-bar-off-and-on. He knew they were listening. Hopefully, they'd stay out of sight and not scare Archer away with their incessant bitching.

Lev had made the attic space of the Compostela into an apartment for himself many, many years ago. Still, it had taken him decades to make changes. They had come slowly as he'd become rooted in the place. When he'd taken over the church, the ceilings had been open all the way to the rafters. He had closed off half of it, liking the airy effect for the main floor. From the former apse back to the alley, however, he'd closed up the ceiling to create an attic. He had finished the walls with salvaged paneling; they had their own peculiar beauty. He had covered the floors over the reinforced joists with pine heartwood, gathered in odd times and different seasons; the boards didn't match perfectly and were of varied widths and colors. It stayed warmer up here than it often did in the bar due to him rerouting a boiler pipe from the basement. At the end of a day in December, his apartment would often be sweltering enough to dry laundry in an hour, and he'd be tempted to open the small stained-glass window at the north end facing the alley for ventilation—which always turned out to be a very cold mistake. He'd put industrial ceiling fans at the roof peak to circulate air in the summer, and it had always stayed comfortable for him. He thought of it as his light-filled aerie on those rare occasions when he was feeling more poetic or the even rarer ones when he invited a woman in.

Like his construction, his sense of decor was somewhat eclectic, but there was a theme: nothing up here was new. Lev found things that were freshly manufactured to be curiously blank and soulless. His walls were covered in bits of art and knickknacks he'd found at the local pawn shop or thrown out in the alley: saw blades that he fancied for the pattern of rust on the spokes, some elk antlers that had been carved with a pattern of leaves that reminded him of the art of scrimshaw, a watercolor of a paint horse. The painting had been done by Bridget, many years ago. If Archer recognized it, he hadn't remarked on it.

"Yeah," Lev said, parking his feet on the coffee table that was made from a sawed-off tree trunk. "They were going to tear the place down. The last church congregation that had been here had dwindled to three members, and then the priest gave up. He packed up his bags and left town without his Bible." Lev shrugged. "I felt like the place was beautiful, that it could use a new life."

"It's cool," Archer said. His eyes drifted around the walls, paused on the picture of the paint horse, and continued. "Did the priest live here, too?"

"I don't think the last one did," Lev said. "And I think that contributed to the church's downfall. In previous decades, a priest would have lived in a rectory, probably the space behind the bar where the cooler and storage now is. He should have been part of this church, literally . . ." He trailed off. "I don't think it will ever be a church again."

"It's nice as a bar." Archer leaned forward. "So. Why did you come to Temperance?"

"Temperance is a weird town. It's a good place for getting away from things, for forgetting. Starting over. I had a lot of things to get away from."

Archer was clearly trying to be nonchalant, but everything about the young man showed subtle tension. He took a drink of the root beer Lev had offered him. Lev had gone back and forth on that—should he be the cool dad and offer the kid a beer? In the end, he had told Archer to get a drink from the fridge, and Archer had picked a root beer. Lev shrugged and poured himself a glass of milk.

"Were you like, on the run from the law or something?" the young man joked.

"Heh. Not in the way you think."

"Witness protection program? That was Mom's best guess. That, or you owed the Mob back east some money."

Lev smiled. "You really want to know? Even if it's completely bizarre?"

"Yeah. I wouldn't have come here if I didn't."

Lev decided to come clean. "Long time ago, I had a family. In Czechoslovakia. They were killed by Nazis, and I . . . I couldn't stop it."

"Nazis?" Archer's brow wrinkled, and it was clear that he was trying to do the math in his head. "But how old are you? Were you a child?"

"I'm old. Very old. And no, I wasn't a child. I was as you see me now."

"I don't understand. That's imp—"

"I know. At least, I know how it seems. I'm asking you to just listen, okay? Besides—you hear ghosts, and you're saying something is impossible?" he asked with an amused look.

"Yeah," Archer said, chuckling weakly. "Sorry—go ahead."

"I'm very old . . . because I am one of a race of old magical ones. The Romans considered us minor household gods, the *Lares*. The Czech and Russians called us *domovoi*. To the English, we were hobs or brownies, and in the north, we were *dísir*. Regardless of our name, wherever we roamed, we were household guardian spirits."

Archer was silent. His gaze slipped once to the door, then returned. Lev figured that he was trying to determine how crazy the old bartender truly was.

But Lev had decided to lay his cards on the table. If Archer fled, then he'd have a good story to tell his friends, his mother would roll her eyes at the adventure, and there would be no harm done. His son would live out his natural life, and then a lot more, and would eventually circle back around to Lev in another eighty years. If he stayed, then there were many things Lev could look forward to teaching him.

"So. You are . . . immortal?"

"We age slowly enough that that's pretty much true, for most intents and purposes. I looked to be around your age at the heyday of the Roman Empire. By the time it became the Byzantine Empire, it wasn't nearly as fun. But that gives you the general idea. I expect that since you're half human, you'll age more quickly. How much so, I'm not certain. You have to understand, this having a kid business doesn't just *happen*."

Archer looked at him. "So are you like the Highlander, then? You can't be killed?"

"Oh, I can be killed. Long life doesn't really have anything to do with invincibility. It has much more to do with living intelligently. The dumbest *domovoi* could be dead tomorrow, if he took up skydiving or driving his car into a wall. There's a reason we're household spirits. Staying home generally causes one to stay out of trouble, avoid drama, and to live a lot longer." Lev took a drink of his milk. "And those around you age and die."

"Like your family in Czechoslovakia?"

Lev made a bitter face. He drained his glass and then wandered into the open kitchen for a refill. "They were my family because I was their guardian. I failed them miserably. I served their family for centuries. I lived in that house when it was built of mud and straw and fieldstone. I tended the hearth, and they grew in prosperity. They were good to me, and I was good to them. I watched generations be born and die under that roof. I showed them how to make offerings to the old gods, how to work with the moon and the sun to harvest both the fields and their own ambitions. Seeds were sown, and there was laughter in that house. I brought what minor luck and magic I could, and I always had a place to sleep by the fire.

"One night, a knock came at the door. For a long time, we thought we were safe from national politics, as isolated as we were out in the countryside. We didn't concern ourselves with the outside world—it was the world, and it was outside of us. I had seen empires rise and fall, and largely those events were of no consequence to the families I served, because we had the good sense to stay out of the way.

"But the men in black came knocking. When no one answered, they forced their way in. I drew the sword I still had from the Roman days, but I was no match for their numbers and their guns. The family was slaughtered before my eyes and the silver taken from beneath the floorboards. An officer had shot me and left me for dead. They set the house on fire, for good measure." Lev lifted his shirt, showed Archer a white scar on his ribs. Time had faded it greatly, but not entirely.

"How did you survive?" Archer asked.

"I crawled into the fieldstone fireplace with the smallest child. The fire washed past us. I survived, but the little girl did not. When morning came, all that remained standing was that chimney, black with soot.

"My family was gone. The house was gone. I could not simply wait for another family to move in and continue where I had left off. Everything I had loved was gone. I stayed there at the burned site for weeks. I sorted the bones into piles and buried them under cairns. I healed."

Lev stared into the contents of his glass. "But I was uprooted. I wandered into Western Europe. I killed some Nazis along the way. I never was much of a fighter, so I killed many of them after they got drunk in bars and wandered out to the alleys to piss. I struck down a straggler here or there in the battlefields as I passed through the lines. But I never found the ones who killed my family. I eventually kept following the sun, going west . . . and I wound up here."

"You stopped running," Archer said.

"It seemed as good a place as any to stop. No one asked any questions about my past. Nobody but you, that is."

Archer stared at the floor. "That's a lot to absorb."

Lev smiled at the understatement. "You don't have to believe me. Door's that way."

Archer stayed seated, though he bounced the heel of his hiking boot on the floor. "I don't know what to think. Being able to hear ghosts is one thing . . . but . . ." he faltered.

"The ghosts are part and parcel of it. All spirits of place can hear the dead. It's so that we can drive the unwanted ones out of the houses we occupy."

"I guess that's why I like being out in the wilderness. In nature." Archer stared up at the ceiling. "It's quieter."

"Yeah. Cities can be difficult, even for an old *domovoi* like me. To be honest, I have no idea what that means for you . . . being half *domovoi*. I can't stress this enough—I've *never* heard of a *domovoi* having children. *Domovoi* always search out their own families and never actually, you know . . . make them. Our families aren't blood."

Archer seemed to think for a while. "But you did."

"Maybe so." It hadn't occurred to him that way. But he'd been around long enough to know that patterns tended to reassert themselves. It wasn't lost on him that he'd created his own home. Maybe, on a subconscious level, he'd summoned the magic for a family to fill it.

"You said you were magic," Archer said. "What kind of magic? Like, pulling quarters from ears?"

Lev shook his head. "I haven't practiced magic since that time. The magic that the *domovoi* practice is simple magic. It's not the fancy magic that ceremonial magicians use. We use dirt, spit, blood, and rocks to accomplish our goals. Our magic is the magic of the earth and the dead. At the beginning of time, our purpose was to keep the dead in the ground and protect the living. Some branches of our family tree still take these responsibilities very seriously. One of our distant cousins, for instance—a hob in a Whitechapel cemetery—keeps Jack the Ripper in his grave."

"I thought they never figured out who Jack the Ripper was," Archer said.

"The hob knows. He poses as a groundskeeper, and he's the only one who knows the Ripper's true identity. Apparently, the Ripper was annoyed at eternal anonymity and yaps endlessly. I can't imagine the shitty conversations the poor guy has to listen to on the right side of the crypt. He's got to use muffling magic every day to shut that madman up."

Archer listened, eyes wide.

"In twelfth-century Bohemia, I lived with a family whose father was interested in ceremonial magic. I watched him, but never participated. He was interested in many odd things. Mostly, he was convinced that he could birth a unicorn from a goat, and spent more energy trying to get that to happen than preserving his family. His wife eventually fled with the children, and he didn't notice for days. Eventually, despite my best efforts, he forgot to eat and wasted away. Even the cats wouldn't gnaw on his scrawny bones. Frankly, that surprised me."

"You sound a lot less attached to that family."

"Eh. They survived. The wife went to her mother's house in Alamannia, and they fell under the protection of a curmudgeonly kobold who rather enjoyed rapping on tables with the little girls and moving around their tea sets when they played with their dolls. They were in good hands. The husband . . . he was something of a self-centered dick, as most magicians are."

Lev reached forward for a wooden bowl on the coffee table. It was full of polished stones and geodes he'd hammered open, fragments of quartz. He'd found each and every one of them in his walks through

Temperance and the surrounding areas. Most were native rocks. Some might have fallen from the pockets of tourists. He fingered through them until he picked up an amethyst geode, about the size of a Ping-Pong ball. He showed it to Archer, spat on it, and closed it in his fist.

He breathed in, breathed out, and concentrated on the stone, feeling its age-old matrix of elements in his hand. The brittle structures moved, reorganized. When he opened his hand, the geode had changed.

A small violet flower sat in his hand. The petals were bruised from his fingers. He hadn't realized which flower it would be, but the stone must have remembered it.

Archer leaned in and picked the flower out of Lev's hand.

"Careful," Lev said. "Monkshood is poisonous."

"That's cool," Archer said.

Lev wasn't sure how impressed he really was. *Domovoi* magic wasn't terribly dramatic, and he was pretty sure any sideshow party charlatan could do a similar small object swap with simple misdirection. It would be up to his son to decide if he wanted to believe or not. It wasn't like he could call down a lightning bolt or transform a frog into a princess.

Archer turned the flower over in his hand. He put it in his jacket pocket.

"Do you have a place to say?" Lev asked. "My couch is open. For as long as you want it."

"You know, I'd like that." Archer's face split open

in a grin. "I think you've probably got tons of stories to tell."

"Many stories," Lev agreed. "Things that I saw and things that the ghosts have talked about."

"I'll go get my stuff together. Be back later?" Archer said, climbing to his feet.

"I'd like that," he said, echoing his—could he admit it? Yes—son. "I'll leave the door open for you."

The two men looked at each other for a moment, then shared an awkward embrace. Archer turned away first. He reached into his jacket and gave Lev a thick manila envelope.

"What's this?" Lev turned it over. It was sealed, with just his first name written on the front.

"It's a letter from my mom." Archer shrugged. "I said I wouldn't open it."

"Thanks."

Archer nodded and waved as he headed for the back door.

Lev watched him go.

Wilma and Caleb appeared, lounging on the couch.

"I hope I didn't scare him," Lev said.

Caleb shook his head. *"You did well. He'll be back."*

"I hope so."

Lev stared at the envelope. It was lumpy and uneven-feeling in his hands. It felt like an envelope full of secrets. After a moment, he opened it and reached inside. He pulled out a letter, folded around a sheaf of photographs.

Lev began with the letter. He recognized Bridget's flowing handwriting.

> *Dear Lev,*
>
> *It's been quite some time, hasn't it? I'm sorry to reach out to you this way. It must be quite a shock to have Archer on your doorstep.*
>
> *I always intended to tell you. Truly, I did. And I'm sorry. Time just . . . slipped away from me. You know that I worshipped Laima when I met you—remember the necklace that I always wore. She's a goddess of fate and guardian of pregnant women. And she apparently has a sense of humor. I hadn't been expecting to have a child. But Laima brought this child to me.*
>
> *I discovered that I was pregnant about a month after I left Temperance. I thought I'd tell you after I was further along, when I was past the danger of miscarriage. I didn't think that there was a point in getting your hopes up or disturbing you, either way. That time came and went, and I thought I'd tell you when I had the baby. I went on a retreat to think, and I had Archer with the help of a midwife in a cabin surrounded by redwoods. He was a beautiful baby. He had your eyes. He was the quietest baby I've ever met. He just watched and absorbed everything around him.*

Lev's fingers stirred the pile of photos. On the top was a picture of Bridget, her hair pulled back from her face, cuddling a tiny infant wrapped in flannel. She looked radiant, and he felt a pang of sorrow for not seeing this in person. He turned his attention back to the letter.

I adored him, obviously, and you have to under-stand he became everything for me. Life happened, and it kept happening. We moved to an ashram and focused on day-to-day life. I painted. He played. He loved people and loved nature.

We moved several times over the years, and I saw that Archer reached for a community, every-where we went. He made families of goats on farms, played guitar with his friends. He made straight As in school. He saved baby ducks from sewer grates and grew gardens. Wherever we went, he grew a gar-den. County fair prize-winning pumpkins. I think he can become a horticulturalist. And a musician. And a veterinarian.

He is a wonderful, wonderful person. I'm sure you'll see that.

Lev flipped through pictures of a little boy with a wagon full of dirt. A boy holding a giant white pumpkin. A young Archer with long hair, playing in a garage band. There were pictures of Archer and a group of young men and women, holding skate-boards over their heads. There were dogs and cats sleeping on the boy, tangled in hand-crocheted af-ghans. A picture of Archer driving a tractor, his filthy face beaming at the camera. In another photo, a teenage Archer stood in a muddy river, lovingly holding a giant salamander to his bare chest.

It looked like a wonderful childhood. A perfect one. Lev smiled at that, feeling an emptiness in his belly as he turned to the next page:

But there are things I can't help him with. When he was sixteen, he started hearing voices. I thought the worst. I took him to a psychiatrist, who thought he might be having signs of schizophrenia. Schizophrenia! I couldn't accept it. I gave him the medications, but they didn't help.

I took him to a shaman. I didn't know what to do. The shaman said that he was a "hollow bone"—that spirits spoke to him. The shaman said he was hearing ghosts. And I believed him. So did Archer. Things got better. But I saw him withdrawing from people, from places.

When he was eighteen, he hiked the Appalachian Trail for nine months. I was in a frenzy of worry. He checked in when he could. But I think he needed that, that solitude. Away from ghosts and the people he loved.

When he came back, he was glowing. He was tan, fit, serene. I thought we were over it. Over the ghosts.

But they came back. He enrolled in college, a beautiful historic campus . . . and he dropped out after a semester. He said that there were ghosts everywhere—in the library, in the study halls, in the dorm where he tried to sleep. All that vigor that he'd gained from his walkabout on the Appalachian Trail had fallen away. He came home a shell.

He kept busy, though. Got a job at a greenhouse. But he needs something that I can't give him. He needs someone who had a finger in the Otherworld to teach him.

I know that you thought I didn't know. And to be honest, I tried to talk myself out of it. But on some level, I always knew that there was something Otherworldly about you. Maybe you know how to help Archer, what he needs to know to live serenely in this world.

I have brought him as far as I can. He needs you now to teach him to be the man he can be in this world.

> *With love,*
> *Bridget*

Lev carefully placed the letter on top of the pictures.

"What does it say?" Wilma asked quietly.

Lev was silent for a moment. "It says that he's mine. And I have to help him."

Lev plucked another rock from the bowl on the coffee table. He spat on it and closed it in a doubled fist. When he opened his hands, an oxeye daisy bloomed.

CHAPTER 12

Red Rain

She walked in her sleep.

She had some dim knowing of this. She remembered that she had done so often as a child, and she had done it again at the hospital. When she was a child, Petra knew it was fear of the dark mixed with a deep dreaming sleep that she hadn't been able to shake off. She'd awaken in her mother's arms under the scalding hot kitchen light. Petra knew that the hospital sleepwalking came under the influence of too many drugs and an undertow of hallucination that sucked all the light out of her consciousness. This was the same as it had been then; a sense that her head floated in a balloon a half mile above her body, with some background music playing in her head that nobody else could hear.

Maybe now it was Maria's potions and exhaustion comingling in her gut. After Petra had nearly passed out digging in the refrigerator for lunch meat for Sig, Maria had sent her to bed. She'd poured a liquid into her throat that smelled and tasted like violets.

Or maybe it was getting close to the end, and she was just dreaming in Maria's bed, clutching Gabriel's papers under the pillow. Then, it had been afternoon. But the hours were bleeding together.

Either way, she could distinctly remember letting herself out of Maria's house at what seemed to be night. Sig had wound around her legs, his fur soft as feathers around her calves. Barefoot, she walked out into the sharp gravel, then into the field. The tactile sensations should have woken her, pulled her awake and what bit of her soul seemed to be persistently floating above her body back in.

But they didn't. A remnant of a dream moved through the fields, a familiar shadow.

Gabriel!

She shouted in her head, but she couldn't make her lips move. Rain speckled her face, warm and soft as blood. It spattered on the ground as she stumbled forward in his wake, trying to follow that silhouette as it wove through the grass.

At her side, Sig whined. Did he see what she saw? He seemed to always come into the spirit world with her and back again. Could he cross into dreams and nightmares? She knew, on many levels, he was a spiritual creature, what Maria would have called a guide. But she wondered how far and how long he could follow her. When she died . . . would he be able to visit her? Or would he be lost forever, and she'd be chasing his memory in dream fields, like Gabriel?

There was no color in this field. Nothing but black and white and grey, stretching forward before her as Gabriel's shadow flickered beyond her. Only the rain had color—a brilliant red that soaked into the ground, clinging to her bare feet and Gabriel's shadow. She followed that shadow to the Eye of the World. Instead of its soothing, familiar turquoise color of day or the black mirror of it at night, it churned a restless, luminous red.

Gabriel! she howled with all the force in her head.

He was walking into the waters of the Eye now, into that unnatural red water. He was knee-deep, the water seething around him. He turned, and she saw him in three-quarter profile then. He was as she remembered, *everything* she remembered: that silence and that stillness poured into a human form. Once upon a time, she thought him indestructible. Now, she knew better.

Gabriel. Don't leave me. Not yet.

He wasn't completely the same, though—he was changed in subtle ways. Where the reflection of a man should have played in the water beyond his knees, there was the shadow of an inverted tree. The Lunaria—she recognized it at once. Its branches reached out, black in the water, spreading over the pool with rapacious speed.

Gabriel closed his eyes and . . . melted.

He just disincorporated, sliding into the water. Where his flesh hit the water, feathers pooled on the surface, spinning out like an oil slick. Hammered by the rain, they began to sink.

Gabriel . . .

And he was gone, and she was standing at the water's edge with the warm red rain pounding the back of her scalp.

Only the shadow of the tree remained, that reflection under the surface of the water.

She sucked in her breath, stalked toward it, and then into it.

Sig pulled at the edge of her nightdress, growling, but she continued. He let go, whining. He turned and ran.

She was alone. Just her and the tree and whatever death was coming for her.

She waded into the water, feeling its warmth taking over her, and reached for the churning branches of the tree . . .

IN THE DARKNESS, in the stillness, it was easy to lose grip on reality.

Gabe had heard stories of contraptions, consciousness deprivation tanks, used to harden soldiers for battle and to torture prisoners. He had thought it an odd idea when he'd first heard it. It sounded like being closed up in a bathtub or in a water-filled coffin.

And while that seemed bad, it didn't seem as horrible as all that. He had never fully appreciated the dimensions of the idea, until now.

The water wasn't frigid, merely unpleasantly chill. That sensation faded; he got used to it quickly, though his hands and feet had gone numb. Once the temperature was no longer an issue, it was hard to even differentiate between the water and the air, leaving him with the sensation of floating in pure darkness. His mind had begun to play tricks on him, creating white flashes of stars in his peripheral vision. There was no sound here, and he began to lose perception. He couldn't tell if he was speaking his thoughts aloud, or if they remained in his own head. He felt his consciousness spilling outside his body, blending with the blackness of his surroundings, like ink in mud.

He wondered if perhaps he had died. He'd lost track of the passage of time. Thoughts drifted in and out of his mind's eye, white shimmery shapes that didn't fully take form. Hallucinations, dreams, visions dredged up from the river and Muirenn's magic . . . they were all the same. He wandered through the dark landscapes of memory and the spirit world.

He did not wander these lands as a man. He was a white eagle, a white shadow upon black. He sensed that, many months ago, when he had become human, he had evolved. That was the nature of living alchemy. He had moved beyond the fermentation stage in which he'd been trapped as a Hanged Man. He had turned from raven to eagle, approaching the perfection of the Great Work. He knew that part of the work was the sloughing off of the physical skin, moving to spirit. Wind slipped under his feathers, making him light and insubstantial. His connection to earth broken, he skimmed through the sky, observing without attachment.

Though it was an evolution, he knew that it took him farther from Petra, from the physical world. She needed him. And he needed to get back to it, to her. He searched for a door, soaring over mountains, through forests, and at last a grassy field, ruled by a mighty oak tree.

The Lunaria.

He knew it at once. It had come for him, or he for it. He was not certain, tangled together as they had been for more than a century and a half.

It spread out below him, with golden roots digging deep into the earth. Its branches spread far above him, into the sky. He felt a pang of elation at that, elation and fear. The tree, he suspected, existed in all planes at once: the upper, middle, and lower worlds. And if it did so, perhaps it existed in all times. Whether this was the tree's memory of itself as it had been in its glory or some imagining of its future form, he couldn't be certain.

But he knew it recognized him. He landed before it, folding in his wings to gaze upon the tree with his sharp sight that saw beyond what he had ever seen as a man. The branches bent in an unseen breeze, and the roots rustled underneath his talons. It would know him. It *had* to. He had been wound up in its destiny since he'd first laid eyes upon it.

And not just him. Golden fruit dangled from the branches, shining softly. They were husks, like milkweed pods, six feet long and half as wide. Gabriel fluttered up to land on the nearest, digging his talons into the rough, dry surface. It pulsed beneath his touch, a living thing.

Gabe reached for a seam in the seed pod and pulled it open a foot. Hanging upside down, in the golden light cobwebs of the pod, lay one of the Hanged Men.

He shouted his name, but it only came out as a raptor's scream.

The Hanged Man slept, refusing to be awoken.

Gabe reached into the pod to free his fellow. But the man was tangled in that deceptively strong gossamer gold. He was not yet ripe, not yet able to be pulled from the grasp of the tree.

Gabe flew to the next pod and tested it. Another Hanged Man lay within, immobile and sleeping. He counted the rest. All of the Hanged Men were here, in this . . . suspension? Gabe had read a science-fiction story about humans in suspended animation, in hibernation on a space ship. This reminded him of that, this utter stillness.

Only the tree moved. The roots rustled a bit, as if covering something. Gabe peered at the translucent ground.

There was indeed something there. A knot of roots fussing around something that lay still as a peach pit at the bottom. It was man-shaped, that much Gabriel could discern at first. His eyes adjusted, and he gazed with his eagle sight at the luminous body that lay underneath the tree. It was familiar . . . male, with a sharp profile and slender-fingered hands. He might have been anonymous except for the tree's light burning around an opaque object at his chest, like dense tissue on an X-ray film. The light twined around a chain and hands . . . a pocket watch.

Gabe recoiled in dread, his feathers ruffling. Lascaris had owned a watch like that. This magic tasted of him. He had created the tree and somehow he had remained entangled in its spirit. Was it like the others, sleeping, or . . .

He lit on the ground, cocking his head. He couldn't hear the watch ticking. That could be good, or it could be very bad.

He straightened, gathering himself to fly away. He knew he had to warn someone who was still in the physical world that something had happened . . .

He leaped into the air, beat his wings three times. But the branches reached for him, trapping him in a cage. He beat his wings against them, feathers descending in a flurry of snow. But he couldn't escape. Branches pulled him close to the trunk of the tree. He struggled against them, the branches snapping, crackling strings of golden light. The trunk of the tree pressed against his spine, sprouting branches high into the sky, shimmering. He was part of it, as he had been before; he could feel the sap moving underneath the bark as easily as he could feel his own blood. He was both comforted and panicked. Comforted, because he had missed the tree, the touchstone of his unlife. Panicked, because he was afraid for what this meant, for himself, for the Hanged Men, for the Lunaria . . . and everyone in the physical world. For Petra and Sig.

The tree would take over everything it could reach. He knew this.

A figure approached, walking through the field. A figure with a coyote. Petra. She was still searching for him, and his heart lifted. He screamed at her from his tree prison, but she, like the Hanged Men, seemed not to hear him.

She was different from the last time he'd seen her. Her physical body had faded, leaving a spectral suggestion of light that smeared away on all the things she touched, an overexposed photograph that was slowly melting.

She was peeling through pages of maps that he had drawn, thick blocks of text. She turned them this way and that, trying to orient herself in the black landscape. There was no moon overhead, no stars to navigate by, just that dim inner glow.

He shouted at her. But all that came out was that same raptor cry. He ruffled his feathers and tried again, but emitted only a hoarse squawk.

She looked up through the branches at him. This time, it seemed she could see him. "Where are you?"

Perhaps if he flew, she could follow him. He knew

she was fading, and he wanted to see her one last time, hold her hand in the physical world, no matter the cost.

But the tree held him fast. It wrapped around him, a tightening cage of golden light. He melted into it, his pale feathers sinking into it.

He fought it. On a cellular level, he rejected this change with all his might, this evolution that took him away from her. He fought hard, fought until his feathers darkened. He fought until his body couldn't take it—he felt it ripping—and then his being split apart like blood spilled in water.

THE EYE OF the World swallowed her.

She had fallen too deeply in it, and she couldn't climb out again. She'd reached down for the tree roots, through the sludge of wet feathers on the surface, hoping to find Gabriel. She'd gone deeper, deeper, and then the tree's branches started pulling her in. She didn't have the strength to struggle. She held her breath and looked up, through the red surface of the water.

Funny how the algae gathered here, like clouds scudding across the glass-like surface.

Consciousness was slipping beyond her fingers. As far as ways to die, this was not the worst. There was no pain. No racking sobs of grief. Maybe the Lunaria would take her to Gabriel if she went willingly.

She exhaled, her lungs emptying of air, and felt

herself beginning to drop like a stone. She closed her eyes and inhaled. The water of the Eye of the World soaked into her brain, bright with salt and magic.

She heard distant barking, far overhead.

All was silent for a moment. She could only hear her own pulse thundering in her ears and feel the grip of the tree wrapping around her legs.

But the calm surface of the water overhead shattered in an awful cacophony, a crash and bubbling. The tree retreated into the depths—she could feel it letting go. Petra hung, weightless for an instant before hands hauled her out of the water.

SHE WAS DIMLY aware of Nine and Sig splashing into the water, pulling her to shore, shaking her. She couldn't move, her limbs as leaden as the stone sentinels shadowing the pool. Droplets of water spangled her face.

Nine was pushing water out of her lungs. She muttered something in another language. Petra wondered if that was one of her father's spells, some bit of practical magic he'd taught her. Nine pushed until bile came up and Petra gagged. Sig circled around the women, whining.

Nine's dark eyes peered into hers, and Petra began to shiver. Sig licked her face.

"Coyote came to get me," Nine said.

"I fell in," she whispered, lying. Her sinuses burned with too much light and the water from the Eye. She felt unanchored in her body, as if she should have stayed in the water, continued to look for Gabe there. She glanced back at the pool. It was silent, dark. No red, no tree, no sign of Gabriel.

Sig washed the hypnotic water from her face with his tongue, whimpering. She looked at her still wet hands—it wasn't blood anymore, just water.

"Come home." Nine pulled her to her feet, and she stumbled. "You will have time enough for the spirit world later."

Without another word, Nine put her arm behind Petra's shoulders and her knees. Too exhausted to fight, Petra let Nine carry her through the grassy field to the little yellow cottage beyond.

EVENING HAD WASHED the creek in orange and gold.

Muirenn took a deep breath, drinking in the sunset as she washed her hair and braided it. Her hair was losing its straw-like texture. Near her scalp, it was soft as algae. She felt more fat along her ribs than she'd had in her far-distant memory. She felt strong. The bruises on her body were fading. The greenish-blue tint to her body was fading. Even her gums had stopped bleeding. Where she was missing a few teeth, she could feel sharp edges of new ones growing in, and she ran her tongue over their fresh, serrated edges. Magic was stirring in her, healing her quickly—she had not cast away all her healing magic on Owen.

She had given herself over to some small luxuries, out here in the wilderness. Away from Owen. Away from that troubling relic of her past, Gabriel. Involuntarily, she scrubbed her tongue across her teeth at the thought of him, at the memory of that terrible bitter taste. Every time she remembered it, she couldn't shake the idea that he had tasted like sour magic from Lascaris's time. Like poison. She hated that she was denied her desired revenge, and hated even more that she had not yet decided what to do with him. She couldn't eat him, so any reason she kept him around would need to be strategic. And if she killed him, she'd need to do it in such a way that she either hid it from or justified it to Owen. Was the former Hanged Man in the middle of some sort of alchemical process? She couldn't put her finger on it. Was he finally decaying? She would have to analyze him, even if it meant taking him apart to do it and examining the pieces in the sunlight.

Preferably if it meant taking him apart . . .

She had spent the last few hours grazing. She'd found some wild onion, the tender bulbs and leaves tasting sharp on her tongue. A bear had dropped a piece of beehive, and she'd gleefully scooped out the honeycomb within. She could taste the labor of the bees inside, nourishing her at a deep, invisible level. She licked the honeycomb clean, crunching up the hard bits of it. She pulled herself up on a bank to pick up a speckled egg that had fallen from a bird nest. She cracked it open and devoured the yolk and white in one delicious gulp. She'd found some dandelion greens and ate them by the fistful, savoring that tang of their greenness.

In between foraging, she made it a point to watch and observe people from a distance. She'd seen some people walking from far away, on trails that wound away into the flat grasslands. She spied a black ribbon of road in the distance, on which silent carriages ran at impossible speeds, carrying people in odd clothing. The wildlife seemed unconcerned by the people and their machines; beavers building a dam didn't seem to pay any attention to the walkers. And the vultures didn't stop to peck human meat from the carriages, simply focusing on the carcasses the machines left behind on the road.

From the river, she spied some morel mushrooms growing on the land. Her mouth watered. She hadn't had those since she was a human woman. But they were far up the bank, at least twenty feet, sprouting in the shade of quaking aspen. She examined them a long time, looking at their tantalizing umbrellas from every angle she could reach. They were true morels, she was certain, not poisonous. Her memory of these delicacies was still sharp.

She contemplated the risk. Twenty feet was not far in the water, and she would have gobbled down water forage quickly. But on land, she knew that this distance—coupled with her tail—rendered her vulnerable to the men and machines she'd seen.

She listened carefully. She heard no one around,

no sign of a threat. The birds sang overhead, and the squirrels showed no sign of alarm.

Taking a deep breath, she sank her fingers into the muddy bank. She hauled herself up with her arms, moving out of the water on her elbows. She slashed her tail right and left for leverage. It wasn't elegant, and her approach was pretty noisy, but her attention was focused on those delicious morels.

After some minutes of effort, she reached the stand of mushrooms. Greedily, she ripped them out of the soft, black soil and stuffed them in her mouth.

Her eyes closed in pleasure. The mushrooms melted in her mouth, and she barely needed to chew them. They were perfect. She had dug almost all of them out of the ground before she looked up to take full stock of her surroundings.

The bank was short and steep. In the distant past, this creek must have swelled to the size of a large river, cutting through mud and sandstone and tree roots.

Above her, something rustled.

She sucked in her breath.

A group of wild turkeys surged over the ridge above her, running past her in a flurry of warbling and feathers. They ran to the creek, a cackling mass of alarm.

She whipped back, her braids striking her in the face.

A man had started down the bank after the turkeys. His expression, looking after them, was one of playful wonder, almost the expression of a child. He carried a heavy pack on his back with a bedroll, and he reminded her of an illustration of a Tarot card she'd seen a long time ago: The Fool. Then his eyes fell on her, and his brows shot up.

He slipped in the spring mud, sliding down the embankment with his arms spread out and hands grasping for the puny grasses growing in the shade. He landed about six feet from Muirenn, gaping like a fish at her.

Two impulses warred in Muirenn. Her first instinct was to flee, knowing that she was at a disadvantage on land. It was a cerebral impulse, born of fear.

But the second one was deeper and more primal. It came from rage and hunger.

She sat, coiled up as tight as a spring in the mud. She could lunge for the water, or she could spring for the man.

Hunger won.

She launched herself at him.

He fought back, battling with a great deal of strength. But Muirenn had been growing stronger herself, and unlike the man, she delighted in this fight. They rolled in the sparse grasses and the mud and gravel and last bits of mushroom. Muirenn snapped at his throat with her teeth as he tried to push her away. He scrambled back on his elbows and feet, crab-like, and tried to climb to his feet. With her tail, she knocked his feet out from under him, rolled, and pressed him to the mud. She planted her hands on his shoulders.

He sucked in his breath and closed his eyes, as if he could ward her off by sheer thought, as if she were some vain imagining or hallucination.

She leaned forward and ripped his throat out.

There was no imagining that.

Greedily, she dipped her head to drink.

She fell back, pressing the back of her hand to her bloody mouth. She thrashed her head from side to side. Like Gabriel—though not like him at all—this man was polluted, his blood burning her mouth with the foul tang of magic.

Hissing, she crawled to the creek and plunged her head beneath the cooling water.

The world was much different than it had been when she'd strode through it on two legs.

It was poison.

CHAPTER 13

Here and Gone

Petra and Nine didn't speak about what happened at the Eye of the World.

To Petra, this was a relief. She didn't know how to explain what had happened. Weird things had always happened at the Eye, but Petra had the sense that this was something more than that. That time was getting short.

Though Nine wasn't talking, Sig gave her plenty of grief. He followed her everywhere. He scrambled inside the bathtub as she took a shower. He tangled in her legs when she went to the laundry room. He had sat opposite her while she used the toilet, ears pressed forward with an *"I'm watching you, you fucking moron"* expression.

"Thank you," she told him.

He just huffed and his canine eyebrows worked up and down in worry.

Petra turned her attention back to Gabe's papers. He had left behind maps, a dozen of them.

They were puzzles, she had decided, designed to confuse Owen. No compass rose had been drawn on any of them. No landmarks. No markings of scale or distance. They were squiggles of scribbles on the paper, turning back on themselves like the trails of termites. Petra suspected that these were the tunnels that stretched below the Rutherford Ranch. The only markings were alchemical symbols. Some she recognized—the symbols for air, fire, water, earth, mercury, and salt. Some were astrological symbols. She wondered if they might have anything to do with alchemical processes, and compared them to what she saw on the Locus. The Locus had stubbornly refused to help her in this, however, as it had decided that notebook paper and pencil were nonmagical, meaning she was on her own. So she'd looked as many of the symbols up on the internet as she could find and made notations beside them. There were symbols for brimstone and antimony and sulfur. Hell, there was even an alchemical symbol for horse shit.

But none of it made any sense. She layered the maps on top of each other, spread them out on Maria's floor in tiled fashion, trying to fit them together as if they were a sewing pattern that would eventually add up to the shape of a body. Try as she might, she couldn't figure out which end was up, where the entrance and exit to this labyrinth was. She resolved to take them to her father during the next visitor's hours. Perhaps he would be lucid enough to give her some insight.

She felt mentally fuzzy. Not at her sharpest. Maybe it was just the fever she felt pulsing behind her brow. Or the ache in her ribs from where Nine had resuscitated her. Nine had left behind bruises that had blackened, almost as if they were oxidizing. Nine had popped a couple of her stitches, and Petra had tried to put the wound back together with some butterfly closures from Maria's medicine cabinet. Unless Sig was talking, no one had mentioned what had happened at the Eye of the World to Maria, though Petra had caught Maria looking at the top of one of the bruises when she was doing laundry.

She held her head in her hands, staring at the pages, spread about her on the living room floor. Pearl, the cat, picked her way among the papers, refusing to step on them in a game of floor lava.

She ran her fingers through her short hair. "I don't know shit about this stuff," she said.

Nine watched her from across the floor. She was eating a sandwich, feeding half of it to Sig. "Have you asked the west wind?"

"I don't know if the west wind and I are on speaking terms." The west wind seemed like an abstract entity for serious magicians. Petra was pretty sure that they had never been formally introduced, much less friendly enough to ask for favors.

Nine unfolded herself, stood, and stepped around

the pages with bare feet. "Sometimes, in our wanderings in the backcountry, we would get a little lost," she admitted. "Most of the time, we navigated by sun and stars. But when one got truly lost, the wind could sometimes be asked for guidance."

"I'm open to anything."

Nine stood by the door. "Brother Wind, please lend us your guidance." She took a deep breath and flung it open to the dusk.

The force of the door flying open scattered the papers in a swirl as wind kept at bay behind the chipped door swept in. Petra instinctively snatched at the papers. They slipped from her grasp like birds.

When the breeze settled down, the papers were scattered in a seemingly random pattern.

Nine stood over them and pointed to the kitchen window. "That way's north."

Petra bit back questions. She'd seen Nine perform magic that could kill a man. She wasn't going to quiz her right now on her mapmaking skills. Petra took her pencil and meticulously marked an *N* on each page as it fell, aligned with the kitchen window.

It was still a gargantuan puzzle, she thought, stacking the pages on top of each other by Nine's true north. Yet this was still better than nothing—perhaps even the key that could unlock the secret Gabe had left.

But if Petra had learned anything as a scientist, it was the need to shift perspective in approaching a problem, to strike at many angles and begin fresh.

Maybe it was time to look at the rest of the evidence and then return to the maps.

She had been reading Gabe's stories since she'd stolen them from Owen's basement. There was really nothing else to call them—they were fantastic accounts of what had unfolded in Temperance 150 years ago.

She read them, one by one, pacing around the house, sitting on the couch, sprawled in bed with a bank of pillows behind her. Nine eventually made her go to bed, and she took the pages with her. Nine sprawled at the foot of the bed, rubbing Sig's ears, while Pearl had taken over her usual post on Maria's down pillow.

"I can't imagine what he went through," Petra murmured. She passed the pages to Nine as she finished them.

"It seems like he knew a lot more than he ever told anyone," Nine agreed.

"You read English?" Petra blurted.

Nine shrugged. She propped her head against the footboard, pulled up her knees, and propped the pages against her belly. "My father made sure we knew all the languages of men."

"You really should think about working as a translator. I mean, seriously. You could go work for the United Nations."

Nine gave her a sidelong look. "The United Nations."

"Yeah. Where a whole bunch of representatives

of different countries get together to argue about stuff. Usually about punishing this country or that or who's bombing who. And war crimes. Lots of war crimes."

Nine shook her head. "No, thank you. I would rather talk to the dogs."

Petra grinned. "It's mostly asses in politics. Besides, I'm not actually sure you could pass the background check. I'm quite certain that you wouldn't show up in anyone's database. Though, that could be a plus."

"My background is just fine, thank you."

Petra knew she'd hit a sore spot. There was a deep sadness in the young woman's posture, a longing. She hadn't wanted to become human. The concerns of humans were not her concerns. She wanted to go back to the wolves and focus on the true business of living: hunting, sleeping, and chasing sunshine.

"When we find Gabe, I think you two should talk. He knows about alchemy. If there's a way to bring you back to your pack, I know he will try to find it."

Nine flicked her a glance. "I am counting on it."

That startled her a bit. Petra had assumed that Nine was acting out of canine loyalty to her human friends, that she was like Sig in that way. But her first loyalty would always be to her pack, and her interests in finding Gabe surely went beyond wanting to help Petra find her husband. That was more than fair. No one in or around Temperance had simple motives.

Sig yawned and snuggled up closer to Petra. She

rubbed his belly. Maybe Sig had pure motives. Lunch meat was as pure as motivation got around here.

Petra flipped to the next page of Gabe's account and began to read.

I did not come to Temperance expecting to be hanged.

I had been investigating Lascaris as a Pinkerton agent for many months by the autumn of 1861. I had come to town posing as a merchant from Boston. I presented myself as a dealer in iron, seeking to expand my business west with the railroads. I came with the right clothes on my back, the right credentials, and the right amount of money to spread around.

When a stranger comes to town, there is always some measure of curiosity. So it was not surprising that the moment I stepped off the train in Temperance, I felt eyes on me. The eyes of pickpockets on my purse. The eyes of socialites on my luggage, assessing my marriageability by its weight and quality. The eyes of the local priest, wondering if I had a soul worth saving.

And of course the eyes of Lascaris were upon me—though I did not know it at the time. Lascaris had a vast network of prying eyes and furtive whispers that observed and reported everything of import in Temperance, not to mention most pieces of minor gossip. Information, no matter how benign it seemed at the moment, was currency to him, to be pieced together and used as leverage later.

Temperance was in the middle of a building boom. The streets were dirt, the townsfolk were a little grimy around the necks, and the whole place smelled like fresh sawdust and avarice. But those were all signs of growth. Logs had been freshly sawn from the nearby pine forest as lumber, hauled in, and used to build a general store, a train station, and a church. The walls still bled sap. I had arrived in town on a Sunday afternoon, just as church was letting out. All of Temperance's society poured out into the street— the ladies in their finest dresses, dour gentlemen staring at pocket watches, and the priest glowering over them all.

I tipped my hat at him. Some of the ladies lifted their eyes at me and looked away, smiling. The priest continued to glower. A shame; a priest could be a great ally in these sorts of investigations concerning supernatural happenstances. A priest who was sensitive to the work of the devil, as he perceived it, was worth his weight in gold. When I worked on an off-the-books assignment in Rome years before, a priest had been invaluable to me in hunting down a killer who believed himself to be Judas Iscariot. The deluded soul filled a wine chalice over and over again with the blood of murder victims.

The way this priest looked at me, I wondered what he would think about a chalice filled with my blood.

There was one inn in the bustling little town in 1861. The Dogwood Inn shared a wall and more than one door with the whorehouse next door. Prostitutes slipped in and out of the halls like ghosts, sliding through passages and cellar doors. Their soft laughter could be heard through the walls late at night. I didn't avail myself of their services, pleading that I was a freshly married man. The women at first were skeptical. But as I settled down at the inn, they became used to my presence. I overheard much gossip and was told more than a few secrets about men who are now long dead. Priests and prostitutes know all the truths of men, I am convinced.

As I made my way about town, I began polite inquiries about real estate, population growth, and the regularity of the train schedule, as a good businessman surveying his prospects would. All the business in the town, I noticed, was conducted in gold nuggets. There was just too much of it in circulation, in pockets, in cash drawers, and left behind on the bar.

Gold had been faked in societies ever since it was discovered. For many ancient alchemists, like the Egyptians, the transmutation of base metals into gold was considered complete if the appearances were similar. If it looked like gold, it was considered to be as good as gold. Much the same was true for medieval alchemists. More than a few passed off brass as the real thing. I had suspected this kind of pale chemistry to be at work in Temperance, to find a community of people trading in brass or plated metal.

I got a few sample pieces from around town and tested them, etching the samples in nitric acid. To my shock, all of them retained their color.

That had been my mission in coming to Temper-ance. Lascaris's investors back east were suspicious of the amount of gold that had been coming from the town. There had never been anyone who reported back from a mine. It simply appeared to be conjured from thin air. It was my mission to assess where it came from. I had an inkling that the idea of conjuring it from air was no exaggeration.

But pure gold had not been conjured in such a large scale before. I began to wonder if some alche-mist, somewhere in the past, had figured out how to do it. Maybe Paracelsus. Maybe Cleopatra. If anyone had figured it out, though, they had kept the secret well, hid the formula in long-rotted skulls or indeci-pherable codes. They hadn't been so bold as to spread it about in the town whorehouse or to use it to pay for steak. It was the reckless act of someone either brilliant, lucky, stupid, or a combination of all three. Whoever was doing this might have information about those ancient processes and deciphered their cryptic notes. That was a fearsome enough thing. But what might be worse was a modern alchemist who had figured out the process independently. That would take a magical talent and an intellect that was even more dangerous. If he knew how to make gold, what else might he know how to do? What other experiments had he conducted along the way? The alchemist would be a dangerous man.

It did not take me long in town to realize that Lascaris, of course, had been watching me. That was confirmed when he sent a message, asking me to dinner at his home. I accepted, but I went armed, as I always did in those days. No Pinkerton agent ever went out and about unarmed—to be fair, most people in the West at that time wouldn't be caught without some means of protecting themselves, lawman or no. But in addition to the standard arsenal, no one investigating the supernatural, such as I was, ever went out without a collection of more arcane weapons: a silver dagger, a pocketful of rock salt, and a bottle of powdered sulfur. I did not carry holy water or other such nonsense. I had seen it work in the hands of capable priests and nuns, but my belief in a good and just God was not strong enough to support its use. Instead, I limited myself to less temperamental tools, those weapons that could be relied upon without reference to the mental state or delusions of the user.

Thus armed, I made my way to Lascaris's home. It was close enough to the main street to walk there without hiring a carriage. It was a pleasant evening, and I enjoyed strolling down the street and the dirt road to his home, over a mile beyond the town proper.

From the edge of town, I could see light burning in the windows. It was the finest house in the area— even I could see that much from a distance. A stable and other outbuildings surrounding a house that was two stories tall, shingled in whitewashed cedar and roofed with slate. Roses had been imported to grow around the foundations of the house, an outrageous and thirsty luxury in the West. For a second I puzzled over how they would survive outside of a hot-house here, but then I took in the mansion as a whole, and it made more sense.

Though it was a fine house, there was definitely something amiss beyond the roses—though there was more to that as well, such as the fact that the clusters of rosebushes stood in the cardinal directions, too thorny and lush-growing for autumn. Balanced with that, the house itself had been strictly situated according to the compass directions: the front door faced east, and the back of the house west. Then there was the low fence surrounding the courtyard, made entirely of iron, a powerful material in the alchemical world. If that wasn't evidence enough, the stone path leading to the house was pockmarked with salt, and I also found bits of salt stuck between the floorboards of the front porch. The crystals had blackened, as if they had absorbed something terrible. Obsidian stones sat unobtrusively above each window and door lintel, like warding black eyes. Protective symbols were hidden in the elaborate decorative carvings supporting the porch. All of it said clearly to someone used to such things:

The owner of this house knows magic, and he has designed this place to be a fortress against eldritch intrusion.

I noted, too, that the house had been dug out with a basement, which was very unusual for the hasty architecture of the West. Most houses were put up quickly and not subject to this degree of care. Here, *though, the foundations were made of stone, and there were small, shuttered windows reaching below-ground level. As I approached, I spied a salamander slipping out from behind one of those shutters and scuttling into the night. The fire elemental was quick and stealthy, but I knew that they only gathered in places of magic.*

I was something of a quiet expert in these things, you see. I had been fascinated by the supernatural since an unfortunate childhood incident that claimed the life of my brother. Though I had spent much of my time in libraries, researching the supernatural, I had made a better career of quietly debunking false prophets and sorcerers for Alan Pinkerton. There was no shortage of so-called magic in this age of science and industry. Men—myself included—still wanted to believe in the strange and unnatural. Most of what I investigated, from Europe through the Americas, was sheer fraud. I was sent to rescue rich men and women who were spending their fortunes to peer into the crystal balls of charlatans.

But sometimes, just sometimes, something would happen that I could not explain. These events were rare. Yet, when they occurred, they added to my world view that there was more going on underneath the surface of everyday life than we could know or understand.

Lascaris, I knew, was a powerful magician of some stripe, though I didn't know where he drew his power from. Most magicians were limited by their available funds or were slaves to their lusts. The former group were too weak to manifest the monies they desired to do great works, and the latter were forever funneling their energy to bottomless pits of obsession. I did not have a sense if Lascaris was subject to that weakness. And he certainly had plenty of money. But every man had a chink in his armor. It was my duty to find and exploit his.

I screwed up my courage and rapped at the door.

A servant appeared and let me in. I was led to a sitting room illuminated by candles and oil lamps. I seated myself on a velvet couch to await the master's arrival.

I glanced over Lascaris's belongings in this room. Some expensive art, portraits of young women. Perhaps they were his weakness or he was showing off his virility. There was a standard assortment of globes and other knickknacks that men often furnished their rooms with to demonstrate status: leather-bound books, maps, spyglasses. The books were old classics, nothing interesting. And the maps were outdated drawings of far-off oceans. Nothing he'd bothered to keep current, and there wasn't enough of any given category to hint to true scholarship.

Window dressing, all of it. So what lay beneath?

The walls were freshly plastered, which was unheard-of in this part of the country. Bits of horsehair even still protruded at a corner. I leaned back and fingered it. It was too fine to be horsehair. I frowned.

In the corners of the room lay precise pinches of

salt, turning grey. A teacup of salt sat on a fireplace mantel. It hadn't been there long enough to accumulate dust, but it, too, was greying. I glanced at the fireplace. A fire danced in the grate. When I looked away from it, bits in the depths would flicker green. The fire seemed to hiss more than it popped. I wondered if there were other salamanders in the house looking to escape.

The place had an oppressive air, as if the windows had never been opened. I looked forward to buying a hot bath at the inn later tonight. If I got through the evening, that is.

"Mr. Manget?"

I stood immediately. I had not heard footsteps.

A man stood in the doorway. He was impeccably dressed, about fifty years old. His hair was greying, but shiny as silver. His eyes were dark and glittering, but he wore an affable smile as he extended his hand.

"Mr. Lascaris." I shook his hand, noting that it was stained black and green in places. He'd been fiddling with powders and potions. Maybe lead and copper. "Thank you for the kind invitation."

"I regret that it took me so long to welcome you to Temperance," he said. "It has been a busy season here."

"I see that the town is bustling. Very promising."

"You are involved with ironworks, I hear?"

"Yes. Most of our work is with the railroads, though I see you have impressive taste in decorative iron." It would only be polite to remark on the fence.

Lascaris gave a smile. "Yes. That was an indulgence. Very difficult to source that kind of craftsmanship out here on the frontier . . ."

We chatted about the town, first over drinks and then dinner. I learned that Lascaris had been in this location for only a few years. At that time, there had been no town, not even a railroad stop.

"It was dust and grassland," he told me over dessert.

"And now it's a thriving town. With such a lovely name . . . biblical?" I thought not. Temperance was an image in an arcane set of Tarot cards that circulated among magicians. The image was of a haloed angel pouring water and fire together at the edge of a river, creating a transcendent third element.

He chuckled. "No. That was the name of my deceased wife."

"Ah, I'm terribly sorry for your loss."

Lascaris shrugged. "It's been years, but the loss of a wife does linger."

I wondered how much of that was true.

"Well, the house is beautifully appointed," I remarked, gazing up at the hand-painted wallpaper.

"Thank you. I like to have a bit of civilization out here in Temperance. But not too much. Just the right amount." He steepled his fingers before him. "So. I am quite curious about your intentions toward my little town. I feel quite protective of it, as its father of sorts."

"Understandably so," I said. I had suspected as

much. I also suspected that I would only be able to remain in town if I was useful to him. "May I be frank with you?"

"Please."

"My employer has been struggling under the shadow of a poor reputation since the Ridgewater train accident. I assume you heard of it?"

"I heard something of it. That some flawed iron was found to have been implicated in a train derailment in Pennsylvania. Very unlucky."

"It was. Business has suffered, and much has fled to our competitors. My employers are searching for new markets where we might effectively demonstrate that we have improved our production techniques."

Lascaris paused. "I see. And the product has improved? I would not like to see such a happenstance in Temperance."

"Of course. The incident in Ridgewater was unfortunate, not to be repeated. However, it has left us, shall we say . . . limited in capital. There are outstanding debts, and the owners of the company are doing their best to save it."

I left that idea there, but I could see that Lascaris was thinking. I wanted him to consider that the situation could be turned to his advantage. That advantage being . . . a way to launder money out of Temperance under the noses of his existing investors, without attracting attention.

"Of course," I said, "we would not wish to do business in any market where we were unwelcome.

*And you no doubt have many existing business re-
lationships to contend with."*

*"That's true," he admitted. "But I think that you
and I might be able to come to an agreement of mu-
tual advantage."*

*We retired to the sitting room and talked late into
the night. A servant brought absinthe, which I had
not had for many years. By the time the moon was
high overhead, it was decided. We worked out the
terms and percentages. I was honestly surprised that
Lascaris would be this quick to deal. I had figured that
the idea would be danced around for many weeks.*

*But there was something impulsive about Lascaris.
And maybe just a little bit desperate. I couldn't figure
that part out at the time.*

*But later, I knew what it was. It was both impulse
and desperation, but also a sheer madness that threatened every man, woman, and child in Temperance . . .
and stranger creatures than I could ever have dreamed
of in a thousand years and a thousand bottles of absinthe.*

SUNSET PLAYED THROUGH the stained-glass windows of the Compostela and faded.

Lev waited. He waited in darkness and finally
decided to light the lamps. His heart jumped every
time the door opened, but only a couple of regulars
straggled in.

Perhaps Archer had let himself in the back door

and had crashed on the couch. But Lev's hearing was too keen; he was certain he would have heard footfalls on the back stairs and steps above from his vantage point at the bar.

His ghosts waited with him. Wilma busied herself with blowing in the ears of her favorite regulars and insulting the rest, while Father Caleb fiddled with his rosary beads as if he expected someone to answer him. Lev appreciated this show of support, on some level.

At dusk, a shadow in a hat came to the front door. Lev instinctively distrusted men in hats. That probably came from his time during the war. But it was a visceral pang of dread that he felt from his gut clear through to his spine, not just remembered foreboding.

The man approached the bar, wearing a park ranger's uniform. Lev recognized him, greeted him as the man removed his hat and placed it on the bar.

"Ranger Hollander," he said.

Mike Hollander nodded, looked away, then looked back. "Do you happen to know an Archer Harker?"

"Yes." Lev didn't elaborate. Maybe the kid had pissed in the wrong pool, but Lev wasn't going to give the ranger more to go on than he had to. He mentally calculated how much money he had in the cash register and the safe for bail money.

"I'm sorry to say it, but . . . we found him dead a few hours ago beside a creek in the southeast portion of the park."

Lev stayed rooted in place. Blood rushed through

his ears. He gripped the edge of the bar so hard his knuckles cracked.

"Oh, no. Hell, no," Wilma said. She was on his left, Father Caleb on his right. He could feel their cold shadows pressing against him, trying to fortify him. Father Caleb made the sign of the cross and muttered to himself.

The ranger continued. "It looks like foul play. He was apparently packing up camp when it happened. A hiker found him. Your name and address were in his wallet. I, uh . . . were you close?"

Lev whispered, "He was my son."

Was. For maybe a day.

And now he was dead. Here, and then gone.

CHAPTER 14

The Madness Season

These pages had taken time to write. As Petra sifted through them, she felt creases and wrinkles pressed into the paper, as if Gabe had tried to wad some of them up and throw them away. Others had hesitation marks carved in the margins, broken dashes that she imagined came from him pressing the pencil on the paper, thinking. Some were filled with lead, others empty. The pressure and vigor of the penmanship bloomed and faded, as if he had slept, woken, and written again and again.

She read and slept, waking with the pages pressed against her cheek. She drank Maria's potions and let her fingers graze over his writing, trying to imagine what he had felt living these events, recalling them.

This was the closest she'd been to him, she realized, this account of his past. And she might never get that close to him again:

Lascaris was mad. I had been drawn into his manipulations. Foolishly, I thought I had the upper hand.

I was terribly, terribly wrong.

Lascaris tested me, in many ways. First, he tested my ability to fulfill my end of the business bargain. Pinkerton sent a shipment of pig iron to make things look authentic, and I sent away bags of gold nuggets hidden in wine bottles and flour sacks. Cash would come back through a courier. This went back and forth a few times over the next months, without so much as a hitch. I feared a train robbery setting all these carefully laid plans awry, but we were lucky in that respect.

The financials up to snuff, he tested my loyalties. I was invited to Lascaris's home often. He was quite the entertainer, throwing parties for the townsfolk, visitors he found interesting, and whichever ladies he fancied at the moment. There was a revolving door of them, and none of those short-lived romances ever ended happily. And by happily, I mean that most of those women were never heard from again.

In the winter of 1861, a woman stepped off the train who I thought might have been his match. She was a singer from Ireland. She'd run out of money, and the conductor refused to take her any farther. She got kicked off in Temperance with only the clothes on her back. In most situations, she would have wound up immediately at the brothel, wandering half-dressed through the secret doors to the hotel in search of gold nuggets.

But Lascaris had seen her crying in the street and spitting on the train tracks. Something about that intrigued him, apparently, and he brought her home with him. The deal was ostensibly that she would cook for him. I am certain Lascaris knew nothing of Irish cooking, but he learned.

Muirenn turned out to be much more than a domestic servant, of course. He heard her singing in the kitchen, and he was entranced. She sang at his parties, and Lascaris fell for her. As much as a man like that can fall for a woman, anyway. But it was more than her voice; Muirenn was a witch, and that was irresistible to Lascaris.

By that time, Lascaris had dropped his guard a bit around me. He would play little card tricks for Muirenn, pull coins from behind her ear. Simple sleight of hand. One day, she surprised him by snatching the coin from his hand. She put it into her palm and closed her fist over it. When she opened it, the coin had turned into a tiny frog that hopped out onto the floor. The frog wound up under the chair in which I sat. I scooped it up and let it out the door.

Lascaris laughed uproariously at that. "You must tell me how you did it!"

Muirenn looked him straight in the eye with her hands on her hips and announced, "I'm a witch."

This was my opening, the one I'd been waiting for. "There's no such thing as witches," I declared. "You and your party tricks."

Muirenn waved me off. "You do not have to believe in something for it to be real. Tell me, do you believe in God?"

I shrugged. "I don't know if there is or isn't a God. But I do know that witches and demons exist only in the mind of the priest."

Lascaris only grinned, though. "Show me more, Muirenn."

She took off her shoes. She stood barefoot on his freshly polished floor. She clapped her shoes together, and they were suddenly full of water, cascading out on the floor in a puddle.

Lascaris clapped like a child. "Brava!"

Her chin lifted. "Show me a better party trick than that."

And that began an evening of one-upsmanship, the likes of which I had never seen. I think that I am relatively good at debunking most magicians. I have exposed a great many false table-tippers and fraudulent mediums in my time. But Lascaris and Muirenn were inexplicable. I thought I could have explained the frog as simple misdirection and the shoes as a bit of hypnotism. But it all went terribly, terribly insane.

Lascaris started a fire. He went to the basement, and there was a rattle of locks. He returned with an assortment of glass bottles. He threw an apple into the fire with a pinch of black powder, and it rolled back out as an orange. He bit into the orange and spat out mercury onto the floor.

Muirenn was not impressed. She muttered over the fire, and the fire took on the shape of a great lizard or a dragon.

"Salamander, salamander," she chanted. "Come to me from the ether."

The fire-being crawled out of the fire. Muirenn reached toward it and stroked its ill-formed head without getting burned. The fire coalesced into a tiny lizard-like creature with a pattern of stars on its back, which turned and fled back into the fire.

I sat down on the couch and feigned confusion.

"Don't faint," Lascaris said, clapping me on the back and shoving a brandy into my hand. He was delighted. "You are among friendly magics."

By hard and bitter experience, I knew better. There is no friendly magic.

Lascaris began to reveal to me more truth. Once he had an audience for his feats, his ego soared. He would start to hold séances, the three of us, in his home over a black mirror. Many strange visions bubbled up in the glass, things my mind now still struggles to comprehend. I demonstrated appropriate naïve curiosity and fascination. He asked me to source odd things for him in addition to the iron shipments: a peacock and a pair of peahens, volcanic ash from Italy, coins from ancient Rome, a jar full of shark teeth.

I knew that he was using these materials for more than party tricks to impress Muirenn. Gradually, I was invited to their odd after-dinner rituals: attempts to summon spirts and such. They'd send away the servants for the night and draw arcane symbols on the floors in chalk to dance on. Creatures would come knocking at the windows or peer back from the glass in mirrors. By the ends of these sessions, the chalk would be worn away, but the creatures would linger.

Real magic was ruled by Lascaris's pocket watch. He insisted that the most powerful times to work magic were at noon and midnight, that spirits were most restless then. He would work the most bizarre magics at those times, the ones calling for blood, spite, and sacrifices.

On my walks back to the inn, you can be certain that I kept one hand on my pistol and another on my silver knife. Shadows seethed on the road between his house and town. I jumped at every coyote howl and every flicker of bats across the sky.

There was a particular coyote I remember. He would walk with me along the road from Lascaris's gate to the edge of town. No monster of the dark ever bothered me in his company. He would keep pace with me, my escort in darkness. He would walk to the end of the dirt road, then stand and watch from the edge of night as I walked to the main street in Temperance. Then, he would always vanish.

I wondered if my strange escort was a summoning of Lascaris or Muirenn. But no. I didn't think so. The coyote merely ferried me back and forth, like Charon over the River Styx. Why, I never figured out. Perhaps he was some kind of genius loci, a spirit of that place and that dirt road.

I had enough suspicion that Lascaris was conjuring gold by this time and not mining it. Gold and other, more fearsome things. He began to ask if I would send for more morbid and dangerous things for him: the severed hands of an executed prisoner, a rare book that was rumored to be cursed, a cornerstone from a building destroyed in a fire. Once, he asked for a pair of fresh human eyes, and they had to be green.

I'd been sitting on his porch when he asked for them. I blinked and blurted, "What do you want the eyes for?"

"For the Great Work, my friend." He blew smoke from his cigar into the darkness, where it writhed uncomfortably before dissipating.

"I don't understand."

"The Great Work is the greatest conjuring, beyond even the creation of gold. It is the culmination of the works of the seven stages of alchemy, perfecting each process until immortality can be achieved."

I pretended to be shocked into silence. He had confessed to the gold. I just needed proof to bring to Pinkerton.

"I will get you the eyes," I said. "Green."

That took some doing. Back east, Pinkerton's men combed the undertakers for a green-eyed dead man.

They cut his eyes out and pickled them in a jar, sending them to me carefully packed in a crate with some silks for Muirenn.

Lascaris was pleased. He did not ask where they had come from, and I did not volunteer.

But I felt I now had better standing to ask him more about the Great Work. I wanted to gauge how far along he was in this endeavor. The gold was fascinating enough, but I confess to having more curiosity about what his ultimate aims were, since the gold seemed like a mere means to an end.

In hindsight, I realize I was already being shown another spell: the one I was under.

He took me for a ride one day. We packed up two of his horses and headed east. On that ride, he told me that he was working through the alchemical stages, and that he thought he was close to perfecting them. We were on our way, he said, to show me the thing that he felt was key to accomplishing this.

We passed through the lands that now surround the Rutherford Ranch. At that time, there were no buildings or fences or cattle. Just grassland and bison grazing in that sea of green whipped by the wind. We rode until we met a massive oak tree, standing alone in the field.

"Behold," he said. "The Lunaria."

It looked to be an ordinary tree to me. But I noticed that the land around it was dark, with the unmistakable rusty scent of old blood in the soil. I did not ask if the stain was cattle or human—I was certain I didn't want to know . . . or that it even mattered to me at that point. There were chalk marks on the tree, alchemical symbols. The ground was littered with black feathers, puddles of mercury, and silver powder.

I dismounted and touched the bark of the tree. It was warm, like an animal. "How is this the key to eternal life?"

"The Lunaria is the embodiment of the 'As above, so below' principle of alchemy. Its roots dig into the earth and its branches reach into the sky. It is a perfect mirror, conducting energy from the earth to the cosmos in a perfect circuit.

"I have been working on this tree for many months. Feeding it. It will soon be ready."

I made a point not to ask him what he had been feeding it. The smell of blood was enough to let my imagination fill in the blanks.

Pinkerton was ready for me to pull out by that time, to come back east and report to the investors. I was torn. I felt the tale of Lascaris's wealth and madness was too fantastical to be believed, that I needed hard evidence to deliver to the men in grey flannel suits. I also dreaded leaving Lascaris to his own devices. As things stood now, when he demanded body parts, I could scavenge those through back channels without harming anyone. If I was not there . . . I knew that he would subscribe to more direct methods.

You see, he was making other friends. One such man was Joseph Rutherford. He was a shady man, a gambler and a thug who'd recently come to town to

run a gambling operation. He'd ingratiated himself to
Lascaris. I had heard him threaten some of the women
at the inn to the point at which he was no longer
welcome there or the brothel. I'd seen him rough up
men in the bar who owed him money, and a couple
of those men never came back. I had no doubt that
were I to leave, Rutherford would step in with more
sadistic means.

Oddly, I will admit the thought made me a bit jealous. There was something that drew me to Lascaris
and his strange powers. Perhaps more than anything,
that disturbing emotion was what woke me up and
made me realize I had to leave. It was getting too dangerous to stay.

I wrote Pinkerton a letter, telling him that I would
be on the train back east within a week with a full
report.

In the meantime, I waited for my chance to gather
evidence, which came soon enough. With the aid of
my spyglass from my vantage point on the second
floor of the inn, I saw them leaving the house one
evening. Though I couldn't tell for certain, I was betting that both the witch and the alchemist were no
longer inside. My moment had come.

I struck out on the road toward his house, walking
as briskly as I could. No lights were on. This boded
well for snooping and thievery.

Once again, the coyote had come to walk beside
me. He seemed jumpy, whining as he trotted along.
I should have listened to his warning, but I trudged

up to Lascaris's fence. The coyote stopped at the fence and turned away. He would not wait for me.

I knew the evidence I needed was in the basement. All secrets wind up underground. So I tried the basement windows first. They were all locked behind the shutters. I rounded the house to the back door of the servants' quarters. I knew that the servants kept a key, for their convenience, under a spittoon at the back door. I found the key and let myself in, wandering into the kitchens.

After some fumbling and searching in the dark, I lit a lamp and quickly located a door beneath the stairs. Predictably, it was locked with an iron hasp. I was not without some lock-picking skill, but it took me longer than I would have liked to work it open.

Such little setbacks would prove crucial.

For the time, though, I had just lifted my lamp and headed downstairs.

I don't know what I expected to find when I went into Lascaris's basement, but what I saw was beyond any of my wild imaginings. It was a fully equipped laboratory, with glassware stretching on a table from one end of the basement to the other. A dim fire burned in an athanor in one corner, and powders and elixirs gleamed in amber glass bottles on shelves. Everything was meticulously labeled: sulfur, mercury, potash, fingers of an elderly woman, frog eyes, swan hearts . . . it was a dizzying collection of science and cruelty behind glass.

I had to work quickly. Lascaris must have kept

notes, and that would be the evidence I needed. I searched the lab tables and quickly spied a stack of leather-bound journals. I flipped through them. Lascaris's wandering script covered the pages. Skimming the dates, I gathered he'd been working alchemy for at least thirty years. I turned away from the pages outlining experiments on humans, searching out the operation for gold . . . there. The most rumpled pages were the most used ones. I saw a thick section of pages, stained by carbon black, that were studded with the alchemical symbols for gold and the sun. This would have to do for evidence. I could translate it later, once I was on a train going east and could gather my thoughts.

I had no sooner slipped the journal in my pocket and turned to leave when I heard the door at the top of the stairs open.

I drew my pistol, fearing there was no way of getting out of this without bloodshed. While I had no desire for it to come to that—and though the investors would very much want Lascaris alive—I valued my own hide over his.

When he came downstairs, there was a profound look of disappointment on his face. "It took you long enough," Lascaris said. "Everyone betrays me in the end."

I aimed my pistol at him. "I am leaving now."

"No," he said with a sigh. "You won't."

Something grabbed my ankle. I looked down, and the shadows on the floor had congealed into a tarry *mess. I moved to extricate myself, but the mass grew arms, reaching up to drag me down.*

I shot at it. The bullets and the sound were swallowed up by the cold darkness of the floor.

I shot at Lascaris. I know I hit him, but the last thing I remember as the darkness devoured me was him standing over me, uttering, "You will be part of the Great Work."

It was the most chilling threat I'd ever heard.

PETRA CLOSED HER eyes, thinking of the tree, Lascaris's Great Work, his attempt to create a nexus of above and below. The Lunaria had, when she first met it, seemed inquisitive and playful. But when she'd encountered its burned roots at the Rutherford Ranch and its spiritual image in the Eye of the World . . . she knew it had changed. It had grown grasping. Bloodthirsty. Maybe it had begun that way, and time had gentled it? Or maybe it had begun gentle, and the loss of the last Hanged Man had driven it mad?

She pressed her hand to her mouth. She had the sense that the Hanged Men had been the Lunaria's children. It had treated Gabe and the rest of the men with an almost loving attention . . . when there had been men. Now that they were gone, maybe the nest was vacant, and the mother driven mad, staring at the empty shells of what had once been alive.

In her lap, Sig sighed.

Petra echoed it with one of her own.

When I came to, I was outdoors, a cool breeze pushing against my body. We were at the foot of the Lunaria. A rope was around my neck, and Joseph Rutherford was propping me up against the trunk. I stunk like chemicals—like lime and sulfur. My skin was crusted with the powder, and it stung my watering eyes. I wondered what spells had been worked on my body while I was unconscious. I felt weak, as if I had no blood left in my veins.

Still, I came out swinging . . . or I would have, if my hands hadn't been tied. Joseph stepped back, holding the length of rope, a look of pleasure on his face.

Lascaris was there. The side of his head was bandaged heavily. I drew some small satisfaction that I'd managed to hit him. And Muirenn, always beside him, gazed upon me with curiosity.

"It will be glorious, my friend," Lascaris said to me. "You will be part of the Great Work."

Again, those words chilled me. "People will be looking for me. Alan Pinkerton knows I'm here."

Lascaris laughed. "Pinkerton can do nothing to stop me. I have unlimited gold and eternal life. He is just a man. He is nothing." He glanced at his pocket watch. I could see that it was now noon.

The rope tightened around my neck. Muirenn stood before us, singing a lullaby. I don't know if it was part of a spell or a touch of her own madness. Above me, a raven lit in the branches and cawed. Other ravens came, joining in the screeching.

Lascaris tried to wave off the ravens with his hat.

He was shouting at Joseph to do something about them, to frighten them off with a gunshot, I think—between the caws and the singing and the lack of air, words were losing meaning.

But Joseph was pulling the rope, and no gunshot came. I dangled, suspended between heaven and earth. Breath was driven from my body, and I felt the blood strangle away in a haze of stars and black.

The last thing I heard as a human man was Muirenn's lullaby, drowned by the ravens' screaming.

But that wasn't the end.

I remember bits and pieces of sensation from then on. Lascaris later explained that the fermentation process he intended to work had failed, due to the interference of the ravens. He decided to leave my body to hang, like fruit, overnight. I think he had the intent of cutting me down in the morning, to see what was left. Or perhaps he intended to abandon me there, as an example, some kind of scarecrow to intimidate his enemies. I'm not certain which it was, to this day.

But it didn't matter—the tree had its own ideas. Sometime in the night, the rope must have broken. I felt the roots of the tree creeping up out of the ground, consoling me, drawing me down into the earth.

And I stayed there, underground, for a full moon cycle. I was still somewhat connected to my body, though in a stupor. I was conscious of rotting, of pressure, of the tree roots digging into me, of honey-colored light. I could hear the squawk of ravens in the tree above during the day, as if they wondered

*what happened to me and gossiped among them-
selves about Lascaris and his unnatural workings.
The gossip would be interrupted by the discovery of
something shiny and subside, only to begin again. At
night, the roots shifted and turned. There was space
here in the darkness, and light. The tree had its own
world it was building, underground.*

And I was part of it, from the beginning.

*I surfaced in a warm spring morning, blinking rot and
dew from my eyes. The tree had pushed me up above
the grass. My clothes were disintegrating from the rot,
and the whole world smelled like grave dirt. Above
me, in the tree, ravens cawed and churned. One fluttered down to pluck the last button from my shirt.*

I was not alone.

Lasacaris and Rutherford were standing over me.

*Lascaris looked disgusted. He flung his hat on the
ground. "It didn't work. Look at him."*

*I looked down. My body was studded with the quills
of pinfeathers, and I was coated in some kind of albu-
menic goo. The pinfeathers seethed and retracted in and
out of my skin in time with my breathing. I felt as if I
were an egg not fully cooked, runny and incomplete.*

*"Shoot him. Take him out of his misery," Lascaris
ordered.*

*Rutherford had squatted to squint at me. "He may
still be of some use to you."*

"How?"

Rutherford just shrugged, eyeing me thoughtfully.
And thus began my service to Lascaris and my tie
to the Rutherford lands.

PETRA PUT THE pages down. It had grown dark, the last bit of daylight drained out of the day.

"Maria will be home soon," Nine said, and she began to gather the papers to hide them.

Petra gave them to her. She glanced sidelong at Sig, who was sleeping on his back with all four feet in the air. She wondered how much he had gotten around, if he came from a family of coyotes who had become fascinated with humans who traveled the road from Temperance to her trailer. She rubbed his belly and sighed.

"What's wrong?" Nine asked her.

"I just wish . . . that Gabe had told me this himself. In person. I thought we had time, time to resolve all the questions between us and leave things in a good place. I really did."

Nine paused to put her hand on Petra's arm. "You have his stories. That *is* his person."

Petra looked through the window to the purpling sky on the horizon. She thought about Nine's words, but shook her head. She didn't have him. Not really. These pages were cold consolation, a hollow reflection of what he had once been. Though they would likely outlast them both.

CHAPTER 15

The Pearl

There was not much time.

Lev had to act quickly. He strode into the front door of Harrington's Funeral Home, a Victorian house decked out with heavy-duty gingerbread architectural trimming just outside the county seat. The county coroner, Susan Harrington, was also a funeral director, as so often happened in rural places like these. There were, after all, only so many places one could legally keep a body fresh outside of a hospital. Lev had checked with the nearest hospital about his son's body, but then got referred to the funeral home for inquiries. Some business about running out of room.

A viewing was in progress for an old woman. He'd seen it in the paper. Raina Sue Carpenter. She'd passed away at home, peacefully, survived by a metric fuckton of relatives and friends that took up a whole newspaper column. He would have preferred to come to the funeral home when no one was around, but he didn't have much choice. There was a long line to sign the guest book, and Lev stared forward, listening to bits and pieces of gossip:

"You know, I heard she took too many hydrocodone tablets."

"I heard that she went to that Pain Management Clinic. Those places are always scams. The one she went to got raided by the DEA last week for Medicare fraud."

"Can you believe that she didn't leave her money to her daughter?"

"Her son said that she left it all to the humane society. How selfish is that?"

"Yeah. What about her children?"

Lev rolled his eyes. Gossip always came to him, no matter how much he tried to avoid it. He rubbed his forehead as the people at the front of the line were complaining loudly about the guest book pen being out of ink.

He felt a voice close at his ear, a spectral voice. He glanced to his left, and there was the ghost of an old woman wearing a velour jogging suit standing there, giving dirty looks to the mourners. Her hair was tightly permed, and she was wearing sunglasses. *"Fuck this. I got no peace from these assholes while I was alive, and now this bullshit?"*

Lev snorted, causing an elderly man beside him to give him a sour glance.

"I'm not kidding," the ghost of Raina Sue said. *"When my cat died, I was ready to shuffle off this mortal coil. I sure hope that there's a section in heaven of cats where I can get away from these fucking people."*

Suppressing more laughter, Lev slipped in behind a family with children whining about wanting water. Instead of signing the guest book, he slipped down the hallway, past the restrooms with the patterned carpet designed to hide stains, to the part of the funeral home where the filthy work of preparing the dead to be seen by the living went down. The ghost of the old woman followed him.

"What are you up to, young man?" she asked.

"Don't you have a funeral to attend?" he muttered.

"The service isn't until five. Besides, I don't want to hang out with that motley crew of liver-spotted dicks."

He rolled his eyes and continued down the hallway. He wished he could introduce her to Wilma. They might be able to have a swear-off that would send Father Caleb into ghostly apoplexy.

There was a little morgue tucked away in the back, hidden by a nondescript door with a sign that announced FUNERAL HOME PERSONNEL ONLY. He let himself in and flipped on the lights. Raina Sue's ghost drifted in behind him.

The fluorescent lights buzzed to life overhead, illuminating in cold light an area that might have originally been a kitchen. Stainless-steel sinks and cabinets lined one wall, and there was a garden hose attached to one sink fixture. A floor drain pierced the center of the tiled floor. A stainless-steel coroner's slab was perched in the middle of the room, spotlessly clean. Various mismatched file cabinets stood around shelves of chemical bottles and plastic tubing.

The place was organized in the physical world. But it was chaos in the afterlife. The ghost of an elderly man paced around the floor in a circuit, mumbling to himself. The ghost of a young woman in a hospital gown sat on the coroner's slab, holding a baby.

Raina Sue was at his elbow. *"What are you doing here, anyway? I don't think you work here."*

Lev took a deep breath. Best not to acknowledge them. Best to get in and get out.

A large steel door, like the kind Lev had behind the bar, signaled that there was a refrigeration unit humming at one end of the room. Lev opened the heavy door latch and peered in.

Ghosts were crowded in here, especially for such a rural place. The county must be having a run of very shitty luck. The ghosts from the freshly dead were always stronger. There was a man rubbing his hands over his chest, hollow with what looked like a gunshot wound. A middle-aged woman was plucking at a seat belt embedded in her shoulder, ignoring the fact that her legs were missing.

And a dark shape was folded up in the corner, sitting on the floor. Lev knelt before it.

"Archer?"

The young man looked up, confused. *"Dad? Where am I?"*

Lev assessed the strength of the ghost's aura. It was weak. There wasn't much time. "I'm getting you out of here. Come with me."

"Okay."

He stood and counted five body bags stacked on metal and wire shelves. He flipped through the toe tags, found the one he was looking for. "John Doe 32" had been crossed out and replaced with "Harker, Archer."

Lev took a deep breath and pulled the zipper, just to be sure.

His son's face was quiet in repose, pale. His neck, however, had been torn out. His clothes were stained the color of dark corn syrup.

Lev groaned inwardly. Those injuries . . . but he reached forward to touch the young man's brow.

"Is that me?"

"Yes. I need you to do something for me. I need you to get back inside your body, as deep as you can get."

The ghost's brow wrinkled.

"Just lie down and rest for now. I have this in hand. Go to the body and don't let go."

The ghost reached for the body. As if he was climbing into a sleeping bag, he lay on the shelf. Soon, Lev could not see the spirit at all.

"Good."

Lev zipped the body bag back up and slung the

body on his shoulder. He retreated to the main room, looked about.

He heard a rustling from inside the body. Faint, like a bird fluttering in a cage.

Good. It hadn't escaped.

"What the hell are you doing?" Raina Sue stood before him, her tiny fists planted on her hips.

Lev cast about. A large plastic trash can, about forty gallons, stood in the corner. Unceremoniously, Lev dumped the body into the can and did his best to cram the bulk of it inside. To obscure its contents, he arranged a sheet on the top.

"Are you trying to steal that body?" Raina shrieked. The other ghosts turned toward him, eyes narrowed.

"I'm taking him home," Lev said simply.

But the ghosts were getting agitated. The ones in the cooler stepped through the metal door to the floor and had begun waving their arms around, as if trying to shoo away a bird caught in a house. A woman stepped through the wall, drawn by the commotion. She must have been in the process of getting makeup—her face was half-painted, and her hat was askew.

"He's a thief!" Raina Sue pointed to him.

Ordinarily, Lev just ignored ghosts. But when they got agitated, really agitated, sometimes they could draw attention from the outside world. If they got wound up enough, sometimes they could knock over objects or mess with electricity. New ghosts, the kind that passed right on to the light, usually didn't have the power to do these sorts of poltergeist tricks. But there were some traumatic deaths here, and Raina Sue was stirring the pot.

Sure enough, the fluorescent lights overhead started to flicker. Then a bottle of chemicals on the counter fell over, the cap breaking, and the room began to fill with a scent of something like formaldehyde.

Enough. He needed to escape attention. He lifted his right hand into the shape of the Horned Hand, pulling his two middle fingers down, as if he were at a Metallica concert. He turned to the nearest ghost, the woman with the half-done makeup. He flicked her on the forehead as if she were a misbehaving dog.

The ghost dissipated, like smoke.

He lifted his hand to Raina. "Back off."

Raina made a face and backpedaled, eyes wide and earrings jingling. She didn't know that the Horned Hand wasn't a permanent fix. The woman with the makeup would re-collect herself in a matter of hours. But these were naive ghosts; they didn't know that. And they didn't *need* to know that. For all they knew, Lev was a powerful necromancer who could send them on a freight train straight to the circles of hell.

Keeping the Horned Hand up as warning, Lev glanced about for a way to escape. He covered his face with his other sleeve to shield against the fumes. Funeral homes always had a back door, wide enough to accommodate coffin trucks and large vehicles, and he spotted it quickly enough. Lev wheeled the can to the doors at the opposite end of the room, pushed it outside on a concrete loading dock.

"Stay here," he told the ghost of Archer.

He shut the door behind him and turned back to the morgue. He'd let the funeral home employees figure out how to turn on the venting system to clear the chemicals out; there certainly wasn't anyone living there. He held his breath as he came back through the morgue without the can, glaring at the ghosts giving him the stink eye, threatening them with his flicking fingers.

He threaded his way back to the main hallway. He started coughing and covered his face with his elbow. The air out here was fresh, clearing the chemical stink from his lungs. A funeral employee outside the men's room asked, "Are you all right, sir? Is there anything I can get for you?"

"No thank you," Lev said. "I'm just . . . stunned."

"There's water over here . . ."

Lev took the water and felt forced to drift through the line to see the old lady, Raina Sue. He nodded and made small talk about how peaceful she looked and how Harrington's had done a lovely job with her makeup. He thought he saw her peeping through the wall at him. He lifted his right hand and she receded.

He drifted out the front door and walked slowly to his truck, heart hammering. He started it, pulled it around to the side of the building, and nonchalantly loaded the trash can in.

"It's gonna be okay," he muttered to the bin.

He cranked the engine and had to remind himself to go slow on the way out, not to attract attention. It was agonizing as he drove down the freshly black-topped drive, surrounded by pedestals with fern baskets. When he got to the highway, he hit the gas.

He didn't have much time.

A spirit could only linger around the body for so long before it escaped for good.

SPIRIT AND MATTER were pretty much subjective categories.

At least, that was the way Gabe saw it now, suspended in darkness. It seemed that there was a somewhat arbitrary line drawn between them that didn't always make sense in his world. Weird things precipitated from spirit, and matter had a way of spontaneously dissolving.

He was pretty sure he was disincorporating now. His awareness had lost its center point within his skull, and it began to wander. Not far enough to reach Petra, wherever she was, but far enough that the disorientation was overwhelming. He was going to die here, for good, as his consciousness bled out, diluted, and dissolved into the water.

Something glimmered in the blackness, moving within his chest. He tried to squint, but wasn't sure if it was a hallucination. Perhaps he was sliding back into the spirit world. The movement within his chest glittered gold under his shirt, and he felt it squirming behind his lung, clawing through the skin in his back. He felt a brush against his shoulder, a thread, like a root. He snapped to full alertness as the pain chewed into his body. Hot blood trickled down his shoulder.

He sucked in his breath as a lance of pain pierced the back of his neck. Rock cracked behind it. A tiny, spidery root dug its way beneath his scalp, boring into the back of his skull.

This was not the spirit world at all; he was submerged in the underground river, and something was chewing out of his body, seeking earth beyond.

The Lunaria. He knew that touch anywhere. He dimly wondered how it had gotten this far, how it had traversed these many miles. He had no doubt, though—this was unmistakably its influence, that feeling of liquid sunshine. But this was not the tender, loving touch of the tree that he'd known for decades. This was angry, insistent, excruciating.

He glanced down. A root blossomed out of his chest, slipping through a rib, questing. He realized then that the tree had not traversed this distance to chew on him. It was *part* of him. It was *from* him. He had carried the seed of it inside his body. And now it was reestablishing itself, taking root here. Perhaps the original was failing, and this was its last-ditch effort to survive. Perhaps Lascaris's influence from the spirit world had either poisoned that one or inspired this new growth.

Whatever the reason, he had no way of knowing if the tree meant him good or ill.

The root burned into the back of his brain, reaching for the retina of his blind left eye.

Ill. He was guessing ill.

PETRA STARED AT the pearl on Maria's kitchen table. She rolled it back and forth between her thumbs, inspecting its perfect glimmer. It was large, very large—as big as a gumball. And the color was unusual—that blue sheen, almost an aqua. She'd seen black pearls that were a peacock, iridescent blue, but never anything like this.

It was likely worth a fortune, she thought as she looked at it. If it was the real deal.

"What is that?" Nine asked, bringing a bowl of cereal to the table. She'd been poking at it with a spoon for the last fifteen minutes as it grew soggy, as if she couldn't decide if it was really food or not.

"I found it in Gabriel's pickup. I think whoever took him left it there. It's a pearl. Typically, they're formed when there's an injury to the inside of a mollusk. Aragonite forms, and then the pearl forms of layers of calcium carbonate. I mean, if it's real. It could be cultured. Somebody could have stuck a bead in a mollusk and pulled it out after a while, and there might only be a few layers of nacre on it. I guess dye could account for its color, but . . ."

Nine's eyes had glazed over, and she absently scratched behind her ear. She pushed her cereal

across the table, where Sig sat in a chair. He stuck his
face in the milk and began to slurp noisily.

"You could always take it to a jeweler. They might
be able to tell. I mean, once their eyes stopped bug-
ging out of their heads." Maria was making a salad at
the counter. Petra wasn't hungry in the slightest, but
had promised to eat a salad for Maria in exchange for
the chance to use Maria's washer and dryer.

"It would likely be sent out to be X-rayed," Petra
said. "That could take weeks." She pushed the pearl
back and forth across the table. Sig watched, his nose
wriggling back and forth as he tracked the pearl's
movement. He eventually grew tired of it and turned
his attention back to slurping cereal milk. He took
his fill and jumped down. Pearl, the cat, hopped up
on the table and began to lap up the rest. The coyote
stretched out at Petra's feet and belched.

Maria set the salad and a bottle of homemade salad
dressing before Petra.

"Thanks."

It should have looked delicious—spinach and green
lettuce with tomato, hard-boiled egg, avocado, and
carrots. But Petra felt indifferent to it. She drizzled the
salad dressing on the leaves but paused, staring at the
bottle. An idea tickled in the back of her head.

"Vinegar," she said.

"There's vinegar, red wine, some oregano . . ."

Petra dropped the pearl in her palm, held it over
the salad, and poured the vinegar all over it.

"What on earth are you doing?" Maria clearly thought she'd lost her mind.

"Calcium carbonate dissolves in vinegar." She held the pearl in her hand, in the warm dressing. "There was a legend about that . . . that Cleopatra, operating on a dare from Mark Antony at one of her fancy dinner parties, dissolved one of her pearl earrings in a goblet of vinegar and drank it."

"You mean to tell me that you're dissolving a pearl worth a fortune on my kitchen table?"

"Yeah. Kind of?" It sounded immensely stupid. No one in the room was Cleopatra. That pearl could do a whole lotta good for a whole lotta people. She stared at it, hesitating. The vinegar would take hours to work . . . she could rinse if off right now and make it part of her bequest to Maria. For some reason, though, she hesitated.

"What would you hope to accomplish by doing that?"

"I, uh, I want to see what's at the middle. Like . . . a Tootsie Pop. How many licks does it take . . ."

She shook her head. "It's your pearl."

But Maria did bring her a coffee cup half-full of red wine vinegar. Petra transferred the pearl to the coffee cup.

"What are you going to do if it dissolves into nothing?"

"Feel really stupid. Likely, there's nothing there. Aragonite at the middle of the pearl would probably dissolve in the vinegar, too. But . . . that's an awfully big pearl. I just . . . I have a hunch." She shrugged. "That's all I have to go on, as lame as it sounds."

"I am not judging the lame-sounding things that go on in my house."

She glanced at the clock. "Visiting hours at my dad's nursing home are soon. I'm gonna head down there and check with him."

Maria nodded. "I'll drive you."

"I can go by myself. Really." She was feeling helpless.

"You passed out. You have no business driving."

Petra glanced across the table at Nine, who shrugged. Nine must have told her about her last visit to the Eye of the World. Probably not the whole truth . . . "passed out" sounded a lot more benign than "nearly drowned yourself."

Petra didn't tell her that she'd driven to Owen's house to toss the joint. And she knew that Nine hadn't imparted that little adventure, because Maria would have shit a brick at that. Maybe it *was* better if Maria drove—there likely wasn't an APB out on Maria's vehicle.

"Okay. Thanks."

Petra went to the bedroom to find her boots. She shoved the maps into the purse she'd begun carrying. Not having pockets was a bitch, but she had to admit that the purse was more helpful for concealing papers.

Still, she was on edge when they left the reservation. She'd left Sig behind with Nine on purpose; if

Owen's men were out looking for her, she didn't want them to go all batshit and shoot a "wild" animal. Owen was a sneaky man, and she was certain he was plotting to get back at her for invading his little castle on a hill.

To her surprise, the drive to the nursing home was uneventful. There were no cops waiting in ambush in the parking lot. She walked right in, checked in at the front desk, and the receptionist didn't punch the red emergency button under the desk. Maria picked through the glossy magazines in the lobby, while Petra headed back to her father's room.

She knocked on the open door frame. "Hey, Dad."

Her dad was sitting up in bed, fiddling with the television remote. He had it aimed in the wrong direction, and it seemed to be changing the channel in the next room, which was stirring up a flurry of cursing from his neighbor.

He brightened when he saw her. "Hi, Petra."

She closed the door behind her, crossed the room, and leaned in to give him a hug.

"How are you feeling?"

"Better," she lied.

He gave her a skeptical look and patted her thin cheek. Good. He was lucid tonight.

"Did you talk to your mother?"

She sat on the edge of his bed. "Yes."

"Good. You should see her."

"Dad. I won't tell her where you are if you don't want me to."

His eyes darted right and left, as if he was contemplating escape. "It doesn't matter. You just . . . see your mom and do what you need to do."

She shifted the subject. They were adults. She was not in charge of their relationship. "I wanted to ask you some questions about alchemy."

His head snapped around. "You're not screwing around with alchemy, are you?" He shook his finger in her face. "I told you that there are no magical ways to cure cancer. Just like there aren't any to cure Alzheimer's. You'll just wind up locked away in the spirit world. As much as it pains me to say . . . you have to let nature take its course."

Petra flinched. "Dad. I'm not looking into alchemy to cure myself. I'm trying to find Gabe. He's missing. Remember?"

His eyes clouded. "Yes. He's gone. You were looking for him."

"Right. I found some things that might be clues. These maps he drew . . ." She pulled them out of her purse. "I don't know what they mean."

He took the pages from her with palsied hands. "These are the roads to ruin. Spirit tracks. The symbols are alchemical symbols. This is the sun . . . the moon . . . lead . . . and silver."

"I got some of that. I just can't translate them to actual geography. I think they are maps of the world underneath the Rutherford Ranch. But I can't orient them, or tell what they lead to. Or even if they're still valid. That place changes from minute to minute."

"What do you remember about the ranch? Any landmarks?"

"There's the ranch house. A barn and some out-buildings. Mountains to the west, and the Lunaria in the back forty."

He turned the maps back and forth. Petra dug into her bag for a pencil and gave it to him. He began to scribble on the maps, and she didn't stop him.

"Mountains are earth. These symbols"—he pointed to some symbols that looked like an upside-down tri-angle with a horizon line drawn through it—"might be the mountain. The water symbols . . . those might be rivers. I'm betting that your Lunaria is the sun . . . there's only one on each map."

Petra nodded excitedly. With Nine's divination of true north, it began to make some sense. If she ori-ented the mountains to the west, there was a sun in the center of each. The Lunaria was the center of this world. The lines radiated outward from that, but she didn't know what they led to.

He paged through them. "There's no telling scale or how far these run. But that might be a starting point."

"Yes! Thank you. Also . . . I found something that Gabe's abductor dropped. A pearl."

"A pearl?"

"Do pearls have any meaning in alchemy?"

He rubbed the stubble on his chin. "I suppose a pearl could symbolize the full moon, the ripeness of light. The moon governs water, intuition, things hidden."

"I keep coming back to water. When Owen and Gabe and Nine and I were on the Sepulcher Mountain this winter, he was muttering about a mermaid. I wasn't sure what to make of it."

He seemed to think. "There was a myth of a mermaid, Melusine. She had the two tails, the tails of a serpent, and symbolized duality. She's been immortalized on the coffee cups of those fancy coffees.

"Anyway. Melusine was both human and Other . . . a man pursued her mercilessly. She agreed to be married to him, on the condition that he not watch her bathing. Her husband didn't adhere to the bargain and saw what she was. She devoured him and took off, living happily ever after."

"That is . . . really bizarre."

He shrugged. "Alchemy isn't clean or neat."

"Clearly. But I need to find this mermaid."

"My initial thought is to follow the moon and the water. But my more considered opinion is that you should rest."

She leaned forward and kissed her father on his forehead. "I will, Dad."

I will, she promised herself, *when Gabe is found.*

CHAPTER 16

Behind Glass

Lev took the body back to the Compostela. He parked in the alley and hauled the trash can inside. Wrestling the can up the stairs was unwieldy and difficult, and he winced at every bounce and creak on the stairs.

Unfortunately, Wilma and Father Caleb were awake.

"*What are you doing?*" Father Caleb demanded. "*Hauling bricks? Are you finally going to finish that backsplash? Exposed brick would really be lovely . . .*"

Lev ignored them, focusing his energy on maneuvering the trash can upstairs and dragging it through the living room to the bathroom.

Wilma flitted beside him. "*What the hell are you . . . oh.*"

She had peered into the trash can and disappeared. She'd been around the block long enough to know that she wanted no part of this nonsense.

Father Caleb was oblivious, nattering on about the backsplash and something he'd seen in a magazine. Lev knew that their world was small, and that they got excited over little things.

"Not now, Caleb," he snapped.

The ghost of the priest sputtered.

Lev turned the trash can on its side and pulled the sheet away. He wrestled his son's body out, struggling to get a grip on the awkwardly slippery bag as he kicked at the can on the bathroom floor. Eventually, he got the bag on the floor and unzipped it.

"Lev. What have you done?"

Lev got the body into the bathtub. It was in really bad shape. It looked as if his son had been attacked by an animal. Most of the blood had drained away. Fortunately, the coroner had not begun cutting the body or putting embalming fluid into it. That would have made his work much, much more difficult. Not that this road was easy. It couldn't be. Magic always had a cost, and the price for what he was thinking was *very* high.

He leaned over the body. "Son. Are you still there?"

"Yes." The answer was faint. But his son was doing as he was told; he was staying in the body.

Caleb stood in the doorway. *"What are you doing?"* he asked.

"Leave us alone."

Caleb shook his head so hard his rosary beads rattled. *"You're interfering with something you shouldn't. If God has taken that boy, you . . ."*

Lev straightened, his hand curling into the Horned Hand. Before the priest could say another word, he flipped him in the forehead. The priest fell through the floor and vanished.

He glanced around. At least Wilma had enough sense to step away. Maybe she would convince Caleb to butt out . . . he shook his head. That was unlikely. He'd have to take measures against Caleb's interference. But first things were first.

Lev turned back and rolled up his sleeves. He undressed the body and discarded the clothes. He washed it, careful to rinse the wound thoroughly. His son had clearly bled to death on the forest floor. Something terrible had happened, something that Ranger Hollander hadn't been able to wrap his head around in his report. Lev had suspicions, but this was not the time for them. Dealing with the dead was the first and only consideration. For now.

He applied oil to the body—mint, eucalyptus, sage. He filled the mouth of the body with sage, closed the mouth tenderly. He rubbed the body with sage leaves, tied the limbs with twine, yew, and still more sage. That would help keep the spirit interred in the body. Finally, he wrapped the body in a clean white cotton sheet, tied with more twine and herbs.

He sat beside the body in his bathtub when his

work was done and placed his hand on the shrouded brow.

"Dad?"

The voice was faint, but there. "I'm here, son."

"What happened? Am I . . . am I dead?"

"Yes."

The spirit voice of his son was silent. *"What happens now? Are you going to do one of those green burial things?"*

"This is not the end. Stay here, with me."

"I don't understand."

"I know. But you will. I promise you."

"I'm scared."

"Don't be. Just stay here. Conserve your strength. I have this well in hand."

Lev lit a jar candle and set it in the porcelain sink. It cast a soothing orange glow in the small room. It was not a good idea to leave the freshly dead in darkness; without a light to focus on, they wandered away easily. He drew a line of salt across the doorway to keep Caleb and Wilma out.

"I will be back," he promised Archer.

He went to his bedroom to change his stained clothes. He smelled cigarette smoke.

"Wilma," he said.

"I'm not judging you," she said, after some silence. *"I know you didn't kill him. I won't interfere. I'm just asking you to back the fuck off and think about this for just a minute."*

"I've thought about it. And this is the only way."
He grabbed his jacket and stepped into his shoes. He
had work to do. "Tell Caleb to mind his own business, if he knows what's good for him."

There was a soft sigh. *"Caleb is going to be an ass.
He's a professional ass. That's what he does. Doesn't mean
he's wrong."*

At least he wouldn't have to listen to Caleb carping
for a few hours. The Horned Hand would drop him
out of sight for at least that long. If Caleb persisted
after that, Lev might have to take sterner measures,
even kick his frocked ass onward to the Light. Which
would break Wilma's heart. But he didn't have time
for this.

He locked the door behind him and headed downstairs to the bar. He emptied the register and the safe,
stuffing the money in his pockets without bothering
to count it. His brow furrowed as he dredged his
memory for a hundreds-year-old recipe. Lev hadn't
kept notes on this type of thing, thinking he'd never
need it. But his memory was long and well-etched . . .
he hoped.

First thing he did was dig around in the basement
for a massive glass aquarium that he'd bought ten
years ago. He had the thought of adding an aquarium
to the bar and getting some fish, and had gotten far
enough that he'd set it up. He abandoned the idea
when a drunk patron barfed in it before he'd even
gotten the tank filled. No sense asking for trouble.

He locked up and jumped in the truck parked in

the alley. He cranked the engine and squealed rubber leaving the alley, heading to the feed store just outside town. He got himself the largest feed tank money could buy without a special order, a two-hundred-gallon black plastic oval container that was larger and deeper than his bathtub. He added to his order several glass windows, glass sealant, and a glass cutter. He drove back, and it took him three trips to the truck to get things unloaded, even parked in the fire lane. He put the items just inside the back door, leaning against each other.

He then hit up the hardware store for five bags of garden sulfur and one bag of quick lime. The teenage girl behind the counter lifted an eyebrow, as if he'd accidentally hit upon a combination of items that was on a homemade bomb watch list. But she didn't say anything—this *was* ranching country—just took his money and went back to reading her paperback novel.

Last, he stopped at the Gas 'n Go and cleared the shelves of whole milk.

Bear, the owner of the Gas 'n Go, looked at the countertop full of milk with raised eyebrows. "Someone got a baby? Or you doing some baking?"

"Yeah. Lots of baking. An old recipe. Cookies."

"You rock on with your bad self and all those cookies, then."

Lev put the milk in the back of the truck and headed home. He parked in the back alley and unloaded all of the newly acquired treasures into his living room. He huffed and puffed, taking the milk first, juggling four gallons at a time. Then, the bags of sulfur and lime. By the time he got to the aquarium in the basement, his arms and legs were shaking. But he was determined to get it upstairs without fracturing it. He wrapped it in a blanket, placed it upright, and slid it most of the way, the bottom of the aquarium sliding smoothly on the worn steps with the aid of the blanket. The windows were awkward, but he got those in without much trouble. He was glad he left the rubber tub and the small bags for last. He was getting old and weak, and he didn't want to admit it.

He locked the door and sat down on the floor to catch his breath. His shirt was soaked with sweat.

"That's a lot of shit." Wilma was sitting on the couch.

"How's Archer?" he panted.

"Still in your bathtub." She gestured with her cigarette. *"Caleb hasn't shown back up to proselytize to him."*

"That's my worry," Lev admitted.

"That Caleb will convince him to head toward the Light and not . . . do whatever it is you're trying to do?"

"Yeah. Men with closely held principles can really be dicks if something offends their sensibilities."

Wilma nodded, and the sunlight shone through her Gibson-girl silhouette as she smoked. Lev wished that he could bum a cigarette off her.

"I'll do my best to keep him the hell out of the way. But you know he doesn't listen to me. If he listened to me, he'd have gone to the Light a long time ago." She gazed out the window.

"You aren't afraid of going to the Dark?"

She laughed, a throaty, sad laugh. *"Hon, there's nothing I could do that would send me deeper into Dark. Besides, I'm curious about what exactly you're gonna do with that crazy collection of farmboy shit. You gonna keep goats in here or something?"*

Lev smiled. These were the easy things to procure. The rest would require some doing.

He thought about the best way to accomplish this while he worked on the aquarium. He cleaned the dust from it with vinegar and paper towels. He rolled his toolbox out of the closet. He disassembled the cheap windows to create a crude lid for the box. It wasn't the glass coffin from *Snow White*, but it was good enough for his purposes. He carried his son's body into the living room and put him in the box.

"What's going on, Dad?"

"It will be all right. It will."

Lev sounded more confident than he felt. He had seen this done only once. Whether he had the capability to carry it out remained to be seen.

Wondering when Caleb would be back, he picked out a canister of salt from his spice cabinet and laid down a thick circle of salt around the glass coffin. He couldn't entirely protect Archer from the sound of Caleb's voice without kicking Caleb out of this plane, but that would hopefully keep the priest from meddling too much. At least the priest would know he meant business.

He called up the slaughterhouse that supplied steaks for the bar.

"Hello. This is Lev at the Compostela. I need something special delivered. Yes. Yes. A rush delivery. It's a little unusual, but I'm having a Bavarian theme night. I need about ten gallons of calf blood. I know, right? It's for blood sausage. Uh-huh. Yeah. It's easier to make than it sounds. Okay, thanks."

He hung up the phone.

Wilma hadn't moved from the couch. *"Curiouser and fucking curiouser,"* she said.

He left the lights on, locked up, and headed out again.

He'd obtained the materials he needed so far through legit means. He opened his wallet, and only ten bucks and some lint was left. He was out of money and out of credit. The rest of the things he needed, he'd have to get creative.

He jammed his hands in his pockets and walked down the street to Stan's Dungeon, the local pawnshop. The shop was open. He pushed through the door, and the cowbell tied to the handle moved to jingle. Lev cupped it with his hand to keep it silent and slipped inside. He locked the door behind him and flipped the sign to read CLOSED to passersby.

The store was cluttered with a never-ending hoard of merchandise. This spring, Stan had gone to an office building auction and had picked up a truckload of weird office artifacts: fax machines, Selectric typewriters, intercom phones, and file cabinets. They warred for floor space with Wild West memorabilia, old vinyl records, militaria, electric guitars, and odds and ends. Lev wove around them to the counter. There was no one behind it. More of the office junk was crowded behind the counter.

He paused and listened. There was humming in the back, a splash, and a contented sigh. Stan was in the bathroom.

This worked for Lev. He slipped to the back, to the closed bathroom door. Casting about, he spied a bungee cord on top of an old file cabinet. He wrapped it around the doorknob and looped it tightly around a file cabinet next to the door. Stan would have a helluva time getting out of the can—the door opened swinging inward, and that door wasn't going anywhere soon.

He heard flushing, then water running. Stan tried the doorknob. It turned, but wouldn't open.

"Hey." Stan pounded on the door. "Hey!"

Lev stifled a smirk. He'd never liked Stan much. The guy blabbed endlessly about everything. But he knew he had to move quickly. Stan rejected the idea of cell phones, so there was no danger that he'd dial for rescue from the bathroom. But Lev disliked the idea of thieving in broad daylight.

He stepped to the jewelry case and peered in. He spied what he needed immediately: a diamond ring, a bracelet with some rubies in it, and an emerald ring. He reached in, pocketed them quickly, and then went to Stan's antiquated surveillance system behind the cash register.

A black-and-white television showed an unwavering image of the shop floor, and an old VCR was jerry-rigged to it with a bunch of yellow and red wires, looking like an '80s-villain version of a bomb.

Lev popped the tape out of the VCR and stuffed it in his jacket.

He headed outside, heart hammering.

The street was deserted. He forced himself to walk nonchalantly back to the bar. Once back home, he heard Caleb's voice booming from the attic in full-oratory mode:

"You have to go to the Light, to God for your salvation. There's no future for you here. You can't . . ."

Lev ran up the stairs and burst into the living room.

Caleb was standing before the glass coffin, just on the right side of the salt line, holding his rosary before him. Archer was sitting up in the coffin. Rather, his body was still lying down, shrouded, but his faint spirit was sitting up, like a child in bed. He had his hands over his ears, as if trying to block Caleb out.

"You get away from him." Lev lunged for Caleb. His hands knew more lethal signs than the Horned Hand. Caleb was way over the line, and Lev was having none of it.

Wilma threw herself between Lev and Caleb. *"Don't. Please. He doesn't fucking understand. He's never had a son—"*

Lev's eyes narrowed. He tangled his fingers between them and muttered in Latin, *"Abiurare."*

Both spirits blew apart, as if they were made of water vapor.

He sucked in his breath and released it. He would see no more of them until moonrise. He hated wasting that bit of precious energy even to deal with them. But he would not be disturbed. He would not tolerate them interfering with his work, whether intentionally or unintentionally.

Wilma was right—Caleb *didn't* understand. And there was no time to explain things.

He turned his attention to his stolen jewelry. He pried the gems out of their settings with his pocketknife and cast them into the bottom of the cattle trough. He cut open the bags and dumped the sulfur and the lime in. It reeked, even after he added the cold milk. The blood would be coming, soon, for him to add.

He stared down at the brew. It was still missing things. Some of the materials he had on hand—mixtures of common and rare herbs that had legitimate culinary purposes. Others he should be able to lift without much problem. Lev didn't want to get arrested for something as bizarre as stealing human hair from the barber shop, so he'd have to be careful. Still, ingredients like cows' hearts and human hair and ram's horns could be found in many places. His odds of finding these things were high. If he failed to snag enough human hair from the barbershop, he might have to resort to ripping off the postmaster's screaming-red wig, which he was pretty sure was made of well-tortured human hair. Point was, he had options for most of these things.

But the hardest ingredient to acquire would be alchemist's gold. He pinched the bridge of his nose.

There was only one way to get that. And that was from Petra Dee.

The woman wore a gold pendant around her neck, depicting the green lion of alchemy devouring the sun. Lev doubted that she really knew the significance of it. Her father had been rumored to be an alchemist. Lev was counting on the idea that it came from him. She had worn it whenever he'd seen her prior to her illness, and he wondered if she had lost it. Maybe she pawned it to pay for her treatment, but he hadn't seen it in Stan's shop. Maybe she had taken it off because she hadn't been allowed jewelry at whatever hospital she was being treated at. Maybe the chain had just broken and she hadn't had time to fix it. The last two possibilities were strongest.

Whatever had happened to cause her to put it down, Lev needed it. Alchemist's gold was critical to this operation.

He descended from his attic once again, to look down the road. Petra Dee's trailer was within sight in the fading light. There was one truck parked before it, in the same position that it had been for days. With luck, nobody was home. Hopefully, Lev would strike it lucky, and she had left the pendant in a jewelry box somewhere. He wanted nothing more than to get in and out without drama and without anyone getting hurt.

He struck off down the road. In the distance, he

heard yelling. Sounded like Stan. It had taken him
less time than Lev had thought to get loose. He
glanced back. Stan was standing outside his shop,
his rant unintelligible from this far away. The girl
who worked at the hardware store had taken his arm
and was leading him inside, likely to call the sheriff's
deputies.

It was reckless to commit two robberies in a day,
but Lev was desperate. He looked away and shuffled
quickly down the gravel road.

This had been a weird road, he knew. Though it
had been given a charming rustic name when it had
last been surveyed—Snortin' Ridge Road—it had
clearly once been something more. Lev knew that the
original alchemist of Temperance had a house here,
back in the day. And the road leading to it was something of a spirit road tracking a ley line that smacked
right into the Compostela. Before Petra Dee had come
to town, he'd often seen a coyote pacing up and down
the road, sometimes sitting in the dirt, as if he was
waiting. It was no small coincidence that Petra had
adopted that coyote soon after she'd moved in. The
coyote now traversed that road leaning out the window of a slow-moving truck when Petra drove the
Bronco into town.

He increased his pace and came to Petra's front
door. He noticed that her mailbox was full, but he still
knocked politely. If she was home, it would be awkward as hell, but there was nothing for it. He guessed
he'd just announce that he'd come here to rob her.

Regretfully, of course. But no one came to the door. He took a breath, looked behind him, and kicked the door in.

It took a couple of tries; the lockset she'd used was likely the best one that could be gained at the hardware store. But it gave way eventually. Lev shouldered inside and closed the door behind him.

The place was dark and cold, like a crypt. Lev flipped on the kitchen light. Opened mail was spread on the kitchen table. The place was in a bit of disarray, as if no one was really living here, just passing through once in a while to make sure the rent was paid and a bear hadn't gotten into the refrigerator.

Maybe it would be awhile before anyone realized that he had tossed the place. One could hope. He methodically started with the kitchen, going through the cheap silverware and cutlery. He tried not to destroy anything as he went, but his primary aim was efficiency. He swept the cleaners out from under the sink, peered into the fridge at a bottle of expired ketchup and some flat beer.

He moved on to the sleeping area. Nothing under the mattress except dog hair and dust bunnies. The dresser was full of rumpled clothes. Tool cases held geology picks and instruments. Nothing, nothing . . .

He began to panic.

He needed that pendant. However he had to get it, he *needed* it.

He was being stupid—Petra clearly wasn't. There's no way the geologist would leave anything valuable in an easy-to-find place. He began looking in cereal boxes, underneath her stack of towels. He was starting to get a bit frantic—it wasn't as if the trailer was all that big—when he struck pay dirt: a piece of wood paneling peeling off near the bed. He reached in and came up with a zipper plastic bag full of money. He turned it around, inspecting it, and he spied the gold pendant glinting in the bottom. He snatched it out of the bag and—after a moment of hesitation—returned the money.

He checked through the blinds for cops before letting himself out of the trailer. Night was falling, and he cut through the field to the edge of town. A deputy's car was parked in front of Stan's pawnshop. Lev circled around the back of the bar and let himself into his apartment. He had left the doors to the bar locked. A few patrons had already arrived, swearing at a hand-lettered CLOSED sign taped to the door. Lev had taken the long way around to avoid that shit-show. There would no doubt be a run on beer at Bear's Gas 'n Go tonight.

He felt bad for stealing from Petra, much more so than stealing from Stan. From his vantage point, Stan was a dick and deserved a little hassle, while she was suffering some shitty luck. But his son's luck was worse than hers; he had to do whatever he could to turn it around.

"What's happening?"

His son's voice sounded oddly like an echo in the glass coffin. Lev crossed to the glass case and put his hands against it. "It's all right. It's coming together. Just . . . just hang on. I only need a few more things.

"I'm pretty scared, Dad."

He knelt and pressed his cheek against the glass. "I know. I am, too."

MAGIC HAD BEEN relatively rare in Muirenn's time, at least before she'd come to Temperance. Then, magic had been something to hide and obfuscate. She'd used what she knew of herbs to poison her husband in Ireland, had worked it to her advantage as she sang her way across the Atlantic. She practiced this art religiously, but always in secret, until she had met Lascaris. Then, she dared to work magic at noon as fearlessly as she had at midnight, finding an unparalleled exhilaration in the freedom of it.

She assumed that with Lascaris gone, most of his magic would have faded with him. She herself felt like a forgotten relic, gone underground and severely weakened. Indeed, a few decades after the Hanged Men imprisoned her, even they stopped bothering to check on her. She had assumed they, and the rest of Lascaris's experiments, were gone, that time had drained the magic out of them.

But she'd tasted two men with magic in as many days. It had grown insidious here, unpredictable. Muirenn disliked that. Trapped in this form, she could not simply walk away, pack a bag and move to a new continent with fresh land to learn. Her body was as much a prison as the cave she'd been trapped in, and she didn't have the power to change it. Not yet. She had to figure out how to transmute her own form, to regain a human shape once again.

She came back to her lair at dusk, gnawing on the foot of a woman who had been wading in the shallows downstream. She hadn't been greedy; she'd just torn the leg off before the woman had seen her. She'd slipped away while the woman screamed about snakes. She spat out the glitter-painted nails, one by one, on the way. The woman had taken very good care of her feet; they were soft and uncallused.

Muirenn swam upstream, coming upon Gabriel. She had the intention of interrogating him, perhaps taking him apart, even if she couldn't eat him. She liked that idea quite a bit, plucking him apart, tendon by tendon, and making him last for a good long while. Maybe he even knew some magic that she could use to change her shape, some secret she could use to walk out of here. But that would just be a bonus.

She paused as she approached, floating still in the water as a duck on a pond. Something had changed. She'd left Gabriel chained to the rock. But somehow he had moved, obscuring himself from view. She swam up carefully.

Tree roots had split through the ceiling of the chamber, cascading over Gabriel's body in a thick wooden shell. As she examined them, they dripped golden light that congealed to an amber-like substance. She could make out the outline of an arm, a jaw, encased in this mass.

She reached out to touch it, only to recoil with a hiss. *Lascaris's magic.* Old, but vital. He continued to interfere with her, after all this time.

She paddled back, contemplating. She'd thrown her lot in with Owen, since he seemed to be the most powerful force in this corner of the world at this time. Maybe she'd been wrong.

She would have to find out for certain.

She sank below the water and began to swim out, out in search of Lascaris.

Muirenn knew that she was limited in her search. She could not stride out on land, let alone assemble a laboratory of magical goods and materials.

She was far from helpless, though. She swam back out to the river, into the night.

Stars spread overhead in a river. It had been so long since she had seen them. The full moon had risen overhead. Frogs twanged and crickets chirped around her. The only light generated here came from the sky, cold and distant.

Muirenn paused at a still spot in the river, behind a pool created by a beaver dam. Only insects disturbed the black mirror of water. The moon was reflected in the water, a silver coin.

She opened her arms around that orb, feeling the moonlight shimmering through her. She might not have any tools, but she still had the water.

The surface of the water grew hazy, and the image

of the moon turned slowly, as if it were a paper cutout floating on the surface of the water.

Muirenn concentrated on it, allowing her vision to grow fuzzy and the water to grow misty. "Water, mirror of moon, mirror of truth. Nothing is hidden from your light, no secrets, no quarter. Show me the face of my old master."

A face moved under the water, as if a mask moved under some viscous substance. Muirenn held her breath. That profile was familiar, sharp and foreboding, even in this thin image of it. The face turned toward her, as if he had awakened in a bed and turned over on a pillow.

"I am coming."

Her breath caught in her throat. It was true.

Her hands balled into fists. Strong emotions warred in her. She loathed him in the deepest darkness of her soul. He had tortured her, nearly destroyed her. She wanted nothing more than to smash his reflection in the scrying mirror of the water with her fists.

"Forgive me, Muirenn."

Her brows drew together. A plea? From *Lascaris*?

Her fingers fluttered to her throat. "What do you want?"

"I want to awaken the Tree of Life. Protect it for me, Muirenn, and all will be forgotten. I shall restore you as you were before."

Her hand slipped to her mouth. "Legs? Real teeth?"

"I will give you all you ask."

She hesitated. She wanted nothing more than to

be free. But she didn't trust Lascaris. She *couldn't*. And yet . . . what choice did she have? Owen was never going to be able to fix her, and in this state, it seemed unlikely she'd be able to heal herself. She needed help.

Even if it meant that help came from the devil.

Muirenn lowered her head. "I will do this thing for you. Just this one thing."

"I give you a token, a symbol of our bargain." The black head in the water smiled and receded below the surface, leaving only the moon in its place.

For an instant, the moon was more golden than silvery.

Instinctively, Muirenn reached toward the reflection of the moon. An object slid through her fingers, and she followed it down, down to the silt at the bottom. Her hand closed around something cold and round. There was no sign of Lascaris here, no shadowy figure in the water.

Still, she hurried to the surface, to feel the air against her face. She swam up, back into the clear moonlight.

She looked down at her palm and clutched the treasure close to her chest.

It was decided.

CHAPTER 17

Facing the Lion

The last ingredients he needed were difficult to find. But not impossible.

Under the cover of darkness, Lev had ventured deep into Yellowstone National Park, driving until he'd run out of road. He parked and wandered into the night, slipping through the stands of lodgepole pine, looking for his quarry. He'd searched for hours, sweeping the land with his binoculars, but finally had caught up with what he needed.

He lay prone on the edge of a mountain with his rifle, aiming at a bighorn sheep climbing the mountain. It was a magnificent sheep, and he regretted having to shoot it. The sheep was strong and beautiful, curling horns gleaming in the dim moonlight.

But he aimed through the sights, stilled his breath, and pulled the trigger.

The crack of the gunshot echoed through the valley. The sheep's knees buckled and it fell, tumbling down the valley.

If he had wanted it for meat, the meat would be bruised and ruined by the fall. But he didn't want it for that. He watched through the sight until he could determine exactly where it came to rest, not wanting to lose track of it.

He picked his way through the rubble at the bottom of the slope to where the sheep had fallen. At least it had died a clean death. Though its hide was bloodied, its eyes were closed, tongue protruding from its mouth. He'd shot it clear through the neck. The animal's sides were still.

Lev knelt beside it, drew a saw with sharp teeth, and began to saw at the brow of the animal. It took him longer than he liked, but he finally managed to get the horns free.

He raised a ram's horn to his lips and blew. A pure, heavy note resounded over the valley.

He nodded to himself. That was a good sound, one that would summon his son's spirit and bring him back to the physical plane. There was nothing quite like the sound from a fresh horn; old ones, even ones that had been maintained, always sounded like the creak of death.

He only hoped it would call no more malevolent spirits than Caleb and Wilma down on his head.

* * *

"WELL. THAT WASN'T what I was expecting."

Petra peered into the coffee cup that had held the pearl. Nine and Maria crowded in to look, like witches around a cauldron, curious to see what their sister had just conjured up.

She reached in tentatively, with a pair of tweezers, for the thing that had been at the center of the pearl. The vinegar had done its job and had eaten away all the layers of nacre. What remained was a brownish chunk of something that would ordinarily be a bit of aragonite that hadn't fully dissolved. Except it wasn't. She picked it up with tweezers, and they all stared at it.

"What is it?" Nine asked.

"I don't know." Petra turned it right and left. "It looks like something that might have been alive . . . before it drowned in the vinegar, that is."

It looked like some sort of sea creature, about the size of a bean. It had black eyes in an oversize head, a tail, and tiny claws. It could be an embryo for pretty much anything, but it looked most like a seahorse with sets of little T. rex arms.

"So. It's not a pearl . . . it's an egg?" Maria asked.

"Yeah. I guess so." That made sense. Sort of.

The creature began to wiggle. Petra squeaked and dropped it. It landed on the table, and Pearl made to pounce on it. Maria grabbed Pearl, who struggled in her grip as the tiny creature scuttled across the kitchen table.

Petra upended a water glass and tried to trap the creature inside. She was too slow, and it ran off the edge of the table onto the floor.

Before Petra could react further, Maria stomped on it. She lifted her shoe, and there was a flattened scorpion-like creature on the floor.

"There will be no bugs in my house!" she panted. Then she glanced at Petra. "Sorry. Instinctive reaction."

"That's totally okay." Petra crouched on the floor and scraped up the flattened creature with a piece of paper. She peered at it. It was pressed as perfectly as if it had been placed between the pages of a book, all the appendages intact. A small amount of black fluid leaked from its chest.

"I am not apologizing for killing that." Maria still held the cat tightly against her chest.

"And you shouldn't. Your house, your rules. I think I need my microscope," Petra announced. That sounded like an eminently reasonable next step. She looked up from the critter on the paper.

"From your trailer?"

"Yes."

"Okay." Maria squinted outside. "It's dark. I'll take you on the back roads."

Petra began to say something, but bit back her thoughts. Maybe Maria had guessed that Petra had been wandering about, pissing off Sheriff Owen. Maybe it was a good idea that she not say too much more about that, to avoid getting reamed out and banned from using the washing machine.

Maria looked sidelong at her. "Yeah. I know."

Petra began. "I'm sorry. I . . ."

Maria raised her hand. "Don't waste your energy."

Petra closed her mouth. If Maria didn't want to argue with her, that was a bad sign. Maria was either well and truly pissed at her for abusing her hospitality, or Maria was cutting her a whole lotta slack on account of her illness. Pissed, Petra could take. Sympathy . . . not so much. She looked away, feeling ashamed and guilty.

When Maria mentioned "back roads," she meant a series of forestry roads that extended from the far edge of the reservation over moonlit fields. Petra couldn't even see the tracks half the time, but Maria always seemed to know where they were. And Sig was having a good time; he bounced from window to window in Maria's SUV, peering into the dark. That made Petra smile.

The shadow roads finally spat them out north of Temperance. Maria put her SUV into four-wheel drive, shut off the lights, and headed for the dull shine of Petra's trailer. She parked behind the Airstream, so they wouldn't be seen by the road.

Sig was out first, his nose to the ground, circling around the trailer. He paused and yelped.

Petra didn't take this to be a good sign. She climbed the steps to her door with one hand on her gun belt.

Her door had been kicked in. The lockset was broken, and there was a fresh dent in the door. Both the main door and the screen door had been neatly closed, perhaps to avoid notice from the road, but up close it was all clear as day.

Dammit. She motioned for Nine and Maria to be silent, nudged Sig out of the way, and edged the door open.

Nothing moved. She flipped on the light, sweeping her gun before her.

"Fucking awesome."

The trailer had been tossed. She groaned and scanned the kitchen. All the drawers had been emptied, cupboards rifled through. Even her cereal had been dumped in the sink. As she went to the back, she saw that her dresser drawers were open and the blankets flipped. Curiously, there wasn't much damage to be seen. It looked as if whoever had been here was just looking for something, but had attempted to be half-assed considerate about it. Probably looking for money.

Which was when she noticed the paneling . . .

Biting her lip, she reached into the hole behind the paneling where she kept her cash. Shockingly, the money was all there. But her pendant wasn't in the plastic zipper bag. Frowning, she reached into the hole, as far down into the void as she could, up to her armpit.

Her pendant, the one her father had given her, was gone.

She sat back on her heels, fuming.

"What did they take?" Maria asked.

"They left the money. But they took my father's pendant. Damn it, I was stupid to have left it here."

"You've had other things on your mind, to be fair."

Petra was pissed. She'd been pissed for weeks, but things were really coming to a head. The world seemed determined to take fucking everything from her, from large to small: her life, her husband, and now a stupid memento of her father's affections.

"Why would anyone want it?" Nine asked. She had poured a bowl of water for Sig, who slurped noisily.

"It's gold. It's worth good money." She frowned. "Then again, if they wanted money, they would have also taken the cash."

"Maybe they wanted it for a magical purpose," Maria said.

That hadn't even dawned on her. "Goddamn it." She was getting really tired of the negative sway that magic held over her life. It couldn't help her; all it could do was hurt her and everyone close to her.

She yanked the Locus out of her pocket and chucked it to the kitchen counter. It bounced in cereal crumbs. She grabbed a paring knife and sliced her palm open over it, ignoring Maria's squeals of objection. She dripped blood into the Locus, muttering dark oaths.

"Show me where the fuck my necklace is," she muttered at it. It was likely that whoever had taken it was long gone, but maybe there was a clue left behind the Locus could point her to.

The blood burped and bubbled in the compass

groove. Maria snatched Petra's hand up and wrapped it with a dish towel.

The red sloshed in the compass lazily, then turned back in a heavy clot, facing toward the door.

Petra grabbed it and stormed out. Sig was on her heels.

She and the coyote plunged into the night, down the gravel road. She heard the crunch of Nine's and Maria's footsteps behind her, and the ratcheting of a shotgun swept under Maria's coat, glad the two of them said nothing. The compass led her down the gravel road, the stone bleached pale in the moonlight overhead. The moon was full, washing the color out of the world and many of the stars from the sky.

Sig trotted beside her, ears pressed forward. He seemed as intent as she was, searching for the answer. Perhaps he sensed her fury and was doing his best to be a Good Dog.

Tears blinded her momentarily, like leaded glass over darkness. She would miss him. She reached down with her dish-towel-bandaged hand to stroke his back.

The compass led them down the road, directly into town, across the street . . .

. . . and pointed at the Compostela.

Petra's eyes narrowed. "I knew that fucking bartender was shady, somehow."

"Well, it's closed," Maria said, pointing at the hand-lettered sign in the window.

That, in itself, was weird enough. If it was night, the Compostela was usually open. Didn't matter if it was a normal Wednesday afternoon or Christmas Eve.

Petra stormed up to the doors and tried them. Locked. "Doesn't matter," she said.

She walked around the side of the building, to the back alley.

There were two doors here. One likely led to the back of the bar, since there was a half-lit EXIT sign above it to comply with fire code. But the other was a puzzle. It was a plain, heavy wooden door. Both doors were locked.

She consulted the Locus. The drying blood churned toward the wooden door on the left.

"Door number two it is," she said.

She hammered on it with her fist, but no one responded. She gave it a kick, but it didn't budge.

She was standing back to make another kick when Nine moved her gently aside.

Maria stood before the door with her shotgun. At first, Petra thought she meant to go full Clint Eastwood and shoot open the door, but instead she struck it handily with the butt of the shotgun. The knob wobbled on its stem, and another blow knocked it off entirely.

Maria shrugged. "Cheap locks."

The door opened to a landing, before a flight of stairs. Petra fumbled for a light switch. A hazy yellow light illuminated a set of scarred, waxed stairs with a bannister made of iron pipe fittings, leading upward.

"Very industrial-chic," Maria muttered.

Petra put the Locus in her pocket, unholstered her pistols, and headed upstairs. Maria followed Petra to the attic with the shotgun, while Nine remained at the bottom of the stairs to stand guard with Sig.

There was an apartment here, and a very nicely appointed one. Hand-hewn pine boards made up the floor, and the walls were covered in wood paneling. The overhead lights were fixtures cobbled together of metal pans and Edison bulbs. The yellowish light illuminated a strange furniture arrangement in the living area. The lights were on when the women arrived.

"That's not cool," Maria said, stopping in the living room.

"No," Petra agreed, not really able to articulate how much "not cool" was an understatement. "Not at all."

There was a body in a glass box in the middle of the floor. At least, that was what Petra assumed it was. Something body-shaped, at least, tightly swaddled in white cloth and covered in a smattering of what looked like herbs, was stretched out in the bottom of an aquarium. Maria crouched beside it, peering inside. "Someone cared about the person who died," she said, pulling her scarf up over her face, her eyes roving over the mechanical decorations. "Maybe they're preparing some kind of green burial?"

Maybe. Petra really didn't care.

The whole place reeked. Petra put her shirt collar up over her nose, although that did little to block the stink of sulfur and lime and God only knew what else. The smell seemed to radiate from a black plastic cattle trough on the floor. It was massive, big enough to fit a small cow inside. Petra peered in. It was full of a viscous black fluid. She thought she detected the sparkle of pyrite floating on the surface. This concoction had to be incredibly dense to allow the mineral to float. It seemed as if it had developed some sort of current, as the top of it slowly churned. Was there some kind of pump in the bottom, or a slowly leaking drain? She didn't know.

What she did know was that someone was cooking up an alchemical soup. Had her pendant become part of that? She rubbed her face. The fumes were strong, strong enough to make the air hazy and her skin itchy.

But she thought she spied the glitter of gold in the depths, a fragment of chain. She reached into the tank, into that disgusting fluid. To her distaste, the concoction was warm, like bathwater. For all she knew, it was caustic as hell. But that didn't matter.

"What are you doing?" Maria whispered.

She reached farther in, eyes watering from the fumes. Her fingers reached, and it was as if the tub was deeper than it seemed from the outside. She leaned over just a bit more . . .

. . . and Sig barked at the bottom of the stairs. She lost her balance.

Petra fell into the vat.

The viscous fluid seemed to grab her, pulling her in with a hot splash. It closed over her head, and she felt it rushing into her nose and mouth, filling her lungs with warm darkness.

She had a curious feeling of separation, moving apart from her body. She felt no pain, no lingering nausea, not even the cut on her hand. She felt apart, as she had in the forgetting place in the hospital.

Apart and lost.

The disconnected sense of floating intensified, then just as quickly dissipated.

Petra found herself on her hands and knees in soft green grass. Her fingers dug into the blades as she twisted around to assess her surroundings.

She had landed at the edge of a grassy valley, between violet mountains and a pine forest. She guessed that this was some aspect of the spirit world, as this was a place she had never visited. The landscape was too surreal to exist in the real world. A river drifted through the bottom of the valley, reflecting a full moon that didn't hang in the sky. The sky above stretched shades of pink, but there was no sun or moon in sight, just a distant flock of ravens moving in that surreal light that seemed to emanate from no obvious source.

She stood to shout at them, waving her arms. In her few trips to the spirit world, birds always had something to do with Gabe. She jumped and yelled, but the birds were too far away to hear her.

They should have seen her; she became aware that she was glowing, a soft yellow shine that obliterated her shadow. But the birds flew away, oblivious to her presence.

She lowered her arms and gazed at them. How could she reach them? What was her mission in this place? Was there a way to connect to Gabriel from here, or . . .

A deep growl emanated from behind her, from the forest. She spun on her heel, expecting to perhaps see Sig.

It *definitely* wasn't Sig.

An enormous green lion stalked out of the forest, tail lashing. His eyes were gold, but his mane and body were the deep green of corroded copper. Along his back was a pattern of golden stars, undulating along his spine.

"Oh, shit." Petra had encountered a green lion in the spirit world only once before. It had turned out to be her father. But this beast did not have her father's eyes; it had eyes that shone as bright as moons, baring pale teeth as it stalked toward her.

She reached at her waist for her guns, but she was unarmed. She held her arms out in front of her, backing away slowly. "Nice kitty," she murmured. This had worked in a James Bond film with a tiger, right? "Sit?"

The lion growled and lunged for her.

His massive paws knocked her to the grass, driving the wind from her gut and slamming the back of her skull against the ground. She could smell the breath of the lion, sulfurous and thick. Her heart pounded, feeling the massive paws pressing down on her chest and the claws flexing against her skin, drawing blood that rolled down the exterior of her ribs.

The green lion drew back his lips and sank his teeth in her shoulder.

Petra screamed and pushed back at the lion with her fists. Bone cracked and red flowed hotly over her glowing body. The lion, annoyed at the hysteria, severed her neck with a quick bite.

The pain was exquisite, instantaneous . . . then gone. She lay, paralyzed, as the lion devoured her. He started at her shoulder, cracking open her ribs and crunching through her clavicle. She felt the pressure of his teeth and tongue against her lungs, frozen, as he fed. He ate her arms, beginning on her right side and continuing on her left. Piece by piece of her flesh went down, down into his belly.

Her consciousness seemed to reside in her head, and the lion left that for last. He picked up her head in his jaws and snapped her down in two quick bites.

The belly of the lion was red and black, but she still glowed. She didn't have a body, just a gooey mass of energy. The glow that she was moved down the lion's throat to his belly, where Petra lay like a stone.

This is it, she thought. *I'm finished. Dead and eaten by a lion.*

Despair washed over her, and she wondered if her consciousness would flicker out as the lion digested her. Would that be the end of self-awareness? The end of her everything?

The glow in the lion's belly, that glimmer of sunshine, expanded. Her awareness grew from the lion's belly, up to the lion's lungs, heart, along the conduit of his spine. She settled in his brain and opened the lion's eyes.

She wrinkled the lion's nose—her nose?—lifting her head to the pink sky. She drew back her lips and roared, shocked by the strength of her voice and the vitality.

She had become the green and golden lion.

PETRA'S HEAD BROKE the surface, and she sucked in clean air.

"*Roaaawwrrrr . . . Ohmyfuckinggod,*" she gasped, wiping dark sludge from her eyes with paws that were now suddenly hands. She'd found her fucking pendant, somehow—the chain was laced around her wrist and the pendant banged against her cheek. She stared at it, dumbfounded. The green lion devouring the sun . . .

Sig whined. She followed the coyote's gaze to the floor outside the plastic tank.

There was a goo-covered body on the floor. Maria had straddled it and was giving it chest compressions, while Nine was hunched over the head, whispering at it in another language.

Petra crawled to the side of the tank. "Guys? I—oh."

The two women turned toward her, their faces ashen.

The body lying on the floor looked like Petra. Bloody goo had been scraped away from her face, but it stuck in her hair and on her tunic. She looked as if she'd been retrieved from a bottle of deep red ink, smeared on the meticulously rustic floor.

Petra covered her mouth with a dripping hand. "Oh my God. I'm dead."

She knew it. She'd done it this time. She was watching her friends trying to resuscitate her broken body. She'd hit ghost-level, and it was all over with.

Nine and Maria looked straight at her, though, in shock. Maria stood first and came to the tank. She scraped the goop off Petra's face and held her by the chin with one hand. With the other, she aimed the shotgun at her chest.

"Petra? Is that you?"

"Yeah. Yeah, I think so." She still couldn't escape that feeling of being the lion . . .

Maria ratcheted the shotgun, one-handed, against her hip. Her grip on Petra's chin shook.

"Yes! Yes, it's me! Petra!" she yelped.

"Give me your social security number."

Petra would have thought that was funny, until she considered that this was the easiest way that Maria had to identify her in the real world. She recited it back.

"Mother's maiden name?"

"I feel like I'm at the DMV."

"The name," Maria said, the shotgun not wavering.

"Jesus. It's Wallace."

Sig jumped to the side of the tank and licked slop from Petra's shoulder, as if authoritatively confirming her identity.

Maria appeared temporarily mollified, and she lowered the shotgun. But Nine was frozen in place, gawking at her, and then the body that looked like her dripping on the floor.

"Come help me get her out of here," Maria ordered.

Nine climbed to her feet. She and Maria fished Petra out of the slime, holding her by the shoulders while she tried to get her legs under her on the slick floor. She slipped in the mess and landed on her ass. She discovered that she was naked. What the hell?

Then she almost laughed, thinking that the lack of clothes was not the weirdest thing going on right now.

"We have to get out of here," Nine said, shaking her head. "This is wrong. All wrong."

"That sounds like a good idea," Petra said, as Maria wrapped her in her coat. Sig washed her face.

"We can't leave her behind," Maria said, pointing at Dead Petra on the floor. "I'll run and get the truck." Before Petra could say anything, Maria was out of there like a shot, thundering down the stairs.

Petra sat on the floor, taking deep breaths. "I don't know what happened."

"You came back," Nine said simply, wiping gunk

from her face with her sleeve. "That is something that even my father could not have accomplished." She glanced at the plastic pool and the glass case. "This . . . apparatus . . . wasn't meant for you, however."

Petra pressed her hand to her roaring forehead. "That guy is gonna be pissed. So pissed." What little Petra knew of alchemy, she knew that most operations were very complicated and elaborate. Some could take months or years to set up, at great financial and personal price. She'd blundered into the bartender's home brew experiment, and this was not going to end well. There was no disguising this mess on the floor, unless they had hours and a dozen bottles of bleach. That was barely half of it—the magic was ruined. He'd know it.

Overhead, the lights flickered ominously.

"Shit," she muttered.

An engine sounded in the alley, then cut off. Nine helped Petra down the stairs, and she left behind a trail of bloody footprints. Maria had spread a tarp in the backseat of the Explorer, and Petra sat meekly on the blue plastic. Sig clambered in at her feet, getting alchemical slop all over him. Maria and Nine returned to the apartment and came back with a very suspicious package rolled in an area rug. They dumped it in the backseat with Petra. Nine shut the door. It was a mess. There was blood that stank like sulfur and lime everywhere—on the door, in the alley. But there was nothing they could do about any of it.

The two women piled in. Maria cranked the engine, and they tore through the alley.

Petra's heart was in her mouth. "I don't understand any of this."

Maria glanced back through the rearview mirror. "That makes three of us."

Petra looked down at the rug-wrapped bundle spread across her lap. She pulled back the corner of the carpet to peer at Dead Petra. It was horrifying, seeing herself this way. Her face was too thin, ravaged by leukemia, but it also seemed rubbery and swollen at the same time. She touched it, and it felt too cold to be real.

"Fuck," she said. "Fuck, fuck, fuck."

"That makes three of us," Maria muttered.

They took the back roads to the reservation at top speed. When they reached the house, Maria pulled the truck right up to the front porch. No lights were on in the nearby houses, thankfully. Maria unlocked the front door and shoved Petra inside.

Petra tracked blood into the house. She tried to stick to the areas of hardwood floor and not the rugs, not really sure that made too much of a difference—Maria wouldn't be thrilled about a bloody mess in any part of her house. Yet another thing to worry about later. For now, she made a beeline for the bathroom. She put Maria's ruined coat in the sink and hopped over the bath mat into the shower.

With the water going full blast, globs of black-red material came off. She hoped to hell she wasn't going to destroy Maria's pipes, because there was no good way to explain this to a plumber, short of confessing to murder. The crud sluiced off her hair and body in layers, like skins of gel. She scrubbed with her hands under the scalding water, pulling off the scabby material with her hands and scraping at it with her nails.

She didn't hear Maria knock. A pair of hands appeared behind the shower curtain with a bottle of vinegar, a bottle of dish soap, and a mesh scrubbing sponge from the kitchen.

"Are you doing okay?" she asked.

"Yeah. No. I think so. For the Swamp Thing."

"Okay."

Maria disappeared, and Petra continued to scrub. She had the feeling that she'd fucked up something very, very badly. But the process went better with the dish soap, the vinegar, and the nylon scrubber. Bits of skin were revealed, pink from the scrubbing. Her skin looked healthy and normal—no marks. She breathed a sigh of relief at that.

She poured vinegar over her hair and tried to work it free of the muck. To her startlement, hair just kept coming as she scrubbed. It came loose, falling beyond her shoulders, past her waist as she freed it from the goo. Some was even stuck under her arm.

Holy shit. What had happened?

She rinsed again and again until the water ran cold. She stared down at her body. It looked . . . healthy.

Muscular, as she might have been in her prime if she'd been hitting a gym daily, which had never happened. She ran her fingers over her arms and legs. Though red from scrubbing, there were no freckles. No scars on her arms from the handprint of an ex-lover, no acid speckles from a basilisk . . . nothing. Her skin was as soft and unmarked as a baby's.

She stepped out of the shower and dried off. Her hair was like Medusa's, hitting the back of her knees, as if it had never been cut. She swore at it and piled it on top of her head with a towel. Some of it still stuck out.

She stared at herself in the mirror, and what stared back surprised her. Her face was paling since she'd finished scrubbing. There were no sun freckles, no nothing. Just milky paleness. No wrinkles, no laugh lines. She looked as if she'd just hatched from an egg that she'd been living in for decades, as if she'd never seen sunshine, broken a bone, or needed stitches. Even the sewn wound at her side was gone. It was as if she were some . . . avatar or simulation of herself, created in a video game, unblemished and perfect.

"Shit. Shit. Shit." All she could seem to do was swear. She wrapped a towel around her body and came out into the living room.

Nine was scrubbing her bloody footprints from the floor. Maria had leaned the shotgun against the refrigerator, within easy reach, and was halfway to the living room with a bucket.

Both women looked up. Sig trotted up to her and leaned hard on her leg. She reached down to pet him. Some of his fur was stiff with dried gunk.

"Well, I'm glad to see it's you underneath that," Maria said, visibly relaxed. Then she tensed, as she approached Petra. Like a mother inspecting a child who had returned from a long trip, she looked at her face. The towel slid, and out tumbled a waterfall of hair.

"I don't understand what happened. It's like . . . I have a new body," Petra said lamely. Goddamn it, she wished Gabe were here to explain it to her. Or at least, that her father was awake to answer phone calls.

Maria seized her arms and examined them, running her fingers over the formerly scarred insides. They had cooled from the shower to a milky, almost transparent white.

"Jesus. It's like you've been cloned."

"Yeah. That's the only thing I can think of."

"How do you feel?"

Petra stopped to ask herself that question. Her stomach wasn't queasy. She felt . . . normal. Not fragile. Nothing hurt. "I think I feel pretty good."

Maria gave a short nod. "Good."

"I'm glad you're taking this well. My mind is blown."

"My mind blew up a long time ago."

Petra glanced at Nine, who was serenely scrubbing the floor. "Nine?"

Nine looked at her, then at Sig, who had happily glued himself to Petra's knee. "Coyote is happy you're back. I trust him."

Petra sat on the edge of the couch. "So . . . what do we do with, uh, me? I guess? With Dead Petra?"

Maria looked at her levelly. "We do what we've been expecting to do for many weeks. We bury you."

CHAPTER 18

The Elaborate Burial of Petra Dee

The women drove out to the edge of the reservation to bury Dead Petra.

Petra sat in the backseat of Maria's SUV with her dead doppelgänger. Sig curled around her ankles on the floorboards, wanting nothing to do with her double. Maybe that's what she was, a doppelgänger. Petra didn't know much about that legend. Except that the doppelgänger was a magical double of a person who shadowed them and eventually killed the target, ultimately taking over the victim's original life. But Petra was pretty sure that *she* was the original, but inhabiting a doppelgänger body. It bent her noodle, and she was a mess.

She had tied back her insane new hair with a scarf, tying it in six knots before it was out of her way. It was heavy as hell, and she was itching to take some scissors to it. The weird sensation of it helped distract her from the very disconcerting feeling of sharing a backseat with her broken-down body. She hadn't really realized how bad off she had been. Her former body, the shell, looked light and fragile.

She self-consciously ran her fingers over her unmarked arms. She sure hoped that she'd get to keep this body, that she wouldn't be evicted out of it. *I mean, that could happen, right?* The situation was all so far beyond her ken. Her fingers slipped up to the gold pendant around her neck. She'd have to hide it, make sure no one saw that she had recovered it. If the bartender figured out that she had invaded his attic and fucked up his magic, there was no telling what he could do to all of them.

Maria finally stopped the truck in a nondescript field. Nothing grew here except sage and rocks. There were no remarkable landmarks; only the scrub weeds and the mountains in the distance.

"This place is as good as any."

"So I take it you've buried bodies here before? Does Mike know?" Petra joked weakly.

"No comment." Maria cracked a smile.

"No plans to farm it or build on it anytime soon?"

"Not unless the federal government decides to seize it to build a pipeline on it or some such insanity." Maria hopped out of the truck. "All bets are off then, and you'll have to explain your own death."

They had gathered shovels from Petra's Bronco.

They hauled the body and the tarps out from Maria's Explorer and laid out Dead Petra in the moonlight. Beside her, they began to dig a hole roughly the dimensions of the body. Sig stood watch, sitting beside Dead Petra and gazing out across the field, like an incarnation of Anubis.

They didn't get six feet deep; the soil was yellow clay and studded with bits of granite, so they went as far as they could before hitting a chunk of sandstone that Petra estimated would take a two-by-four to lever out of the hole.

Petra unwrapped the body. She stared at herself, at this vessel that had carried her in the physical world for decades. She didn't know what else to do except kiss her forehead and tell her, "Thank you." She pulled her wedding ring off Dead Petra and put it on her finger.

And she made sure to retrieve her purse. It was strapped across her body, and it contained her keys, wallet, cell phone, and most importantly—the Locus. It wouldn't be difficult to identify the body without ID . . . Petra had been fingerprinted for various security clearances in the past, and she was pretty sure that a dentist somewhere had her dental records. But she wanted to make it as difficult as possible.

The three women wrapped Dead Petra tightly and lowered her into the hole. They scooped shovel after shovel of dirt on top of the body, without comment. When the work was complete and the soil tamped down, Maria leaned on her shovel.

"I don't know what happened back there. I'm not sure I want to know."

It wasn't much of a eulogy, but Petra wasn't sure what else there was to say as Maria and Nine gathered their tools and headed back to the Explorer.

In the halo of headlights, Petra crouched by the grave with Sig. Her fingers wound in his fur. Sig thought she was real and that she was herself. That was the only thing she could cling to, as she walked away from Dead Petra. She finally climbed into the SUV, Sig clambering in behind her.

On the way back, she buried her face in his ruff and cried. She wasn't sure what she was crying for. But it sure seemed as if something terrible had happened, something irretrievably lost that she couldn't define, and her soul wept for it.

SOMETHING TERRIBLE HAD happened.

Lev knew it as soon as he'd parked in the alley behind the bar. There was a gooey mess of footprints leading from the door. He immediately forgot the ram's horns getting sticky on the floorboards and jumped out.

His first thought was that somehow the alchemical reaction had occurred without him there. That somehow, Archer had come into contact with that brew to create the homunculus . . . that he had fled into the night.

But the lock was broken from the outside. With

dread, Lev climbed the stairs, two at a time. They were smeared with blood and alchemical albumin. Heedless, he ran up the stairs to see the mess on the floor: a pool of blood, chemicals, and pulp. Something had been in the vat, the vat in which he'd intended to create a new body for Archer.

Father Caleb and Wilma were standing just beyond the mess. Wilma was staring at it, arms crossed, smoking with what was, for her, a deep expression of contemplation on her face. Caleb's eyes were wide, and his chubby, shaking fingers worked the rosary.

"What happened here?" Lev demanded. His hands were already curling into shapes of the Horned Hand. "Did you do this?"

"*No! No!*" Caleb sputtered. "*It was terrible. These women came, they broke in here, and one of them fell in, and . . . and . . .*" He lapsed into speechlessness.

Wilma tapped out invisible ash into the ether. "It wasn't pretty, that was for sure. It was that sick woman. The one who was looking for her deadbeat piece-of-shit husband who took off on her."

Lev came to his knees beside the glass coffin, opened it with shaking fingers. Archer's body was undisturbed.

"*Dad?*"

The voice of Archer's ghost was faint, slipping away. Damn it, the young man had stayed where Lev had ordered him to stay, in his body. Lev reached in to grasp the shoulders of his son's body, as if that action might hold the spirit there, in this plane.

"I'm here."

"Dad, I'm going to go. I have to. I'm sorry."

He lowered his head. He wanted to say, *No, don't.* But he had already expended so many decades of saved magic on this single project, all poured into the plastic vat. He intended to create a new body for his son, a vessel to continue his unnaturally short life. He had seen the homunculus created once before, in Prague. He had doubts as to whether it would work. In that regard, he shouldn't have worried.

It just hadn't worked for *Archer.*

And there was no duplicating this. All the magic was done and spilt, and it wasn't coming back any-time soon. Not within the hours that Archer had left to wander the earth, anyway. Lev's thoughts raced. Perhaps he could bind the young man's spirit here, accumulate enough power to give another try . . .

A rustling sound emanated from the body.

"Dad, I'm going to go. I'm glad I got to meet you. I . . . I love you. Thank you."

It seemed the body exhaled. And Archer was gone, like a brittle leaf blown away.

Lev's hands balled into fists and he roared. Once again, his family was gone.

He leaned forward, head in his hands. He sensed Caleb at his right hand, Wilma at his left, the devil and angel on his shoulders.

"What is . . . was . . . all of this?" Caleb asked.

Wilma shushed him. *"It was magic. Beautiful, brutal magic."*

"It doesn't matter," Lev said. "It's ruined."

Apparently unable to help himself, Caleb sighed. *"Well, at least your son is in a better place."*

Lev lifted a shaking finger. "Do not say that to me. Do not give me that vapid bullshit. So help me, if you utter another word like that again, I will personally see to it that you're banished to the Dark for the sin of pride for eternity."

Caleb shut it.

Lev sobbed. He remained on the floor, staring at the now-empty glass case.

Wilma knelt beside him. She was brave. *"For what it's worth, I don't think she meant to do it."*

"It doesn't matter," he said. "This requires an answer."

"Damn." She sighed. *"What will you do now?"*

"I'm going to take care of the body."

"Can we help in any way? I mean, this is really fucked up, but . . . we're here for you. As much as we can be."

Her sympathy was palpable. He couldn't stay mad at her. Wilma had seen more of the foul underbelly of humanity in her two short decades on earth than most people did in several lifetimes.

"Yes," he said, climbing to his feet. "You can."

He reached into the glass case for the body. He carried it down the stairs. Wilma followed. After a moment, so did Caleb. Lev carried the body to the basement.

The basement of the Compostela had never been finished to be used as living space. It was shallow, and Lev always grazed his head on support beams when he came downstairs. He kept odds and ends of brewing equipment down here: pipes, barrels, bits and bobs that he wasn't using at the moment.

The center of the cellar was dominated by a boiler. It was old iron, painted several times, reaching upward with eight arms of pipes like some kind of mechanical tree. The whole thing was dark and silent now.

Lev laid the body down before the belly of the boiler. Wordlessly, he opened the door to light the stove. He fed it the last bits of winter wood he'd kept around for chilly mornings. When the fire was blazing, the heat was palpable, sticking Lev's shirt to his chest and prickling sweat on his brow.

He gazed into the fire. Fire was the purifier. Fire was the eraser. Fire was holy.

Caleb cleared his throat. *"Would you like for me to say a blessing?"*

Lev was about to snap at the ghost, but then he just slumped and nodded.

Caleb folded his hands. *"Our Father who art in heaven . . ."*

Lev gathered up Archer's body. He approached the shimmering heat and placed the body, feetfirst, into the belly of the boiler. He pushed, crumpling the body a bit. The shrouded form slid inside.

Lev stood back, watching the sage curl and crackle. The sweet scent of it soaked the room, pure and clarifying. He had stopped listening to Caleb.

Wilma stood at his left hand. *"He went to the Light,"* she whispered. *"I saw it."*

Lev nodded, stone-faced as he gazed into the fire.

This act, this thievery of his son from him, would *not* go unpunished.

OWEN WAS STARTING to become suspicious; Muirenn could feel it.

He paced along the shore of the underground river, agitated, kicking gravel and wearing a track in the silt.

". . . people have been going missing, killed," he was saying, rubbing the back of his neck. "People along the tributaries, leading here. If that was you, they're eventually going to put two and two together, and find you."

"It wasn't me," Muirenn said. She wearied of the amount of soothing and reassurance her new master required. Lascaris, for all his cruelty, had needed none of that nonsense. She would rather serve Owen, but she suspected that his time might be limited. "And you are in charge of the law here, no?"

"I'm in charge of the sheriff's office of this county, and I can keep a lid on those investigations. I can re-assign staff and sweep some of these things under the rug. But not the murders in the park. Killings that happen in the park are under federal jurisdiction. And the Feds do not look kindly upon dead tourists. It hurts their revenue."

Muirenn shook her head, and the pearls she'd braided in her hair rattled. "I have had nothing to do with any of this."

Owen stared at her, his hand twitching to his side-arm. "Don't lie to me, Muirenn. Just don't."

"Surely, there are other crimes that need your attention?"

"Of course there are!" Owen said in an explosive exhalation. "Body thieves. Someone stole a corpse from the coroner's office. And weird things have been going missing—theft of jewelry, some butchered live-stock. And of all things, human hair was stolen from a barbershop." He spread his hands out before him. "I mean, who the hell steals hair?"

"You have many criminals in your midst."

"I guess. But there seem to be some connections to the missing people in the park . . . and the river goes from here into Yellowstone."

Muirenn lifted her chin. This tack was starting to bore her. "I promised you the healing of your hand. Show it to me."

Startled at the change in conversation, he turned away, only to turn right back. He was wearing a glove on his once-injured hand. He stripped it off.

It was pink, like fresh salmon. More important, new fingers had formed on his hand, the ring and the littlest one that had once been missing. Dark violet veins were growing in. The flesh looked soft and fragile, but it was there.

"Don't doubt me. Or my power, Owen," she said.

Owen looked away. "Whatever you're doing, you have to stop this. Please."

He was slipping away. She knew it. He was weak. If he had his way, he'd see to it that she was chained and starved. She had been right in summoning Lascaris, as much as she hated him. A weak king was worse than a strong one, regardless of where his moral compass lay.

She said nothing to him. She simply dipped below the surface of the water and swam out into the darkness, a song on her lips.

She may as well eat while she could.

SHE WAS GOING to have to pay for this new body, one way or the other.

Petra lay in bed, but she couldn't sleep. Sig dozed, snuggled up to her belly, snoring softly. He always liked being the little spoon when they slept. That wasn't distracting; what was distracting was the sound of blood in her ears and the way her lungs filled with air. Nothing ached, nothing was disintegrating. All was perfect. *Too* perfect. She stroked her smooth arms in the dark. No scars. No evidence that she'd ever really lived a full life.

It occurred to her that perhaps she should have left the body behind in the attic of the Compostela. Everyone, even Owen, would have believed her dead, and she'd have complete freedom to search for Gabe. But seeing what lay in that attic . . . the bartender would have cleaned up the mess and buried her himself, without sharing the news of her death. He would have known she was to blame. That bartender would have hunted her down more quickly. He would have seen her, and he would have known.

And he would be looking—she was certain of that. Petra stared up into the darkness. It might take him a while to figure out that the gold pendant was missing from his bizarre cloning brew. There might have been other clues left. But no matter what, he *would* be searching for her.

With Owen, she knew that he could be stopped with interjurisdictional lines. He had no authority on the reservation, and Maria and Nine were safe here. The tribal police would relish the chance to kick Owen's ass and drive him off their land, and Owen knew that. He wouldn't come close.

But the bartender . . . that guy had no such administrative geas around him. He would come looking for her, and he'd be on their doorstep before the tribal police could do anything. *And* he knew magic. How much did he know? What could he do? If she had drawn Sig, Maria, and Nine into this mess beyond the extent they already were . . . she didn't want to think about that, as likely as it was seeming.

Petra flopped onto her side, and Sig turned over to kick her in the belly. She didn't believe in fate, that she was scheduled to die of leukemia at an appointed hour. Falling into that vat had been a pure accident. Still, she knew deep in the marrow of her new bones that she'd fucked up something major. Her time in Temperance had taught her something: magic always had a price. The cost for this, whatever it was, was going to be astronomical. She would have to pay it, but she hoped that the debt would be visited on her alone.

She climbed out of bed to wander to the kitchen. Sig flopped over to take her place, uninterested in what she was up to.

Petra turned on the overhead light in the kitchen and picked up a mason jar holding the creature that had come from the pearl. It lay at the bottom of the jar, flat as a squished spider. She realized that she'd left her microscope back at the trailer, damn it. But the hatchling still bore some need for analysis. And there was no better cure for insomnia than science.

She puttered around the kitchen, opening drawers and cabinets. She gathered up an odd collection of items to put on the kitchen table: a laser pointer cat toy, some chewing gum, a white Corelle saucer, tweezers, and a flashlight. She popped the gum in her mouth and chewed it while she looked in her purse for her cell phone.

She sat at the kitchen table and took apart the laser pointer. It unscrewed fairly easily, and she was able to pop the lens out with a pencil. Very carefully, she put the lens on the table and wrapped the gum around the edges of the lens. She affixed the laser pointer lens to the lens of her cell phone camera.

She turned on the flashlight, balanced it on its end, and placed the saucer on top. The white plate lit up like a spotlight. Satisfied, Petra dumped the contents of the mason jar on the plate. The squished bug landed pretty close to the middle, and she pushed it to the exact center with her tweezers.

The next part would be tricky. She grabbed a couple of Maria's phone books and stacked them beside the flashlight. She balanced her cell phone on the edge of the phone books so that the lens was aimed at the bug. Then she turned on her cell phone's video camera and peered at the screen.

The height adjustment took some experimentation. By adding the user manual for Maria's bread maker, she was able to get it at the perfect height. An enlarged image of the bug appeared on her screen.

"Ta-da," she whispered. "Instant microscope."

She peered at the bug. It truly was like nothing she'd seen before. It seemed like a nearly fully cooked embryo of something . . . it looked like its lungs might have been developed before Maria smote it on the kitchen floor. It had tiny eyes that were black, and insectile-seeming claws at the end of arm-like appendages.

And it had a mouth, with teeth. The creature's jaw had been crushed open, and Petra detected dozens of tiny teeth in the mouth.

"Hell," she muttered.

The thing had come in an egg. Perhaps it wouldn't have hatched without contact with liquid. But it was a hardy bastard . . . vinegar would kill pretty much anything else. And the fact that it had come in an egg meant that there were likely more of these things. Things that grew in eggs usually had many, many brothers and sisters.

She had no idea what this little monster was, or what it might grow up to be. But she was very glad for Maria's fast reflexes. It looked as if it might have been in the process of growing a bunch more legs. Long bristles advanced up and down its abdomen, reminding her of legs on a house centipede. It had no antennae, so perhaps it wasn't in communication with a mother ship somewhere—hurray for good news. Its tail was curled tightly up in a corkscrew, but she thought she detected a barb at the end of it. Was that for climbing? Stinging?

Whichever, she was glad it was dead. She put it back into the jar and screwed on the cap tightly. She knew it was dead, but she was proof that around here, dead didn't often mean much.

She reassembled Pearl's toy, put the rest of the odds and ends away, and decided to climb back into bed.

That little bit of science must have been enough to lull her to sleep. She was asleep the instant her head hit the pillow, a dreamless sleep with no creepy-crawlies emerging from mason jars.

THE SKY WAS still grey, without even the smallest bit of pink tinting the horizon, when there was a banging at the door.

Petra sat bolt upright, fighting her unwieldy tangle of hair and reaching for the gun belt hung on the bedpost. The cat slid under the bed as Maria rolled off it, grabbing a shotgun leaning in the corner. Sig jumped to the floor and growled.

"Stay here," Maria ordered. She stepped out onto the floor—barefoot, in her nightdress—and shut the bedroom door behind her.

Petra heard other footsteps in the hallway. Nine, she presumed.

Her heart hammered as she heard the door open.

"What do you want?"

"I have no quarrel with you." It was the bartender's voice, a low rumble like thunder. "Give me Petra Dee, and I'll be gone."

"'Give you'? You're trespassing. Get out."

"You've got a funny definition of trespassing."

"And you're involved in some really weird shit. Get out."

"Not until you give her up. I know she's here. Her truck is outside."

"I think that you don't have any understanding of whose turf you're on." The shotgun ratcheted back. "Leave us alone."

"I'm not leaving. Not without her."

This was going nowhere. Petra grabbed her guns and opened the door. Sig flowed out before her, growling and snarling.

The bartender was standing just inside the door. He looked pissed—the kind of pissed that's beyond a full night of red-eye crying, a carton of smokes, and a bottle of vodka. And he was holding a freaking sword. Maria had aimed her shotgun at him. Nine had picked up a bread knife, and Petra aimed her pistols at the bartender. It was very ridiculous, the three women in Maria's flannel nightdresses, but costumery in a fight didn't matter.

"There's a saying about bringing a knife to a gunfight," Petra said.

The bartender's eyes widened as he looked at her. "*You*. You took what was intended for my son."

She glared at him and gestured at the body she wore. "What, this?"

"That body." He stabbed a finger toward her. "That homunculus. I created it for him."

"The body in your attic—that was your son's body?"

"Yes. And you took what was meant for him." He lifted the sword.

"Dude, I will not hesitate to fill you up with buckshot," Maria said. "Do not test me."

"Look," Petra said. "It was an accident. I was looking for the pendant you stole from me."

"You should have left well enough alone."

"Hey. You don't get to go breaking into my house and then get pissy because I broke into your house, and repay the favor by getting pissier and breaking into Maria's house." Petra's heart pounded in her chest over her tenuous reasoning. It pounded very well, she noticed, much more evenly than the old one.

Sig was slinking across the floor toward the bartender, belly low, teeth bared.

"I'm sorry your son is dead," Petra continued. "But that is not my fault." Usually, when shit went pear-shaped around Temperance, it *was* her fault. This one fucking time, she could categorically say that it wasn't, and she was going to announce it as loudly as she could.

Maria didn't seem all that interested in any of that, though—just the fact that this sword-wielding bas-tard was trying to get into her house. "Listen—you need to get the hell out of here. Because unless you turn around and walk out that door, you aren't walk-ing out of this alive," she said. "You just aren't."

Nine had omitted the trash talking. She'd sidled noiselessly closer to the bartender with the bread knife in her hand, behind him.

"It doesn't matter," the bartender said.

And he ran forward, swinging the sword at Petra.

She shouted and ducked. The dude was under-standably pissed at her for fucking up his science experiment, but she really didn't want to shoot him. Even more frightful was the thought of incurring Maria's wrath if she missed and shot something im-portant, like one of her needlepoint pillows.

Sig had none of those qualms. He lunged, grasping the bartender by the arm. The man flailed right and left, trying to free his arm from the grip of the dog who remembered that he was a coyote. While this was going on, Nine slid behind him and pressed the bread knife to his throat.

Despite all this, the bartender was still flailing,

coyote attached to his sword arm and a bread knife at his neck. Runnels of red ran down into his collar.

"*Jesusfuckingchrist*," Maria murmured. With the butt of the shotgun, she struck at the man's hand until the sword clattered on the floor. Petra hurried to kick it away, under the couch.

"I do not want to pick buckshot out of my beautiful couch." She shoved the shotgun up against his chest. "How about you sit the fuck down and we have a civil discussion? That, or you can leave—with your blood still inside your body. Entirely up to you."

He stood there for a moment, the knife at his neck and the coyote dangling motionless as a towel from his outstretched arm. He looked at the coyote. Sig pulled back a lip and growled.

He sighed and dropped his arm. Sig let go and hopped down on the floor, pleased with himself. He went over to Petra, sitting down, looking up at her.

"Good boy," she said quietly, scratching behind his ears.

Sig's tail wagged contentedly.

The bartender sat heavily in one of Maria's chairs, deflated. "It doesn't matter. It's all over, anyway."

Maria threw him a dish towel. "Do *not* bleed on my chair."

The bartender wrapped the towel around his neck and put his chewed arm in his lap. "This wasn't what I had planned."

Petra moved opposite him, sitting down on the couch. Sig went to sit at her feet, but she kept her guns at her sides. "How about you tell me what you did have planned? I mean, what was the intended upside to the vat of goo you had in your attic?"

He gazed down at the floor morosely. "My son had been killed. I knew I could save him, but the window of time was very short. Spirits only linger for three days around bodies. A very long time ago, I had seen a man make a homunculus."

"That's the second time you've said that. What's a homunculus?"

"It's a magical double, a creature created in a vessel, if you like. It has no mother, only a magician for a father. It grows behind glass, and it takes the shape of the magician if the magician . . . seeds it."

Petra wrinkled her nose. "Ugh." She chose not to contemplate the idea of the bartender as her biological father.

"Yeah, well. I clearly didn't get to do that part." He looked in distaste at Petra. "I had intended to put my son's body in the vessel, to transfer his spirit to it. Until you managed to fuck it all up."

"Look. That was totally unintentional," she said.

He gave her a dim look. "I took the pendant because I needed an item of gold that had belonged to a magician. Your father was an alchemist. It fit the bill, and I didn't have time to sift through shit I could order on the internet."

"You could have just asked. I would have lent it to you."

"Really? Just like that? Like we're great friends,

and you would willingly hand over that pendant to someone who's basically a stranger?"

Petra didn't say anything.

He shrugged. "It doesn't matter—you weren't exactly available to ask anyway, and time was critical."

"Can't you just . . . cook up a new brew?"

He shook his head. "My son's spirit is gone. And I've expended almost all the magical energy I had on that one effort."

"So . . . are you an alchemist?" Christ, they were thick on the ground here.

"No. I am not an alchemist. Merely . . . a minor guardian spirit. Come here to forget." His gaze was distant.

Petra felt a pang of sorrow for him. "Look, man . . . I'm sorry. Really sorry. If I had known, I wouldn't have gone clomping around in your, uh, lair."

The bartender gazed at her with a limpid gaze. "At least it worked."

Petra looked down at her body. "Yeah. I guess so."

The bartender looked as if he were about to say something, then thought better of it.

Petra resisted the urge to poke him with questions. This body . . . how durable was it? What exactly was it made of? Did it have a normal expiration date? Did she have to go and howl at the moon to maintain it? She wanted to know, but this wasn't the time.

Maria broke in: "I'm really sorry to hear about your son. Can you tell us what happened to him?"

"He was killed. His throat was torn out by a predator. Not an ordinary predator. Something that has been here a very long time." He seemed to weigh what to tell them. "I think that he was killed by a creature known as the Mermaid."

"She seems to be coming up a lot in conversation," Petra said.

"What?" he asked, looking at her sharply.

"We suspect Sheriff Owen is somehow in league with her, that he is the one who has kidnapped Gabriel."

The bartender's mouth turned. "Well, if the Mermaid has him, he's as good as dead."

CHAPTER 19

Walking Poison

Gabe. Wake up."

Gabe opened his eyes in the darkness. Above him shone a starry blue-white light. His eyes watered, and he tried to carefully fix his gaze on it, though he couldn't turn his head. He was held fast by a cascade of tree roots, behind a wooden wall constricting ever tighter. There was barely enough room to squeeze out a breath.

"Gabe. Are you alive in there?"

The light came closer. Gabe squinted.

"Okay, you're alive."

The light retreated just a bit.

Gabe blinked, wanting very badly to rub his eyes. It was Owen. He was perched beside him in a kayak, poking at Gabe's prison with a pocketknife.

"What the hell is this?" Owen asked. "Did she do this to you?"

"No. She didn't. This is . . . unexpected." Gabe declined to elaborate. His voice was rusty and thin, and it took too much effort to speak. "What brings you here?"

"I found Muirenn's trophy stash." He flipped the light a bit downstream to Muirenn's pantry. It had grown in recent time. New bits of bone and gristle had been added to it. From this distance, it had begun to smell, like compost.

"This surprises you?"

Owen's face was dark, and he rubbed his beard. "I wanted to believe her. I did. But the killings . . . there have been at least five that I can trace to her. Likely there are more."

Gabe said nothing. He'd already said all he could say about Muirenn.

"But she has to be stopped," Owen continued. "She's going to bring the Feds down on here like flies on a carcass."

"Probably," Gabe said. "Hopefully." If he could have shrugged, he would have.

"I can't let that happen."

"How do you hope to accomplish this?"

"I don't know," Owen confessed. "I was thinking . . . that you might have some ideas."

Gabe laughed. "I'm generally disinclined to help you right now," he said. "You've amply demonstrated that I can't trust you."

And he was guessing that Owen had been trusting Muirenn, allowing her to work her magic on him. It had not escaped Gabe's notice that Owen was all of a sudden wearing a right-handed glove with fingers. Muirenn had been expending a great deal of energy on Owen. No wonder she'd been stocking up on food.

"What if . . . what if I got you out of here? Would that be a good enough expression of goodwill?" Without waiting for an answer, Owen began to saw at the wood with his pocketknife. The wood groaned and bled golden sap. The sap congealed and hardened, a glittering resin tougher than before. Owen tried his knife on the resin, and the blade snapped.

"Gah. Tell me how to get you out of here. What do I need? A saw? Fucking dynamite?"

Gabe laughed again, hollowly this time. "I don't think you can."

The light shone down his body. It was fully encased in tree roots. Only his face and hands remained barely visible.

"Dammit," Owen said. He leaned back in the plastic kayak, and the water sloshed. "I really screwed the pooch on this one, didn't I?"

"Yes. Yes, you did."

The two men sat in awkward silence for a moment.

Gabe sighed. "The only way to kill a hunger like the Mermaid's is to poison it."

Owen leaned forward to listen.

* * *

"THE MERMAID KILLED your son. Wouldn't your anger be better placed in her direction?"

Nine had been silent throughout the morning. She had listened to Lev rant and rave, Petra get defensive about her role in the failed resurrection of his son, and Maria threaten anyone who got blood on her furniture with eternal damnation. The cat had made an appearance. Pearl sauntered through the room, yawning, giving all four of them dirty looks before jumping up on the fridge to watch from a safe distance. But Nine finally spoke up, shocking the others to silence.

Lev turned to her, blinking. "Well, of course. That wasn't going to go unanswered in any reckoning."

"Wouldn't we be better off figuring out where she is and kicking her tail? Not to mention that we might be able to see if she knows anything about Gabe's whereabouts." Maria was pacing the kitchen. The shotgun leaned against the refrigerator, within easy reach in case Lev got spunky again.

"That would get my vote," Petra said quietly. She looked at Lev. "How about it? Temporary truce?"

"Truce." Lev lifted a finger. "On one condition."

"Name it."

"I get to be the one who kills her. You owe me that."

Petra gazed at him with sympathy. Her heart ached for him, it truly did. She never had a child, but she knew what it was like to lose a loved one. To imagine that one would have the power to stop that, and then fail . . . it was too much to bear. "You can have her. I swear."

Lev nodded in satisfaction.

"I mean, I reserve the right to rough her up before delivering her to you, if I find her first."

"Of course. But I have to be the one to kill her."

"Entirely."

"Great. Dibs on the Mermaid have been sorted out. But where do we find her?" Maria continued to pace the floor. Whenever she got close to the refrigerator, Pearl swatted at her hair.

"Well . . . I have some maps. But I don't entirely know what they mean." Petra stood to go to the bedroom. She took her guns with her, awkwardly fitting the gun belt over her plaid nightdress. She hauled her sheaf of papers out from under the bureau and spread them on the coffee table before Lev. "Gabe drew these."

She refused to focus on whether or not Gabe was still alive. Lev had seemed to make a certain pronouncement otherwise. She had to hope. And if Gabe was gone . . .

. . . well, Owen would be hers. Lev could make sushi, and she'd strangle Owen with her new, strong hands.

"Where did you get those?" Lev fingered through the pages.

Petra exchanged a guilty glance with Nine. "I might have possibly, just once, broken into Owen's house to look for Gabe. He was there at some point before we arrived, but had been moved. These were left behind."

Lev scanned the maps. "Many of these waterways are underground. When I first came here, many years ago, I explored the land on foot. I walked from one end of Yellowstone to another. It took months. I remember . . . at the eastern edge of the park, I followed a creek to private land, to the Rutherford Ranch. That was before I knew that I could get my ass kicked for even breathing near that land."

"You lived to learn otherwise, obviously."

"Through sheer luck. I thought about heading back into the park, but I heard singing. I followed a small river to a point where it flowed out from underneath a hill. I found a gate embedded in rock at the bottom of hill, with the river flowing through it.

"There was a woman there. I saw her arms, pale and grasping, extending from the gate. She was calling to me, and I wanted to set her free.

"But there was a gunshot. Sal's men . . . Gabriel's gang. They stopped me. They told me to forget what I'd seen.

"I didn't want to leave—she was clearly imprisoned against her will. But one of the men shone a light into the darkness.

"I saw that there wasn't a woman there. It was a creature that had the outline of a woman. But it had black eyes and serrated teeth, hissing at me like a snake. What I saw wasn't human, and I knew I wanted nothing to do with it. In my gut, I thought she might be some kind of a rusalka."

"What's a rusalka?" Petra wanted to know.

"The rusalki are Eastern European water nymphs. Depending on who's doing the telling, they are the spirits of women who were drowned. They would exist as water spirits, seducing men and drowning them, until they were avenged. Others say that they are simply forces of nature who provide rain to crops." He shook his head. "It doesn't matter. Whatever she was, I wanted to get away. I backed away, hands up. The men let me go, though they could just as easily have shot me and fed me to her." Lev lapsed into silence.

"Do you remember where that was?" Petra pushed at that silence.

"About . . . here." Lev grabbed a pencil and sketched the border of what Petra guessed to be Sal's land, at the foot of the mountain. A thread of jagged water, marked by an alchemical symbol that looked like an inverted triangle, crossed the border. Lev pointed to it. "But if she's loose, killing people . . . she's not imprisoned there anymore."

Maria rifled through a stack of phone books and came back with a tourist map of Yellowstone National Park. "Mike says that there have been killings . . . here. And here. Downstream from the place Lev remembers. She's staying in the same area, venturing no more than a couple of miles away."

"It's a place to start," Petra said. She glanced around the room. "Are we all in?"

There were solemn nods and a coyote yip. The cat yawned and hopped down off the refrigerator to go to the back bedroom.

"Great. Let's go fishing."

MUIRENN HAD RETURNED with treasure.

She had thought that it might be difficult to find prey. Signs that said DANGER—NO SWIMMING had cropped up downstream. Some of the roads in the distance, leading to the water, were cordoned off or blocked with orange sawhorses. Someone was keeping people away from the park.

Well, most of them.

She had found a group of teenagers swimming in the river. They had tied a rope to the lower limbs of a cottonwood tree. They took turns grasping the rope from the bank, swinging into space with whoops and yells, and landing in the water with great crashes.

You could always count on teenagers to defy rules and do something stupid.

She watched them from the deep water, waiting until the smallest boy launched himself into the water. He was probably a good three years younger than the others, maybe one's little brother that they were forced to babysit. Once he broke the surface of the water, she slid into action. She smashed his head on an underwater rock, plucked him from the bottom, and sped upstream as quickly as she could. By the time the teenagers realized that he hadn't surfaced and began looking for him, she was a half mile away, and the boy was a flopping rag at her side.

She would savor this. She would take him back to her pantry with the rest of the meat, reminding herself to chew slowly, to not wolf down her food. Still, she couldn't help but to nibble on the boy as she swam. He was the tenderest and most nourishing thing she'd had to eat yet, the flesh soft as veal.

She was humming happily to herself when she returned to the cave. She installed her leftovers in the pantry. It was getting crowded; she'd have to clean it out or expand the space to accommodate the river bounty.

Beside her stash of food, Gabriel hung motionless. She frowned at this. The tree roots had covered his body. All she could make out now was the profile of his face in the damp wood, like some kind of sleeping Green Man carving. She poked his cheek, and he didn't move. Condensed water dripped from the brow.

She sighed. Maybe the land had a deeper quarrel with him than she did. But she deserved to see him suffer, not be pressed away in the grip of a half-conscious tree. Her next task would be figuring out how to get him out of there. If she couldn't eat him for dinner, she was determined at least to play with him a bit.

A light shone above the black water ahead, far upstream. Muirenn sighed in irritation. Owen was back. What in hell did he want now? Weren't there enough things going on aboveground for him to interfere in? And he presumably had work to do. She had, after all, given him his hand back to keep him busy. Wasn't that enough?

Grumbling deep in her throat, she skimmed through the water to the light.

"Owen." She did her best to lift the corners of her mouth in a smile. "You've returned."

He held the light before him, blinding her. She held her hand up to the light to shade her sensitive eyes.

"I'm back. And I brought you a gift."

He held something in his hands. A rope, she realized, through the blinding light. The rope was tied around a giant plastic barrel. Owen yanked the rope, and the liquid contents of the barrel poured into the river in a thunderous splash.

She ducked into the water to swim away, but she surfaced and screamed. The blue liquid seeped into the water, scalding her gills and flesh. She flipped and howled. The liquid crackled over her skin, forming blue crystals inside her gills and in her skin and hair.

She knew what it was the instant she tasted it. "Blue vitriol," she gasped.

"Copper sulfide," Owen said. He was standing on the bank, aiming a pistol at her. "Gabe said that you wouldn't like it."

She turned to flee, and a gunshot disrupted the water before her. She shrieked and dove under the water, hoping to escape the bullets and the chemical. But the chemical was sinking deeply in . . . it scalded her eyes and her lungs.

She tried her best to swim away, but bullets plowed into the water around her, splashing sand up into her face.

She surfaced, turned, and hissed at Owen: "You don't know what you've brought down on your head."

"I'm just righting a wrong."

"You're just an idiot who couldn't accept the good thing he had. And now you're going to pay for it."

"From you?" He chuckled.

"From *them*."

He turned around frantically, and she had some satisfaction in how wide his eyes became.

The riverbank and the shallows, studded with pearls, began to seethe. Her children, tiny and toothed, broke through their eggs as the blue vitriol chewed into their shells. Like crayfish, they scuttled up the bank and swarmed Owen.

"Gah!" He swung and slapped at the creatures. His flashlight spun crazily, the beam bouncing against the fog clinging to the cavern's ceiling.

Muirenn seized this chance to escape, to head for the gate and cleaner water. Once these chemicals had dissipated, perhaps she could find a new hiding place . . . perhaps. But her priority was getting away from that traitor. She winced, feeling hot blood at her side. She fingered a hole at the bottom of her ribs. Owen must have grazed her. She felt slow, slow and weakened. But she could recover. She had survived much worse.

She paused at Gabriel's grave in the roots of trees.

She had no idea if he could hear her or not. But she put her face very close to his and whispered, "It's a good thing you're dead and in hell, Hanged Man. If you weren't, I'd chase you there."

PETRA HAD NO idea how to chase a mermaid.

She didn't know what she was expecting, really. She'd had a mermaid action figure as a little girl. That mermaid had green-blue hair, a shiny blue tail made of glittery fabric, and she swam with Petra in the bathtub. When she wasn't in the bathtub, she lived in the soap dish until a dog finally ate her. Petra rescued her from the dog, but the doll bore scars on her arm and face ever after. Petra didn't love her any less, but she learned a very valuable lesson about dogs and irresistible hair.

Which was a lesson that she seemed to be relearning now. Petra, Maria, Lev, Nine, and Sig had piled into the Bronco. They were hauling ass to the nearest road access to the Mermaid's lair, which Petra decided was likely going to be a lot more treacherous than a plastic soap dish. Petra drove and Lev rode shotgun on the passenger's side. The women in the back counted out ammunition and divided it among themselves, while bullets rolled around on the bench seat. Beside Petra, Sig perched, chewing on the ends of her hair. She hadn't had time to cut it and had pulled it back with rubber bands. Sig had the end of the ponytail in his paws and was chewing at it vigorously. His eyes were slitted in bliss, as if she'd been reincarnated as the best chew toy ever. Petra decided that she didn't really care; it was getting cut the instant she had ten free minutes. Maybe she'd ask Maria to braid it and give it to Sig.

Lev sat beside her, his sword balanced between the seat and the door. He gazed outside the window, his face an unreadable mask.

"So. Bullets will stop the Mermaid?"

"I don't see why not. Iron bars were able to hold her. I mean, most magical things are not entirely invulnerable. But I only met her once."

Petra felt like a dumb-ass for a brief second, but pushed forward. "This coming from the guy who can violate the boundaries of life and death at will."

He gave her a dark look. "Don't push it."

"Hey. I had to ask. I don't know much about magic and its rules."

She stared at the road ahead, weaving the Bronco carefully around painted sawhorses that had been set up by Mike's colleagues to keep people out of the area.

She hadn't pushed Lev about what flavor of supernatural he was. He said he was a guardian spirit. And while she had other things on her mind, she couldn't help her curiosity. What all did that entail? She'd never seen him guard anything more fearsome than the keg in the back of the bar until she'd wandered into his attic. She was pretty sure she just didn't want to know.

Yet, she really kind of did.

"Turn here," he ordered, pointing to a break at the side of the road between the steel berms.

Petra dutifully pulled the truck off the road. The branches of lodgepole pine scraped the sides of the truck, stones pounded the undercarriage, and she was pretty sure that she was going to drop an axle. She went as far as she could, bouncing to a halt in a clearing before a stream.

"This is the stream that comes from the underground river," he said, popping open a door.

The group piled out. The women bristled with guns. Petra flung her coyote-spit-damp hair over her shoulder and considered asking Nine to lend her a knife. Lev unloaded one thing he'd found in Maria's basement that Petra thought made sense: a fishing net. It was old and moldy, but it was made of strong polyester rope. Lev slung it over his shoulder and shut the tailgate.

"The plan is to follow the water upstream, hope we run into her. As far as we know, she hasn't killed this far west before. Theoretically, she should be upstream."

Lev advanced down to the bank, and the others followed. They walked east along the creek for several yards until he approached a downed tree. He walked over the tree to the opposite shore. He cast one corner of the net back to their side. Nine caught it, and they spread it out. The weights came to rest on the bottom of the stream, and they walked against the current, dredging it. The net was designed for large fish, the size of trout, as the spaces between the ropes were as large as Petra's hand. Frogs bounced out of their way, and a groundhog watched disapprovingly from a nearby field.

"With any luck, we'll get her tangled up and caught quick," Maria said. "You know, before it gets full of debris and frogs and shit."

"When do we ever have any luck?" Petra observed.

"Well. Okay."

They slowly moved upstream, weaving through cattails and soft, marshy land at the foot of the mountain. It was slow going, but they were determined to be quiet. Even Sig was silent as he paused to chase a duck. Unsuccessful, he just huffed at Petra as he returned to her side. They had to flip out the bottom of the net a couple of times to release a couple of hapless turtles and an idiot groundhog who was determined to gnaw on the ropes. Sig kept snapping at him, but he was not impressed.

The creek became more shallow and flattened. It snaked through fields and forest, and in a couple of miles, it emptied out in a wide runnel on a grass plain.

Lev pointed.

The creek seemed to drain away to nothingness. But as they approached, Petra could see the water breaking into a gap in sandstone. It slipped into the shadow of a shelf cave, shrouded by weeds.

And there was a gate there, true to Lev's word, nearly obscured by the weeds. It was old metal, the plain rails speckled with tarnish and rust at the weld marks. But the gate had been broken. The door lay open, pressed by the weight of the water against the opening of a tunnel.

Petra squinted and reached for her flashlight. It looked like there was enough foot-purchase on a shelf for them to proceed inside, single file.

She motioned to Maria to follow her. She mouthed to Lev, *We'll flush her out to you.*

Lev nodded. He tightened his grip on the net. Nine crouched in the grass on the other side of the creek, doing the same. It looked like a good trap from here, a solid plan.

"Stay with them," she told Sig. She knew he could swim, but she wanted him as far beyond harm's hungry reach as she could get him.

Sig growled in response but dutifully parked his ass on the bank beside Nine, slapping his tail on the cattails.

Petra stepped into hollow darkness. The outside light fell away rapidly, and she focused on minding her footing. The rock was slippery, and she knew full well that she and Maria were within reach of anything that might be lurking in the water. So she minced along, holding a flashlight in one hand and a pistol in the other.

Maria had more sense. She clutched her shotgun close, and had switched on a dimmer flashlight that dangled from a carabiner on the belt loop of her jeans. There was no getting around announcing their arrival with light in the monster's lair.

Petra's eyes began to adjust to the cave. She realized that this place was not entirely dark. In the far distance, she could make out a small star of light that bobbed and wove like a firefly. Someone else was down here. Quickly, she doused her light and motioned for Maria to do the same. They remained motionless, clinging to the wall, listening.

Petra thought she heard splashing. And a howl. Reflexively, she moved forward to get to the thin strip of beach that surrounded this side of the underground river. They'd have more room to maneuver on the beach. A veil of moisture clung to her face, like sea spray.

And then there were the gunshots.

Petra raced toward that bright light. Her feet crunched along the sand, and she was forced to turn on her light to avoid breaking an ankle on the jagged rocks. The blue-white light ahead of her bounced around, and there was shrieking. A woman's shriek. And the shriek was coming toward them, like the whistle on a train.

Petra planted her feet in the sand and rock. Maria's light gleamed beside hers, in enough time to catch a dark bluish shape streaking past them toward the entrance.

Petra shot at it. The roar of Maria's shotgun was behind her, but the shape vanished.

"She's heading your way!" she shouted downstream.

She hoped to hell that Lev and Nine and Sig were ready for her.

CHAPTER 20

Witch Creek

Petra turned toward the distant, star-like light that bobbed and jagged in the distance, like a lantern being shaken. But her attention was snagged by another, dimmer light: a faint gold shine on the opposite side of the river.

She swept her flashlight over it. It seemed to be a wall of tree roots, ancient and unyielding, something that had been here for hundreds of years. She moved to dismiss it, but the gold glow dripping down the surface bothered her. It reminded her of the hostile Lunaria, miles distant. And there was something about it . . . something that was vaguely man-shaped.

She ripped off her gun belt and handed it to Maria. No point in ruining perfectly good guns.

"What the fuck are you doing?"

"I'm not sure, but . . . I think that has something to do with Gabe. Cover me?"

"I have a choice?"

She stripped off her jacket and boots and waded into the water. A neon green kayak floated past her. She considered trying to catch it, but let it go. Maybe Lev and Nine could snag it.

The water was cool, but not frigid. She was conscious that the Mermaid could turn back at any moment, and she'd be drowned, chewed, or worse. But she kept her eyes on the mass of roots on the opposite bank. The water felt odd, slippery, and her damned hair kept trying to drag her down. As she approached the mass of roots, she saw blue crystals beginning to form on the wood at the waterline. Her skin stung, like she was swimming in bleach. She struggled to keep her head above the waterline.

Shit. She was swimming in some kind of toxic stew. So much for trying to keep this new body in decent condition. She swam as quickly as she could to the opposite bank and tried to climb the wall of roots. She found purchase with a toe, and her heart was pounding as she pulled herself out of the water.

The roots were warm, like flesh. She was startled by that and nearly let go. But she climbed up higher, her fingers roving over the strange lattice of wood. How had the Lunaria come this far?

She half expected the tree to attack her, as it had before at its home. But it seemed to have other priorities, now, and it ignored her. Dim light pulsed beneath the skin of the wood, as if it was busily digesting something more interesting. Or someone . . .

Petra lifted her hand to a niche in the wall. Her fingers brushed against something that felt like flesh, and she squinted.

"Oh, Jesus."

Gabe's face was embedded in the wood, like a mask jammed in the back in a costumer's wardrobe. His whole body must be under there, somewhere . . .

She slapped at his face. "Gabe. Wake up."

But his face remained slack and his eyes closed. She was too late. Her heart fell to her feet. After all this . . . he was lost to her. Lost to this stupid tree and the idiot secrets this place kept.

Her vision blurry, she tore at the roots with her hands. But they were solid as an iron gate. Small gaps and cubbies pierced the surface of it. They were too small for her to do anything other than try to reach in and see if she could detect a heartbeat under soggy flannel. She couldn't.

She pressed her forehead to the roots. He had always belonged to the tree. No matter what. It had finally reclaimed him, like a jealous lover, and he was lost to her.

She was dimly conscious of an itching feeling at her pant leg, and she rubbed her shin against her other calf. But the itch became a sting, and she looked down.

"Fuck!"

There was something crawling on her . . . many somethings, larger versions of the creature Maria had stomped in her kitchen. She kicked against them. The little bastards were crawling out of the water. Hot blood ran from the back of her knee, and a weird crustacean-like creature fled away with a chunk of flesh.

"Gah! Bastards!"

Maria's flashlight jogged and rolled on the opposite shore, as if she'd dropped it.

She turned back for Maria, and she caught sight of her friend's silhouette slapping at the swarm of creatures. Petra winced again and was reminded of a nature channel show she'd seen many years ago about fire ants plucking a human body clean within a matter of hours.

She tried to climb higher in the tree roots, searching for some means of escape. But the devouring creatures swarmed up and over her in a seething mass, crawling over her legs.

Dammit. This was not the way she wanted to go.

She buried her face in her elbow to shield her eyes.

In that darkness, something glowed. It was warm, like sunshine, and played red against the interior of her eyelids. She cracked open one eye.

The roots were glowing, glowing with a brilliant gold light. The effect was like a bright candle behind a pierced metal lantern, seething and swirling.

Above Petra's head, a bird shrieked.

A raven emerged in a void between the roots and fluttered into the darkness, toward the nefarious little creatures. It snatched one up.

In that golden light, other ravens formed. They flooded out of the gaps and cubbies in the tree, seeking out the crustaceans. Black wings fluttered over her, shrieking in a deafening cacophony, as the birds poured out and began to devour the bugs. Their shadows flickered against the mist clinging to the walls of the cavern, slinging rain back into her face.

They poured out for minutes—dozens, hundreds of them—a black mass that blotted out the golden light, like a swarm of locusts. They plucked the bugs from Petra's body and then scattered into the dark, leaving Petra clinging to the tree roots.

"Oh, my God," she breathed.

She reached inside the tree for Gabe, hoping that there was still one more living thing trapped there. But there was only emptiness behind the roots of the tree. Nothing.

Petra turned back to the bank. The birds had scoured Maria clean, gulping down the bugs in a cloud of black. Before her eyes, they dispersed.

"Are you okay?" she shouted at Maria, desperate to be heard above the squawking.

"Yeah!"

Petra took a deep breath and dove into the water. She swam as quickly as she could to the opposite bank, bracing herself for the stinging bite of those bizarre little creatures. To her surprise, she didn't feel anything. Just water and whatever crud was in it stinging her wounds.

She dragged herself out of the water, and Maria helped her. Her friend's face was dripping blood on one side.

Petra put her hand on Maria's shoulder. "Really? Are you okay?"

Maria lifted her hand to her forehead. "I got chewed. But nothing fatal. What the hell was that?"

"Those biters . . . I figure that more of the Mermaid's eggs hatched." She jammed her bloody feet into her boots and laced them. "The birds . . . I think that was what's left of Gabriel."

Maria's hand fell on her back. "Oh, God. I'm sorry."

Petra shook her head, choking back a sob. "We gotta help Lev and Nine get that bitch. We have to . . ."

She was cut short by a yell upstream, where she'd seen the blue-white light.

"What the hell is that?" Maria muttered.

"I have no idea." And she didn't. Her imagination and emotions had been stretched to their limits and broken.

"Probably something that needs to be shot." Maria ratcheted back her shotgun.

"I'm in the mood for that. Yeah. Let's go shoot some things." She reached for her gunbelt.

The women moved down the beach. The sand was gritty, containing bones and fragments of what Petra guessed were pieces of pearl shells. Here and there, a fat raven could be found, gobbling down a little biter. A black feather poked up from the sand. Petra reached down and clutched it to her chest. It was the last part of Gabe she'd ever hold. She knew it. She stuffed it into her pocket.

"Look at that."

Maria's light reached a shape huddled on the beach beside a blue plastic barrel, surrounded by a stain of red. It was a man, covered in blood. Gingerly, Maria reached down and turned the man to face them.

It was Owen. Or what was left of him. His face was pale, and it was clear that the little biters had been chewing on him. But he was still in one piece. Mostly. His right arm was jammed under his armpit. He pulled it out. His hand was just a bloody stump, from the wrist down.

"She took it," he whispered. "She took my hand."

Petra regarded him with narrowed eyes. "Yeah, well, you deserved it, you son of a bitch." Owen deserved this, and much more.

Owen didn't dispute it. Petra figured he was in shock. Didn't matter. She unholstered one gun and pointed it at him.

"Because of you, Gabriel is dead."

Owen tucked his stump under his arm, bowed his head, and waited for her to shoot him.

Petra shifted her weight from foot to foot. Before she'd come to Temperance, she'd never turned a gun on a living thing. Now, now she was considering plugging Owen Rutherford and kicking his body into the river. She pulled back the hammer.

"The Mermaid," he said. He didn't beg—it was just

quiet resignation. "Gabriel said that to kill her, you must put her back where she came from. You have to cut out her heart and deliver it to Heart Lake. And her head to Witch Creek."

Petra shook her head. "You gave my husband to that swimming bitch. You kidnapped him, and you gave him to that bitch and now he's dead."

Owen hung his head. "If it matters at all, I'm sorry."

"No. No, it doesn't *fucking* matter. We three had a deal. Gabriel was going to tell you what he knew. He would have accepted you as his new master, since you own the ranch. And you would have left us alone. Why was that not good enough for you?" She was shouting at him, and her face was wet.

Owen said nothing.

Petra shoved her gun into Owen's face and hissed, *"Why was that not good enough for you?"*

Owen licked his lips. "Because I wanted more. She promised me everything."

"And now you will have nothing. Nothing."

Petra stood back. She didn't want his pathetic brains splashing on her.

"Petra."

She glanced back.

Maria stood behind her. Her shotgun was lowered. "I won't stop you from killing him. He deserves it, and I support your decision to smear him off the face of the earth. I just want you to think about what that means for you. You've been given a new life.

Scrubbed clean to do anything you want. Just be sure you don't waste it on a piece of trash like him."

Petra took a deep breath. Owen was slime. She felt at this moment what she'd felt at the hospital and in the dark nights when everyone else slept. She felt what she'd felt in Lev's attic, and when she'd seen Gabriel's body in the tree. She felt that closeness with death, that still intimacy with the ever after.

Only this time, she could stop it.

She released the hammer and holstered her gun. "Let's go."

Maria nodded, and they headed back out the way they'd come.

Owen might well bleed out on his own. But she had done no harm to him, and she could live with that.

It began to rain inside the cavern, rinsing the blood and chemical residue from her face. Maria put her arm around her.

They trudged wordlessly to the gate, but increased their pace as they saw Lev and Nine struggling with the net in the light near the river.

"We have her!" Lev gasped.

Petra reached for the net. Inside snarled a creature with blue-green scales, hissing and shrieking. She was gnawing at the polyester cording, flipping and snarling like a swordfish in the ocean.

Maria aimed her shotgun.

The net ripped . . . then gave way, and the Mermaid tumbled into the creek.

"We don't have her," Lev growled.

* * *

LEV GRABBED THE kayak, jumped in, and started paddling. The Mermaid was fast, he would give her that. He would have been unlikely to catch her in a boat on a level playing field. But she was injured. She'd come out of the cave covered in some blue-crystal crud, and bleeding black into the water. Because of that, she was easy to track as he followed that blue-black ink in the water. She'd been shot, he had guessed, as he heard gunshots echoing from the cave.

He followed her for almost a mile. He heard the others crashing through the underbrush behind him. They were falling behind, unable to keep up.

That was fine with him. The Mermaid was his.

He was gaining on her. The kayak cut smoothly through the water, and he paddled furiously.

Her head broke the water at last. She opened her mouth to draw breath, her crystalizing hair curling around her in a miasma. Whether it was to sing, cough, or ensorcell him, it didn't matter.

She turned to him and whispered with wide black eyes, "He's awake."

He had no idea who she was talking about. The only "he" that mattered to Lev was Archer.

"My son is dead."

And with that, Lev lifted his sword and swung as hard as he could. The blade bit into her neck, barely slowing as it severed her spine, and her head came clear off. Dark blood stained the creek, from shore to shore, rendering it as black and opaque as the underground river.

He exhaled for what had to be the first time in days, his heart pounding.

It was done. The revenge he sought. But it had been so sudden, he thought, as the kayak drifted in the suddenly quiet water. Ripples from the violence pushed against the banks, disturbing the cattails. And then all was still.

His mind, though, wasn't.

He was pulling the body to shore by the time the women and the coyote caught up with him. He was up to his knees in mud, dragging the body of the Mermaid by one arm. He held her head by the hair in the other hand like Perseus with the Medusa.

It had been a long time since he'd killed anything. This feeling sang in him, as if it were the righting of some great injustice. He had never been a warrior; he didn't fool himself about that. But this felt as if the injustice was balanced. He rubbed his face on his shoulder, threw the body in the reeds. Where the black blood fell in a slap, the plants curled and withered.

"Wait," Petra panted. "To be truly finished with her, she has to go back to where she came. Put her heart in Heart Lake. And her head in Witch Creek. The problem is . . . I don't know where those places are."

"They are west of here. Many miles west. But I can do that." Lev stood over the body a moment before plunging his blade into the Mermaid's chest. Dark blood leaked out of the wound. He reached in and found the warm heart, cut it from the center.

Maria and Petra looked away. But Nine and the coyote watched solemnly, the way that animals did. Animals never shied away from death.

Lev tossed the head and heart on the skirt of the kayak. They landed with a thick splat. He covered them with his jacket, obscuring them from any passersby that he might meet on the journey.

"Gabriel?" he finally thought to ask. "And Owen?"

Petra took a deep breath, and it looked as if she fought tears. Maria and Nine put their arms around her.

"Gabriel is dead," Maria said. "Owen lives, for what it's worth."

"I am sorry for that. For both of those pieces of news."

Petra blinked back tears. "Thank you. For everything."

Lev put a hand on her shoulder. He nodded at Nine and Maria. Their deal was done. He turned away.

A figure plodded forward in the mud. Owen. He staggered forward, fell to his knees, gaping at the figure of the Mermaid.

"I can fix that second piece of news for you," Lev offered, pausing in wiping black blood from his blade on the cattails.

Owen's eyes were glazed. One hand was tucked under his arm in a spreading red stain. He was mumbling to himself. "She's dead. Yes, she's dead. And you can't . . . I can't deliver you from this place without her. She was our only hope."

Petra gazed at the sheriff with narrowed eyes. "He thinks he talks to a ghost. The ghost of a little girl."

Owen lifted his eyes. "I was never able to solve her murder. The Mermaid said that . . . she could help her move on, to stop this haunting. It's been so many years . . ."

Lev knelt before Owen. He gazed at the sheriff with a deep sense of pity, pity and loathing. "Owen. I speak to the dead."

Owen gazed at him frantically. "You can?"

"I can. Do you believe me?"

Owen reached out and clutched at Lev's shirt with his good hand. "You see her? You know, then. I have to help her. She needs to move on, to go to heaven or wherever good souls go. She's innocent, and she doesn't deserve this. She doesn't deserve . . . me."

Lev looked down at him, his jaw hard. "There are no dead speaking to you, Owen. Only your own mind."

"She's not . . . she has to be real! She has to be! For years, she's been speaking to me." Owen's brow wrinkled.

"The only dead here, Owen, are the ones you're responsible for. Those dead are silent."

Lev shook him off. Owen would suffer more as an insane man than if Lev killed him outright.

Lev strode to the boat and got in. Without looking back, he paddled down the river.

He wasn't sure what to do next. Should he return

to the life he'd conducted a week ago? Strike out on the road again? He knew that he had to speak with Bridget. Maybe a road trip was in order, and he could see where life took him then.

He paddled for days, through forest and mountain passes. He dimly remembered going this way, many years before. He gazed upon the bison in the fields, watched the eagles fish. He emptied himself of his emotions, washing himself in the water and foraging for food by the shore. When he had to pick up the kayak and walk, he dragged it behind him. He slept beneath the pines and listened to the frogs. It had been a long time since he'd set himself upon a path like this, and he felt his ragged emotions smoothing as he worked his muscles and navigated by the sky. Out here, there were no ghosts. He encountered no people. Just him and the land and sky. He remembered how Archer had said he loved the outdoors for just this reason, and it made him feel closer to his son. He picked up stones, held them, allowed them to blossom into flowers, and skipped them across the surface of the water.

By the time he reached Witch Creek, the bundle in the skirt of the kayak had begun to reek, and he would be glad to be rid of it. This part of the water was lovely, on the other side of the mountains in shaded lowlands. It reminded him very much of the places that the rusalki were said to haunt, in Eastern Europe.

He unwrapped the head and chucked it into the

water without ceremony. He felt, though, that he should say something:

"Water, take your servant and never release her again."

The waters closed over it greedily. A tortoise caught one of her braids and towed it deep beneath the surface.

It was the following night by the time he reached Heart Lake. This area was more populated, and he was glad for the cover of darkness. The water shone in the light of the waning moon, lapping waves against his boat. Only a faint shimmer-stripe of sunset shone in the west. Lev took the heart in his hands and cast it into the lake.

"Water, take your servant and never release her again."

Fish swarmed, ripples in the dark water. They ripped the heart to pieces, as if it was the most luscious delicacy they'd ever encountered.

He took a deep breath, the paddle stretched across his lap. It was accomplished. He floated still, serene, on the water.

What would come after was anyone's guess.

THE WOMEN HAULED the Mermaid's body back to the gate, taking turns, two at a time, one at each arm. Sig led the procession, slinking through the blades of new grass. Petra wondered how she would explain

Gabe's death to him, or if he already knew in that mysterious coyote way that he had about him. Owen drifted at the fringes. No one spoke to him. He just shadowed them like a bleeding vulture.

Petra plodded numbly, the sunset bleeding across the sky behind her and driving her shadow before her. She pulled one arm of the Mermaid, and Nine had the other for this part of the journey. The Mermaid's scales slipped and skipped over the grass, while the guts and stump of a neck had the tendency to get caught on things. Petra just focused on putting one foot in front of the other and didn't worry about being gentle with the corpse.

Nine's stomach growled audibly. Petra gave her some serious side-eye.

Nine shrugged.

It was getting late. The gate finally came into view. Maria took over from Petra, and she and Nine hauled the body a few feet into the cave. Petra heard a heavy thud as they chucked the Mermaid's body on the sand. No one had been here in years. Maybe she'd rot in place. Whatever. She was Owen's problem, not theirs.

A faint cawing came from a distance.

Petra looked beyond the gate, to the field above the cave.

An oak tree grew there. The tree was smaller than the Lunaria had been in its full glory. But it had some of that same stateliness about it. Sig loped through the grass to the tree, climbing the hill with his tail up. Petra followed, her muscles aching.

The tree was covered in ravens. They seethed and moved among the oak's fresh green leaves as if they were shadows. One spied her, and cawed. Perhaps that was its way of saying goodbye. Petra felt a lump in her throat at that sentimentality.

Until, that was, the ravens left the tree and swooped toward her in a cloud. Sig barked, and Petra threw her arms up over her head. They swarmed around her, blotting out the light of the sunset like the debris of a house in a tornado, circling in a deafening cloud. Their wings slapped her head and back, and she thought that for certain the magic of the Rutherford Ranch finally intended to kill her once and for all.

A featherlight touch brushed her hair, and the shrieking abruptly stopped.

Petra lowered her arms an inch.

It was Gabriel. Whole, gazing at her with quizzical amber eyes.

She sucked in her breath and threw her arms around him. One of his hands was tangled in her hair and the other wrapped around her back.

"I thought you were dead," she whispered.

"I thought you were dying," he said. His brow wrinkled in puzzlement. "Have I been gone long enough for your hair to grow that long?"

She snorted back tears and snot on his soggy flannel shirt.

"It's a long story. A very long story."

He thrust her hair back from her face and kissed her soundly. He tasted like warm sunshine.

She drew back reluctantly. "The tree. What happened?"

"The tree . . . is changing. It has its own purposes now." His fingers plucked a long strand of hair that stuck to his stubble. He turned it over in his hand, examining it. "It serves another will. I don't understand why."

Grasses crunched behind them. Sig growled.

It was Owen, stumbling toward them.

"Has it imprinted on Owen? Jesus Christ." She pressed her forehead to his chest. Petra was thinking about the tree as if it were a freakishly powerful gosling imprinted on the village idiot.

"No. I don't think so."

Owen dug into his pocket and pulled out something shiny. He shook it at Gabriel. "The Mermaid gave me this. Said she found it."

Gabriel took it from him, and his expression darkened. It was a gold pocket watch that dangled from a short, broken chain. The hands were frozen at twelve, and the crystal was cracked.

"What?" she asked, wanting to know.

"That watch. It belonged to Lascaris."

Petra's gaze slipped to the tree. "What does it mean?"

Gabe followed her gaze. "It means . . . we are all in very serious trouble."

Acknowledgments

Many thanks to the team of literary superheroes who worked on this book with me.

Thank you to David Pomerico for taking on this project, and for your patient and bulletproof edits.

Thanks to Becca Stumpf for all the magic bracelet action. P.S. I have boot envy.

Thank you to Caro Perny for using all the contents of your creative utility belt to help publicize my work.

Thanks to Jason and Marcella, who fight the good fight against dastardly plot bunnies during first reads.